To my father and his brothers, who sought their fortunes here

ALSO IN THE AKASHIC NOIR SERIES

ORANGE COUNTY NOIR, edited by GARY PHILLIPS
PARIS NOIR (FRANCE), edited by AURÉLIEN MASSON
PHILADELPHIA NOIR, edited by CARLIN ROMANO
PHOENIX NOIR, edited by PATRICK MILLIKIN
PITTSBURGH NOIR, edited by KATHLEEN GEORGE
PORTLAND NOIR, edited by KEVIN SAMPSELL
PRISON NOIR, edited by JOYCE CAROL OATES
PROVIDENCE NOIR, edited by ANN HOOD
QUEENS NOIR, edited by ROBERT KNIGHTLY
RICHMOND NOIR, edited by ANDREW BLOSSOM, BRIAN CASTLEBERRY & TOM DE HAVEN
RIO NOIR (BRAZIL), edited by TONY BELLOTTO
ROME NOIR (ITALY), edited by CHIARA STANGALINO & MAXIM JAKUBOWSKI
SAN DIEGO NOIR, edited by MARYELIZABETH HART
SAN FRANCISCO NOIR, edited by PETER MARAVELIS
SAN FRANCISCO NOIR 2: THE CLASSICS, edited by PETER MARAVELIS
SAN JUAN NOIR (PUERTO RICO), edited by MAYRA SANTOS-FEBRES
SEATTLE NOIR, edited by CURT COLBERT
SINGAPORE NOIR, edited by CHERYL LU-LIEN TAN
STATEN ISLAND NOIR, edited by PATRICIA SMITH
ST. LOUIS NOIR, edited by SCOTT PHILLIPS
STOCKHOLM NOIR (SWEDEN), edited by NATHAN LARSON & CARL-MICHAEL EDENBORG
ST. PETERSBURG NOIR (RUSSIA), edited by NATALIA SMIRNOVA & JULIA GOUMEN
TEHRAN NOIR (IRAN), edited by SALAR ABDOH
TEL AVIV NOIR (ISRAEL), edited by ETGAR KERET & ASSAF GAVRON
TORONTO NOIR (CANADA), edited by JANINE ARMIN & NATHANIEL G. MOORE
TRINIDAD NOIR (TRINIDAD & TOBAGO), edited by LISA ALLEN-AGOSTINI & JEANNE MASON
TRINIDAD NOIR: THE CLASSICS (TRINIDAD & TOBAGO), edited by EARL LOVELACE & ROBERT ANTONI
TWIN CITIES NOIR, edited by JULIE SCHAPER & STEVEN HORWITZ
USA NOIR, edited by JOHNNY TEMPLE
VENICE NOIR (ITALY), edited by MAXIM JAKUBOWSKI
WALL STREET NOIR, edited by PETER SPIEGELMAN
ZAGREB NOIR (CROATIA), edited by IVAN SRŠEN

FORTHCOMING

ACCRA NOIR (GHANA), edited by NANA-AMA DANQUAH
ADDIS ABABA NOIR (ETHIOPIA), edited by MAAZA MENGISTE
AMSTERDAM NOIR (HOLLAND), edited by RENÉ APPEL & JOSH PACHTER
BAGHDAD NOIR (IRAQ), edited by SAMUEL SHIMON
BERLIN NOIR (GERMANY), edited by THOMAS WÖERTCHE
BOGOTÁ NOIR (COLOMBIA), edited by ANDREA MONTEJO
BUENOS AIRES NOIR (ARGENTINA), edited by ERNESTO MALLO
HOUSTON NOIR, edited by GWENDOLYN ZEPEDA
JERUSALEM NOIR, edited by DROR MISHANI
LAGOS NOIR (NIGERIA), edited by CHRIS ABANI
MARRAKECH NOIR (MOROCCO), edited by YASSIN ADNAN
MONTANA NOIR, edited by JAMES GRADY & KEIR GRAFF
MONTREAL NOIR (CANADA), edited by JOHN McFETRIDGE & JACQUES FILIPPI
PRAGUE NOIR (CZECH REPUBLIC), edited by PAVEL MANDYS
SANTA CRUZ NOIR, edited by SUSIE BRIGHT
SÃO PAULO NOIR (BRAZIL), edited by TONY BELLOTTO
SYDNEY NOIR (AUSTRALIA), edited by JOHN DALE
VANCOUVER NOIR (CANADA), edited by SAM WIEBE

ATLANTA

VININGS

BUCKHEAD

PIEDMONT PARK

MIDTOWN

VIRGINIA HIGHLAND

WESTSIDE
RESERVOIR PARK

LITTLE FIVE POINTS

CENTENNIAL
OLYMPIC PARK

INMAN PARK

EAST LAKE TERRACE

LIONEL HAMPTON-
BEECHER HILLS PARK

MECHANICSVILLE

GRANT PARK

EAST ATLANTA

CASCADE HEIGHTS

COLLEGE PARK

HARTSFIELD-JACKSON
ATLANTA INT'L AIRPORT

PEACHTREE CITY

STONE MOUNTAIN

STONE
MOUNTAIN
PARK

285

20

PANOLA MOUNTAIN
STATE PARK

TABLE OF CONTENTS

PART III: NOSE WIDE OPEN

INTRODUCTION
Underneath the Scent of Magnolia and Pine

Atlanta, the "city too busy to hate," may be the noirest town in the nation. When I say "noir" I don't mean that we are the murder capital, nor do we strive to be. We are the ninth-largest city in the United States. Our airport is the busiest on earth, hosting over 100 million passengers in recent calendar years. (It is said that even on your way to heaven, you must change planes at Hartsfield-Jackson.) An entire school of hip-hop was born here too. But it is not our urbanity alone that makes us noir. We are a *Southern* city. Margaret Mitchell wrote *Gone with the Wind* both in and about Atlanta. Martin Luther King's Ebeneezer still stands proud on the northeast side of town. Just after the Civil War, six colleges were founded to lift the recently emancipated, and these institutions promote black (Southern) excellence to this day.

Atlanta is rife with contradictions. Priding ourselves on not putting all our business in the street, we shelter secrets for generations. At the same time, we have somehow managed to become a reality television hub. TV personality Todd Chrisley serves up his own brand of "bless your heart" backhandedness and family dysfunction for millions of viewers all over the country, yet gossip magazines hint at a scandal hidden in full view. Most of the "Real" Housewives of Atlanta are not even from Atlanta, nor are they housewives, but they have taken our hometown as their own—and housewifery is a state of mind, not a marital status. These ladies fight at baby showers, marry with the cameras rolling, and divorce in the same fashion. T.I. and Tiny of *The Family Hustle* are ATLiens for sure, and they allow us to be spectators as they negotiate what it means to be recently rich, famous, and black. Kim Zolciak used to be a Real Housewife of Atlanta, sharing the most intimate details of her love life, but drawing the line at being filmed without her blond wig. After the racial tensions on set bubbled over, she moved to her own show, the programming equivalent of white flight—and actually became a housewife.

Atlanta Noir is not a citified version of Southern Gothic. These authors delve deep into the grotesquerie that is embedded in every narrative and character. When we write noir, we don't shine a light into darkness, we lower the shades. There are no secrets like Southern secrets and no lies like Southern lies.

Keep in mind that there are those who still speak of the Civil War as the "War of Northern Aggression," perhaps the biggest lie of all. Bronze markers dot the landscape, lamenting the loss, never allowing the past to pass. Yet, in the early 1980s, a serial killer terrorized the city for two years, murdering at least twenty-eight African American children, but this recent history has been put to bed. No memorial stands in honor of the fallen. No one has forgotten, but nobody talks about it, because this is Atlanta and this is how we do things.

This city itself is a crime scene. After all, Georgia was founded as a de facto penal colony and in 1864, Sherman burned the city to the ground. We might argue about whether the arson was the crime or the response to the crime, but this is indisputable: Atlanta is a city sewn from the ashes and everything that grows here is at once fertilized and corrupted by the past.

* * *

In this anthology, I am excited to share fourteen writers' take on the B-side of the ATL. These stories do not necessarily conform to the traditional expectations of noir as several of them are not, by any stretch, crime fiction. However, they all share the quality of exposing the rot underneath the scent of magnolia and pine. Noir, in my opinion, is more a question of tone than content. The moral universe of the story is as significant as the physical space. Noir is a realm where the good guys seldom win; perhaps they hardly exist at all. Few bad deeds go unrewarded, and good intentions are not the road to hell, but are hell itself.

They call it the "Dirty South" for a reason. Here, Waffle House is more than a marker of Southern charm and cholesterol. Yes, the hash browns are scattered, smothered, and chunked, but narcotics, sex, and cash are available, if not on the menu. Just on the outskirts of the East Lake Golf Club is a neighborhood that is not mentioned on the real estate brochures. Perhaps it's true that servants are just like family, but this is not necessarily an upgrade. Megachurches may save you from sin, but not from the wrath of the past.

That said, this book also engages noir in the old-fashioned sense of the word, hard-boiled and criminal. Judges put hits on citizens, crazy neighbors turn out to be homicidal—and victims of homicide. Drug dealers double-cross each other, and sometimes sweet little girls murder just for the hell of it.

But don't forget that this is the Peach State, and down here, we like to take our poison with a side of humor. Behind every murder, under every drug deal, beneath each church pew, and tucked into the working girls' purses is a moment of the absurd and a laugh to be had at the expense of those who can't handle the truth.

Welcome to *Atlanta Noir*. Come sit on the veranda, or the

terrace of a high-rise condo. Pour yourself a glass of sweet tea, and fortify it with a slug of bourbon. Put your feet up. Enjoy these stories, and watch your back.

Tayari Jones
May 2017

PART I

The Devil Went Down to Georgia

SNOWBOUND

BY Tananarive Due

Buckhead

Monique took the forecast seriously from the jump—snowfall projected in Metro Atlanta and Buckhead. Only a couple inches, but still. She'd hated snow since college, and her childhood in hurricane-prone Miami had taught her to treat meteorology like prophecy, so she spent most of Monday afternoon navigating a motorized scooter through the narrow aisles of her closest Publix to stock up on groceries. The store's inventory was too big for its space, so even a moderate crowd reminded her of the frenzy of her childhood's coming storms, Mom pulling her by the hand.

Monique was only forty-five, but with her left foot in a cast, the supermarket aged her by thirty years. Before the roller-rink debacle that had sent her to the ER a month ago—her punishment for showing off her old South Beach moves for her nephew—Monique had never noticed how many of her favorite brands were so high on the shelf, or how difficult it was to inspect packages of meat from a scooter. She'd never faced the indignity of bumping against aisle displays and knocking items to the floor, or noticed the frustrated huffs from shoppers who wanted her to move out of sight. To disappear. Eyes flitted away in a race not to look at her, to render her invisible.

Who wanted to see a middle-aged woman in a baggy sweatsuit riding a handicapped scooter with her foot in a cast?

She'd long ago stopped going out to clubs where she had to impress bouncers on the rope line, but even in LA, she'd never been as invisible as she was now. Two more weeks, and she would join the ranks of the visible again. She would not just walk, she would *strut* everywhere. A six-week taste of infirmity, and then she would never take her own two feet for granted. She would stand upright as long as she could.

The man behind her in line chuckled at the case of bottled water in her basket. He was in his seventies like her father, but his back and neck were straight, and he didn't use a cane. She regularly envied mobile strangers now.

"People here act like they've never seen snow," he said. "It's not gonna kill nobody."

As she reached the wooded end of the cul-de-sac on her street and drove her car down her driveway—such a steep drop that her seat belt pinched her chest—Monique realized her dream house was a nightmare as long as she was in a cast. With Nate back in LA for last-minute reshoots, the house waited to mock her. And in four months, she hadn't yet befriended a neighbor who might give her a thought; the other three houses at this end of the street were equally shrouded in old-growth pines, oaks, dogwoods, and magnolia trees, set back from the road to discourage visitors. Just like hers.

Monique hadn't expected to have a broken ankle when she and Nate bought this two-story, four-bedroom Mediterranean with a tile roof on two wooded acres in Buckhead. The driveway was steep enough to be a hiking trail. Nate was five years younger, and neither of them had been thinking "retirement" when they signed the papers. But what *had* she been thinking? Now she could only reach the streetside mailbox by car, since her crutches were useless most times. And her four-wheeled "knee walker" with a pad to rest her left knee on so she could glide freely around the house lost its charm on hills—and her yard was *all* hills. Nate had annoyed her with his constant complaints about the house, but now she realized how right he'd been—it was a beautiful show home, but not a good place to live.

It had taken her two years to wear him down—too late to move before Mom died—and only then after he landed regular directing gigs on a series shooting in Atlanta. Her mother's brain tumor diagnosis hadn't been enough to sway him, and the time apart with both of them flying off for weeks at a stretch had started to make them not just roommates, but resentful strangers. In Atlanta, she'd promised, they could have a house worth the million and a half they'd been paying in Santa Monica for a bungalow. They'd both spent the past twenty years bashing their heads against Hollywood to collect a few dollars—him as a director, and her as a producer-turned-screenwriter—so wasn't it time for a place big enough to raise a family?

She'd miscarried three times in ten years, so Nate had agreed they could fill out adoption paperwork by spring for a newborn, and statistics said they could have a black or brown baby nine months after that. She could finally indulge her desire to live in the Big House—wasn't that the secret dream of every black child of the South? If Nate hadn't laughed, Monique's first choice would have been a black-and-white colonial that could have been in *Django*, on a flat green lot only missing a row of slave cabins.

She would camp in the house all day Tuesday, she decided. And Wednesday and Thursday too, if she had to. She didn't want the car gliding down the hill out of control, or to lose her balance trying to maneuver herself around outside. *Hell* no.

Nate called as she was pulling into the garage. She told him her plan over the Bluetooth. The car was now her favorite phone.

"Why not just go over to your dad's?"

Nate still didn't grasp that moving to Atlanta to be closer to her family didn't mean she wanted to become a child again. His parents were long dead, so he idealized her father. What could Dad do for her in a snowstorm? She didn't want to spend two or three days in the house where Mom had gotten sick while Dad sat in front of the TV.

"I'm fine here."

"Will your dad be all right?" Nate had grown up in LA and was suspicious of any weather that wasn't sunshine.

"He's from New York. Please. It's a couple of inches."

But two minutes after she'd convinced Nate she could be safely independent, Monique lost her balance trying to climb the garage step to the kitchen door, her plastic bag now at her feet instead of under her arm, a can of cat food rolling under the car. She was such an absurd snapshot that she took herself in: legs splayed apart, ass on the floor, heart thrumming hard. The tickle in her throat might be a chuckle or a sob. She wasn't in pain, thank God—she hadn't hit her ankle—but her rebellious body was reminding her that she must watch every step. And maybe that would never go away, even once her cast was gone. Her doctor said she might have a few balance issues with her ankle, and *a few* might be Doctor Talk for *You're fucked.*

This is what getting old feels like. The thought came every hour now, the toll of a clock. This was how it had started with Mom: a slow debilitation until she could only wiggle a finger, trapped in a silent body. Mom's constant falls had alerted them that something was wrong, and *something* turned out to be four inoperable brain tumors.

This is how it starts.

"I've fallen!" Monique called out in her garage in a frail tremolo. "And I can't get up!"

Just like the old lady in the wrist-alert commercial, or whatever the hell it was.

Her laugh was loud enough to bring her cat, Midnight, meowing to the kitchen door.

Every time Monique moved into a new home, she had recurring dreams about imaginary spaces hidden from her sight during her waking hours. Her first apartment had a phantom second kitchen that was always clean, unlike her real one; the Pasadena town house she bought with her Fox money had an imaginary third level with entire rooms in disrepair, including a soaking bathtub black with grime. When she and Nate got the overpriced little place in Santa Monica, the dream wing had at least two upper levels, with narrow staircases and twisted warrens and every inch crammed with papers and keepsakes from the previous owners.

In therapy after her third miscarriage, while Mom was dying and life had turned vicious, a shrink had suggested that the missing rooms represented her past, or unfinished business. But Monique didn't think so. She had reasoned that if she finally bought a house the size her mind was truly longing for, she would stop craving spaces to explore. The atrium with a skylight, library, gym with a mirrored wall, master bedroom worthy of royalty, finished daylight basement the size of an apartment, multiple pantries and cubbies, and backyard woods with its own city of raccoons, possum, rabbits, chipmunks, and screaming bird life would let her stop creating imaginary spaces.

But she'd been wrong: instead, she dreamed the new house

had a second basement one floor *beneath* the real basement, with a narrow stairwell with a flickering light, damp, slick gray walls, loose cobblestone floors, and multiple creaky doors that led nowhere good. She often approached the closed doors, but she had never fully opened one—

And in her dream Monday night before the storm, she was nudging one of the imaginary basement doors an inch wide to a pool of blackness when she heard the crash from downstairs.

She woke with a gasp, her heart a drill in her chest. She would not have heard the sound if she'd been upstairs in the master bedroom, a world away from the basement, but she'd taken to sleeping on a sofa in the atrium now that she couldn't manage the stairs—the spot closest to the half-bathroom between the basement door and the kitchen, where she often washed in the sink. Ordinarily, she liked the atrium and the shadowy tree branches swaying above her. But that night, the overall effect was frightened confusion: *Where am I?* The new house. In Atlanta. Sleeping downstairs. *Mom is gone.* (That was always near, a slap.)

But what had made that crashing sound?

The cat, she told herself, but she felt Midnight leap from his usual sleeping spot between her knees, always skittish and ready for some shit to go down. Midnight's feet pattered as he scurried across the living room to hide in the library. Maybe she'd spooked him when she woke up. Monique listened for new noises to confirm that she hadn't dreamed the crash. She held her breath, waiting. And heard . . . nothing. Even the crickets who had invaded the house in the fall were silent, their population long ago killed off by winter.

If Monique had been more certain of which basement had produced the sound—the real one or her dreamscape—she would have gotten up, rested her bad leg on the knee walker's sure cushion, and propelled herself to the basement door to make sure it was locked. (Of course it was, wasn't it? Why wouldn't it be?) She never decided *not* to get up to check the basement door; she just took so long to decide that sleep fell again.

It wouldn't dawn on her until much later, after the snow, that the sound she'd heard was breaking glass.

Like most people in Atlanta, Monique's Tuesday morning began as usual: for her, the English Breakfast tea she'd adopted when her doctor said to give up coffee, her traditional boiled egg, yogurt, and toast at her desk while she caught up on police shootings and social injustices on Twitter. Next, her struggle to tear away from social injustices on Twitter so she could work on her spec comedy script she'd promised herself she would finish by the time her cast was off. Since she kept seeing local weather tweets, she turned on the TV in the living room so the morning newscast could fill up the downstairs with constant updates and companionship.

Nate wasn't home, so she didn't bother to dress or shower (though she brushed her teeth). She propped herself up on the sofa beneath her blanket with her laptop, not even moving back to her desk in the library to sit upright. She didn't love her library office yet, with its bare shelves and unpacked boxes. Still, it was a good writing day: the kind where you start writing at nine sharp and look up and it's nearly noon. For three hours, she hadn't checked social media, gone to the bathroom, or foraged in the fridge out of boredom.

A small sound made her look up at the atrium skylight, and for the first time she noticed the snow flurries. The flakes were coming down fast, bringing debris from the trees down with them. The snow was quickly collecting, obscuring her view with a growing curtain of whiteness.

Only then did she listen to the newscaster: "... *traffic is building up on all of the major roadways and most businesses are sending their employees home ... And it's a parents' nightmare, as we've been reporting: county public schools were open this morning, but parents, in case you're just tuning in, you're being asked to come pick up your children ...*"

What kind of dumb-ass shit was that? Monique imagined her sister-in-law rushing to get her third-grader, Jason, to school only to then have to turn right back around and pick him up. She was so annoyed on behalf of Denise and Michael that she wheeled herself into the open-air living room that reminded her of one of the sets from *Miami Vice*, sparsely furnished with the décor they had brought from LA, their L-shaped leather sofa and classic black art prints she'd seen as a child on *The Cosby Show*—Ellis Wilson's *Funeral Procession* and Varnette Honeywood's *Generations of Creative Genius*.

The TV screen showed a sea of red brake lights against gray skies. It was only midday, but the roads were clogged like it was rush hour, dusted with ice and snow. Not like the clumps in Chicago when she was at Northwestern, but enough.

"Now, lemme get this straight ..." Monique said aloud, her voice tiny and mouse-like in the expansive room, "y'all keep the schools open, then wait till the snow is *falling* to tell people to come get their kids?"

She had not missed Nate all morning—hadn't even thought about him because sometimes they went a day and a half without checking in during long stretches apart—but she missed him now. When it was time to trash talk, there was no better partner than Nate. She longed to call him, but he was probably just arriving on set in LA, since it was right after nine Pacific time. He'd told her it was best to call before nine or after seven.

Instead, she Facebooked with Denise and was glad to learn that she and Michael had kept Jason home from school in Smyrna, and they had canceled their classes at Spelman and Morehouse. But Denise wrote that she'd gotten texts from several friends who had been stuck in their cars for more than an hour. And school buses full of children were trapped in the gridlock.

My people, my people, Monique typed, and got a frowning emoji in response. This was their running gag in any complaint about Atlanta's leadership, echoing Zora Neale Hurston in *Dust Tracks on a Road*—where Monique had been surprised to learn that *My people! My people!* long predated her generation. Mom used to say it too, and the shoe still fit. Hadn't the school board and mayor seen the same weather forecasts she and Denise had?

Between the white heat of creativity and feeling scandalized by the news, it was nearly three o'clock before Monique realized she hadn't seen her cat all day. Not since the middle of the night. *Not since I heard the crash.*

True, Midnight was a shelter cat who had clearly been through some serious shit back in the day, so sometimes he found places to hide in the house and disappeared for hours. But to miss breakfast? As long as Monique could remember, Midnight had never failed to follow her to the kitchen each morning. The disappearance suddenly felt sinister, so for the first time, Monique wheeled herself to the basement door.

The door was not quite pushed firmly into place. *Unlocked.*

With her foot in a cast, Monique hadn't been down to the basement in a month. And Nate, who worked out in the basement gym religiously, had been gone nearly a week. Her housekeeper Sharmanita only cleaned the basement once a month. Had the door been ajar all this time?

A frigid breeze tickled her sock feet. Cold air was sheeting out from under the door, as if her nightmare basement of cool dripping walls were real, no longer her true-life basement with a thermostat set at seventy degrees. She opened the door. Fourteen steps in brown industrial carpet led down. She flipped on the light: bright fluorescent, no flickering.

"Midnight?" she called.

Except for the TV newscast, her house was all silence.

But now the cold was unmistakable—biting and hard. It was about fifteen degrees outside, and maybe only thirty in her basement stairwell. She exhaled and saw her breath as mist. Of course! The hall was cooler too. How hadn't she noticed it before?

"Midnight—come here, sweetness!"

She prayed for Midnight's thin mew and an appearance on the stairs so she could close and lock the basement door. The heat downstairs must be off; the basement was more Nate's than hers. She and stairs did not get along, and these were steep and awkward. But Monique had no choice. She needed to fight her growing alarm that Midnight had somehow gotten into the basement, or even out of the house. Cats fled when they saw an opening, and she and Nate had agreed Midnight would be an inside cat—less prone to injury or animal attacks. Was Midnight outside freezing in the snow?

Damn—how could she raise a baby if she couldn't take care of a cat?

So Monique tied her terry-cloth robe around her waist—yes, she was still in her robe—and sat on the top stair to begin her slow, careful journey bump, bump, bumping her ass down one step at a time. *At least I have plenty of padding*, she'd joked with Nate when he saw her scooting from upstairs once. It wasn't a good look, but it got the job done.

The stairs descended to the gym and its parquet floor, but beyond the parquet's border on the far end, more industrial carpet led to the basement door's decorative glass—and the door's beveled bottom glass panel was shattered. Glass and snow glittered inside from a gaping hole; the entire bottom third of the door was gone. A few dead leaves had blown inside. No wonder it was so damn cold in the basement.

"Shit," Monique said aloud. Had the wind been strong enough to break the glass?

She hugged the gym wall and hobble-walked until she was close enough to touch the indoor snow that powdered the carpet near the rake and outdoor broom, Nate's tools. She peered outside, and she almost forgot her worry for the cat, childlike with wonder at the snowscape that had once been her backyard; every hill and tree branch drenched in white. Nate had sat outside for hours after they moved in, hypnotized by their private wilderness. Now she was too.

She glanced down for paw prints leading from the door and saw none. Not cat paws, anyway—but there *were* some kind of tracks, almost miniature five-fingered human hands in pairs, as if gnomes had walked inside doing handstands. Walked *inside*, not out.

What the hell . . . ?

Something heavy scurried behind her, nails scrabbling on parquet—

"Midnight?"

—but the fur was gray-white instead of black, the two-foot size too thin, too long, and the tail was like a giant rat's, lashing in sickly, hairy pink across the floor. The tip vanished into the darkness of Nate's screening room, adjacent to the gym.

Monique screamed. Only when she closed her mouth did she realize that she had grabbed the broom, wielding it like a Viking's sword. In her cold, trembling hands, the broom shook as if it weighed fifty pounds. Her body wanted to run, but even her primal terror was practical—*Don't hurt your ankle!*—so she stood fixed, still leaning against the wall for balance, panting and nearly dropping the broom. Adrenaline surged in every vein and pore.

Her clogged mind tried to make sense of it: a possum had broken in to get away from the cold. The old pines and oaks canopying her yard were an ecosystem—the house a late intruder. And this creature was no different than the possums her grandmother had hunted in the woods, stewed for dinner, and tried to coax her to taste. In this way, slowly, Monique talked herself down from the panicked ledge where she was frozen.

"Midnight?" she called again. Did possums attack cats? Was that what had happened?

Still breathing hard, Monique waited to see if the animal would come back out, and she heard her mother's voice: *Mo, he's more afraid of you than you are of him.* Mom, raised in the country in upstate Florida, had been fearless about snakes, lizards, you-name-it, but Monique, raised in suburban air-conditioning, had not inherited that trait. A possum in her house was a core violation of How Things Should Be.

She entertained and dismissed plans to find a way to block the door's hole, or to close the screening room door and trap the possum inside. Instead, keeping her eyes on the screening room doorway, she used the broom as a cane and hopped her way back across the floor until she reached the stairs, where she sat and began her awkward ascent the way she had come down. Going up took far more energy, in part because her heart was racing. Her forearms were sore by the time she reached the top step and reunited with her waiting knee walker to lock the basement door. She checked the lock twice. That done, she stopped holding her breath.

Door locked. On her feet. All was right with the world again—or as right as the world felt anymore, in a new house, in a new life without her mother.

She had left the basement door open while she was downstairs, and the foyer was so cold that she could still see her breath as she huffed toward the safety of the parts of the house she had mastered. Her trip to the basement seemed silly and dangerous now. What if she had hurt herself? She hadn't even brought her phone with her.

She found her cell phone charging in its usual place on the kitchen counter and felt an ache when she saw she hadn't missed a single call. Not her father. Not Nate. No one. Mom would have called her half a dozen times by now to make sure she was all right.

So, the tears came. Nine months after Mom being gone, this was her mourning: no wailing or screaming, just tears of fire at unexpected moments—when she heard Al Green's "Let's Stay Together" or any song by Nina Simone; when she saw footage of 1960s freedom marches like the ones her mother had led. Or when she watched any daughter out with her mother, especially if they were laughing.

Monique did not want to be alone in her house with a possum in a snowstorm. She did not want to be alone, period. Grudgingly, she admitted that Nate had been right to suggest that she go somewhere else. Even Michael's house, with three dogs and an eight-year-old, would have been better. Her broken ankle *did* make her a child again, apparently.

Was it too late? Steady and confident on her knee walker,

Monique rolled to the side foyer window to peek out at her driveway, and her hopes of leaving died. The driveway black-top wasn't visible beneath the snow except for patches of ice. Her van would never climb the steep grade out to the street without snow chains on the tires, and she had never even seen snow chains because *you're not supposed to need fucking snow chains in Atlanta*. Her anger at the snow was so powerful that it throbbed her temples.

Tears threatened to turn to sobs, but Monique tightened her throat to prevent this.

Nothing bad had happened. All she'd suffered was the door's broken glass. Midnight would show up. Midnight probably wasn't in the basement—the door had been unlocked, not open. The possum had *not* killed Midnight.

Nothing is either good or bad, but thinking makes it so. Some smart-ass had left Shakespeare's words taped inside the ladies' room at the hospice, and now Monique could never forget the quote, a singsong nursery rhyme when she had trouble going to sleep. Her sleep was more restless now that she'd stopped taking her painkillers, but she'd thrown out the bottle a week ago, when Nate said he thought she was sleeping too much. And she barely noticed her ankle except when she accidentally bumped it, and even then it wasn't pain, just the oddness of the metal plate and screws buried beneath her skin. Now she longed for the pills, just as she had known she would.

So she had a Corona instead, then another, and as her mood lightened she decided to throw herself a snow party. She turned off the news to stop worrying about the thousands of people still stuck in their cars at sunset after six hours, and who might have to sleep in the frigid cold overnight. Instead, she stuck the salmon she'd scored on sale at the Publix in the oven and caught up on three episodes of *Scandal* she'd missed.

And although she rolled back and forth across the three dried leaves on the kitchen floor for hours, she didn't notice them until she'd crumpled them to bits and they were starting to look like a mess. And wondering about the mess forced her to see an intact brown leaf beside the refrigerator, near the doorway to the hall.

On the way to the basement.

She'd always been a slob deep down, even more so now, so she'd started bringing Sharmanita in twice a week. Sharmanita had come in Monday morning to sweep and mop the floors, before Monique went shopping, so the floor shouldn't be littered with leaves.

Monique wheeled herself through the archway to the hall again, where the air was still ten degrees cooler than the kitchen, and flipped on the light to study the floor. The hall chandelier's speckled light spilled across her shiny wood. Monique was relieved the floor looked the way it should—until her eyes tracked to the basement door, just beyond the threshold, where another dead leaf lay like a waving hand. Daring her to ignore it.

Monique's heart understood before her mind caught up. Her heartbeat was quivering her knees before she bent far over to make sure she wasn't imagining what she saw in the dappled light: beside the leaf, a large crescent of mud—the size of the heel of a footprint. Dried mud. Hours old. Sharmanita had mopped the house, and Monique had driven inside the garage with her groceries—her feet had never touched mud.

She had not brought these leaves into the house. This was not her footprint. This was a boot.

That truth toppled her lies to herself: a possum had not broken the glass. Her mother could have told her that no possum, no matter how cold, could have broken through those thick glass panes on the back door, or *any* of the house's glass. The possum had come in *after* the glass was broken. Which meant . . .

Monique stared up at the spiral staircase that spun its way to the second floor, as impenetrable to her as Rapunzel's castle. At least two thousand square feet lay above her—a master bedroom, the hobby room, the guest room, the junk room. The linen closet. The walk-in closets. Her house had a thousand places to hide.

Monique tried to make her mind a calm, blank slate as she slowly, silently wheeled her knee walker out of the hall. She wheeled across the kitchen to the living room, close to the noise of the TV's Verizon commercial, fumbling in her robe pocket for her cell phone, which she'd kept with her since she'd come back from the basement.

She dialed 9-1-2 and had to backspace with her shaking finger to dial 9-1-1.

Someone is in my house. The words were ready, but instead of a 911 operator, she got a busy signal. She tried a second time, jabbing the numbers. Busy again. She dialed Nate next, and a tiny sob broke free when the same busy signal taunted. *How? How could this be?*

The thin ice holding her mind steady fractured, and she crashed through layers of impossibilities. This could not be happening. Like the six-week sonograms when not once, not twice, but *three* times her babies had not had beating hearts (*This can't be happening*), or when the neurologist clamped his lips like he'd eaten something sour and handed Mom the gray-black slides of her brain, pointing out four "masses" (*This can't be happening*), or when her mother's chest stopped rising with breath. *This can't be happening.*

But it *was* happening. The city was snowbound, thousands of people shivering in cars, children camped at schools, and she was trapped in her house. She could not drive out. She could not walk out. Since the only landline phone was upstairs in the bedroom, she could not call out. Her hurricane days in Miami had taught her that sometimes you couldn't call 911, not just in South Fulton and Bankhead and Lakewood Heights, but in gilded Buckhead too—911 *was* a joke, like Public Enemy preached—because everyone was stuck in their private hell, and no help was coming.

A *thunk* came from upstairs. She might not have heard it if it hadn't been directly above her head. Something heavy hitting the plush carpeting. Something dropped.

She imagined the two of them as mirror images, her holding her breath downstairs while he held his above her—yes, that had been a big boot heel by the door, a man's boot, so *he* was up there calculating, just as she was. Did he know her ankle was broken and she couldn't go upstairs? Had he stood over her on the sofa and watched her as she slept?

Monique had turned a bend past scared, past numb, to a whole new feeling—the feeling her mother had described when she was driving civil rights workers to a meeting in McComb, Mississippi, and they saw a procession of cars without headlights following them in the dark. The new feeling made Monique's mind work fast. She picked up the TV remote and inched the volume down ever so slightly. She didn't dare silence it—oh, he'd be sure she'd heard him then—but she needed more quiet. Could it have been the cat? Could it all be her imagination—

Footsteps. Striding. One. And the next. And the next. Just when she hoped no more footsteps would come, another. No longer on carpet, but on the upstairs hall floor. He had been in the master bedroom, but now he was moving toward the stairs. He had been so quiet before, but he was not quiet now. The footsteps carried the tenor of *oh fuck it*, because he had dropped something heavy and knew she had heard him. He *knew*.

Monique gazed wildly around her, looking for a place to hide. The open floor plan spread before her like a great, un-navigable sea. She looked toward the atrium first, where her pillow and blanket waited, but only children believed in hiding under blankets.

The library! Her desk was too small for her to hide under, too exposed, though the previous owners had considered building a bar nook, so in the corner was a marble counter with three cabinets beneath it. She hadn't unpacked her books, and a few boxes obscured the cabinets from easy sight—but she knew they were there. And empty.

Gently, Monique lowered herself from her knee walker, leaving it in the living room—her decoy. She began to scoot herself across the floor, leveraging for speed with her good foot. The wood was smooth as glass, and in her robe she glided like she had wheels. She kept her hand on the cell phone in her pocket so she would not drop it. She jumped when the phone vibrated with a text message—she didn't glance at it, but she noted the information for a safer time: the phone didn't call out, but she could text. Soon. Very soon.

She did not know she could move so fast.

When she got to the library boxes, she heard a mew. Midnight was way ahead of her—not only hiding behind the boxes, but he had partially opened one of the cabinets where he had probably been hiding since he realized a stranger was in the house. Cats didn't raise an alarm like dogs: they had sense enough to hide, and expected you to have sense too.

Midnight brushed and purred against Monique while she

nudged the largest box as quietly as she could to make her path to the cabinet door. She had to open the door fully to fit her bulk inside, and for a horrifying instant the physics seemed impossible—but a heavy footfall from the foyer stairs was motivation to find a way to pretzel herself inside the black hole, feet first. She somehow climbed in without bumping herself or making a sound, as if she had always known this moment of stealth would come. Midnight bounded into the cramped space beside her.

Yes, the cat had been hiding here. She smelled faint cat piss; Midnight's litter box was upstairs with the stranger. Monique reached through the cabinet door's slat, tugging at the corner of one of the boxes to pull it as close as she could, a silent slide. He would only see boxes—he might not notice the cabinets. Then she closed the cabinet door gently, gently. Not a sound.

Hush, baby, Mom used to say, and her voice rang clear in Monique's head. With the dark cabinet humid from her rapid breathing, her skin slick and dripping with sweat and tears, Monique curled herself the way some part of her remembered, knees to her chin as she lay on her side, eyes closed, caressed by the ever-present *THUMP-THUMP, THUMP-THUMP*.

She was calm. So strangely calm.

Shhhhh. Just hush, baby.

Hush.

TERCEIRA

BY DALLAS HUDGENS

College Park

H e felt the warmth on the side of his face. It spread down his neck and across his arms, then ran through his torso and legs. Sweet, enveloping warmth, like death should feel if it truly is a herald of a brighter realm. And then the dog bit Finney's hand, and he realized he was not ascending but lying facedown on a marble bathroom floor.

The dog scampered away, collar jingling. It was small but had drawn blood from the meat of Finney's left hand. He sat up, realized he was naked, realized the marble floor was heated, and realized he didn't know where he was.

And then he threw up.

After he'd rid himself of the bile and foam, he flushed the toilet and lay back on the floor. The quiet hum of the overhead lights made his nerves twitch, and the warm tiles were no match for the cold sweat and chills that came over him.

He had work to do, a flight to catch. He knew the flight was at 3 o'clock. Oscar always scheduled Finney's runs for Fridays at 3, supposedly the busiest time on the busiest day at the busiest airport in the world: Atlanta's Hartsfield-Jackson. Finney had made four of these trips so far. This was his last, a $10,000 payment the reward. The way it worked, he dressed as a businessman, checked in for his flight to New York, and took a wheeled carry-on duffel bag through security. Oscar provided Finney with an extra phone for each trip, to be destroyed afterward. When Finney reached his departure concourse, he'd use the phone to text a number that had already been entered. That number went to an airline employee with security access, also on Oscar's payroll. The employee would text Finney the location of a men's room inside the concourse where Finney would wait in a specified stall for another text. When it came in, he'd slide the carry-on under the stall door and receive an identical but heavier case in return. Oscar never told him what was inside, but Finney knew it was guns.

Firearms had always been Oscar's moneymaker. MAC-10s, SKs, nine millimeters. They were cheap and easy in Georgia, not so much in New York. The gun laws were that different. Finney boarded his flight with the bag and wedged it in the overhead compartment beside laptop cases and overstuffed duffels. Nobody had a clue. His next stop was a parking lot near LaGuardia where he met up with Oscar's partners and handed off the case. Doing the numbers in his head, he figured Oscar was marking up some of the weapons four to five times above what he was paying for them.

He tried to breathe and take hold of the moment. He couldn't remember if it was supposed to be a three count in and six count out, the other way around, or something completely different. Finally, he stood and went to the sink. He washed the dog bite, splashed his face, and slicked back his hair.

The bathroom opened onto a large bedroom in grays and whites. Light pierced the burlap curtains and hurt Finney's eyes. A naked woman lay facedown on pale sheets, blond hair tumbling onto her small shoulders, a skinny arm hanging off the side of the bed. She snored loudly.

Finney found his clothes draped over a chair. He pulled his phone from the suit jacket's pocket. He'd missed three calls from Oscar, and it was 12:28.

"Fuck."

He couldn't find the second phone, the one he would need at the airport. Then he remembered leaving it in the trunk of his car with the dummy suitcase after picking up both at Oscar's office. The problem was, he couldn't remember where he'd left the car. He had a vague memory of riding with the woman in an SUV the night before. Point A to point B, but he didn't know where either of those points lay.

He called Alana instead of Oscar.

"Where are you?" she asked. "Oscar is pissed."

"I'm not sure."

"What do you mean?"

"I mean, I don't know where I am."

He'd noticed the snoring had stopped. And then he heard the woman's voice, slow and hoarse: "Johns Creek." She was sitting up, snorting coke out of her pineapple keychain pendant. He remembered the pineapple.

"What's Johns Creek?" he asked.

"It's where you are." And then she shrugged. "I mean, unless you were asking in a more existential way."

Alana heard the conversation through the phone. "Jesus, Finney. You're in Alpharetta. Traffic is shit out there. It's going to take you at least an hour to get to the airport. You need to leave right now."

He pulled back the blinds. A man in khaki coveralls was walking the front yard, spraying chemicals on the grass. The driveway was empty except for a black Porsche SUV.

"I don't think I have my car with me."

"You rode home with me," the woman said.

"Call Oscar," Alana said. "Tell him everything is fine, that you overslept. Then find your fucking car and get to the airport."

The woman walked to the bathroom and closed the door. Finney let the curtain fall shut. He sat down in a chair; a dull pain had settled behind his eyes.

"I'm moving after I get paid."

Alana sighed. "Moving where?"

He'd thought of a few places recently, but not a damn one of them would come to mind in the moment. "I don't know. I'm just taking my talents elsewhere."

"You don't need another fuck-up," she said. "This kind of thing never happened before. Now, it's every week."

He couldn't deny it. His long run of dependability had reached a horizon, and he'd found nothing beyond that intersection of caring and wanting except a comfortable ditch. Alana could have made a list of his fuck-ups, all similar and rooted in a need to move far away from his current life. The worst to date was almost missing the previous month's flight to New York. That time, he'd awakened in a hotel room with a gash on his forehead and his wallet, phone, and car keys missing. Oscar had not been happy. And it didn't matter how long they had known each other—Oscar didn't tolerate multiple fuck-ups. Finney knew that missing today's flight was not an option.

The woman walked out of the bathroom, still naked.

"Talk to me," Alana said. "Where's your mind right now?"

Finney ended the call, and the woman asked if everything was okay.

"I need to get to the airport."

She offered to call a car service, but he told her he had to find his own car first. She pulled on a pair of yoga pants and grabbed a sports bra and white sweater from the dresser. "I can drive you back to your car."

Finney put on his pants and shirt. "I don't remember where I left it."

She walked over, picked up his suit jacket, and checked the label on the inside pocket. "Tom Ford," she said. "Looks like I brought home a two-thousand-dollar suit with short-term memory loss."

The suit had belonged to Oscar—last year's collection and no more use to him. He'd given it to Finney to wear on the plane trips, filling out the businessman look he felt was required. Finney didn't see how it mattered but had gone to Oscar's tailor to have it fitted. He was glad he'd done it. That suit could carry half the load in a conversation.

"Where did we meet?" Finney asked.

She ran her fingers through her hair and shook her head. Her hair fell perfectly straight at her shoulders.

"Lenox Square," she said. "But I have no idea where you parked."

Lenox Square shopping mall: a parking lot the size of a war zone. He wouldn't know where to start looking.

Over the woman's shoulder, a framed photograph on the dresser caught his eye—the woman standing beside a smiling man wearing glasses and a leather jacket.

"Is that Usher?"

She glanced back. "I sold him a house."

Finney felt the blow of a missed opportunity. "I almost worked with him once."

He told her he'd briefly run a recording studio in town. She was sitting on the side of the bed, tying an orange pair of Nikes. "You mentioned your short music career last night."

It was short, for damn sure. The studio had been owned by Oscar, a throw-in on one of his land deals. Oscar liked to think of himself as a real estate mogul, not a gun trafficker. He put Finney in charge of the studio, and Finney took some online audio-engineering classes and turned out to be a quick learner on Pro Tools and also pretty good at making trap beats on the studio's old 808. The place was making money and Usher's producer had booked some time, but Oscar shut the place down and sold the building and equipment to put a down payment on a condo that supposedly had the largest balcony in Buckhead. Finney took the 808 home with him, an unspoken *fuck you* to Oscar (as if fucking Oscar's girlfriend Alana wasn't already enough). It was also then that Finney started thinking about taking his talents elsewhere.

Finney's headache wouldn't back off, and his hand was throbbing from the dog bite. He asked the woman if she had any Tylenol in the house. She told him she didn't.

"Has your dog had his shots?"

She looked at him strangely. "I don't have a dog."

He offered his hand as evidence. "What's this?"

"You dropped a fifty-dollar bottle of George T. Stagg bourbon in my kitchen last night. You cut your hand, and then you said, *Put it on my bill.*"

He gave the hand a closer inspection. It was a jagged cut, nothing like teeth marks. "Jesus. I thought I saw a fucking dog in your bathroom."

"Don't take this the wrong way," she said, "but have you ever had a brain scan?" She offered a weary smile, which loosened a few memories from the night before. The expression might have been unspectacular, but it was genuine and as warm as her marble bathroom floor, and it made him recognize why he had wanted to talk to her in the first place.

They'd met at a bar inside the mall. He remembered her telling him about her divorce, two daughters who lived with her ex-husband in Charlotte, about her own mother who'd died last year in a small south Georgia house, surrounded by garbage she couldn't let go of but no visible signs of a family. It took the county's public administrator six months to find Monica and tell her about her mother's death. That was her name, Monica. He remembered that. He remembered all those things she'd told him, but he still couldn't remember where he'd parked the car.

Once they were in Monica's SUV, Finney began to get his bearings. Traffic lights, strip malls, gated subdivisions, new high schools with perfectly groomed baseball fields. They passed a sprawling limestone compound surrounded by parking lots. A pond with a fountain glittered in the sun.

"Is that a college?"

Monica swung her head toward the structure. She was wearing large, square sunglasses. "Kind of the opposite. It's a church."

Finney pulled his own sunglasses halfway down his nose to get a better look. "I honestly thought religion would die before disco."

"Well, maybe disco will be resurrected," she said.

Soon enough, they hit traffic—three lanes in one direction, brake lights and chrome in an unbroken chain. The sun and pollen washed out the colors of the cars and trees. Everything appeared in a cataract haze.

The north Fulton suburbs had never been Finney's stomping grounds. Growing up, he'd lived with his grandmother in College Park, three houses down from the airport fence and one of the east-west runways. His grandmother had taught him to play baseball in the small front yard. They used a bowl of plastic fruit and a sawed-off broomstick. She laid down paper napkins for bases. When the flights would take off and land, they couldn't hear themselves talk, couldn't hear the thwack of the apple flying off the stick. The jets rattled the windows, blew away the napkins, and shook his nerves. He could feel their weight and power. They were relentless, every three to four minutes in the middle of the day. His grandmother never minded the planes. She would tell him the guy in row three was a Braves scout and had liked Finney's swing.

He asked Monica to stop for coffee. As late as he was running, he still needed help with the headache. He hoped it might wake up his memory too. She pulled into a Starbucks and settled in the drive-through lane, which was at least twelve cars deep.

"Just pull into a parking space. I'll go inside."

He asked if she wanted coffee, but she took a pass. "I gave up caffeine." She distractedly rubbed the little pineapple hanging from the steering column as she said it.

Almost all of the parking spaces were empty, and when he got inside, there was no line at the counter. He was back to the car with coffee in less than two minutes. The drive-through line still hadn't budged.

She slung the SUV back on the road and into the slog. It was 12:55 now. Lunch traffic. Oscar called two more times, but Finney waited until he had enough coffee in his system. Finally, he answered and let Oscar open the steam valve a little.

"What the fuck? Where are you?"

"Heading to the airport." Finney made a point to sound as casual as possible.

"I've called you fifteen fucking times. Are you drunk?"

Finney sipped his coffee and let the question circle the airspace. "The battery on my phone is fucked up."

"Are you lying?"

Finney told him he was not lying.

"I can't work with someone I don't trust, and I'm having a hard time trusting you lately."

"I got a slow start this morning. Everything is good now."

"You're slow because all you care about lately is drinking and getting your dick wet."

"I make you money, Oscar. I've always made you money. There's something you can trust."

Oscar laughed. "*I* make the money. Let's be clear about that. You're like a room service waiter and I own the hotel. You can be replaced."

Finney reminded him about the recording studio.

"That fucking studio," Oscar said. "You made two nickels running that thing, and you've had a fucking attitude ever since—like you're some kind of rap mogul."

They were sitting at a traffic light amid a large intersection, a baby superstore on one corner and a funeral home on the other. Cradle-to-grave convenience, although it might take a lifetime by car to get from one corner to the next.

"Don't worry about today, Oscar. I'm gonna make this run, and you're gonna pay me, and then we can go our separate ways. I think it's time." Finney was surprised the declaration had come so easily. He waited for a reply, but it never came. Oscar had ended the call. Finney didn't know if he hadn't heard what he'd said or simply didn't give a shit. He tossed the phone on the dashboard, leaned back in his seat, and let out the breath he'd been holding. "Fuck."

"I know," Monica said. "This traffic is awful."

Finney looked around hopelessly, as if a way out might exist. "I've gotta make this fucking flight."

"Why don't you just book a later one?"

"I can't. I've got a meeting."

"So change the meeting."

It made sense. It's what a normal person in normal circumstances would do. But those people didn't wake up on strange bathroom floors or get attacked by phantom dogs. They didn't work for a man who listened to Nietzsche audio books and kept a full-time tailor on his payroll.

This was actually the second tailor Oscar had employed. He'd set up the first one with a storefront that carried Oscar's favorite brands. The boutique's primary business was laundering money for a Mexican drug cartel that Oscar outfitted with weaponry. A lot of cash went through the store, and the tailor couldn't help himself. He skimmed two hundred grand to buy a yellow diamond and a Maserati for his girlfriend. Alana, who kept Oscar's books, discovered the missing money before the cartel noticed. Oscar had to replace the cash from his own pockets. He sent two of his people to kill the tailor and his girlfriend. No bodies were ever found, just the blood-stained Maserati.

Finney felt a wave of nausea, a chill on the back of his neck. He cracked the window for fresh air and closed his eyes and saw himself and Monica sitting in the pews of a bright sanctuary. He drew in a breath and let the image sit there and actually felt better for it.

Monica blew the horn at the driver in front of them. The drive-through at a fast food restaurant had spilled out into the traffic lane. The driver was the last person in line. Monica blew again, and the man seemed to reassess his lunch options and drove away.

"You ever think about moving?" he asked.

"Well, I'm not married to the house." She glanced over at the side mirror, then whipped the Porsche into a gap in the middle lane. "I bought it out of foreclosure. I'm just looking to make a profit when the market turns."

"Where would you go?"

"Somewhere around here, I guess. I mean, this is where I'm from."

"Me too," he said. "But I'm done with it." He sipped his coffee. "Did we already talk about this?"

She smiled. "No."

She might have come to realize he was damaged; a rescue dog with a nice coat but a head full of spikes. She must have at least regretted not ditching him at the coffee place, but she didn't let on. She seemed to be amused instead.

Traffic moved slowly, and the numbers on the clock would not stop changing—from 1:15 to 1:20 at a single intersection. The only thing that comforted him was her presence. He enjoyed hearing her talk, enjoyed the slow scrape of her voice, like boots shuffling across an old sidewalk, enjoyed the slinky way that she steered with one hand, a soft grip on the wheel, while the other tapped a silent rhythm on her thigh. She was the music in that car.

"You see that office building over there?" she said. "They were filming a scene for a movie back in January. I guess the scene was set in the fall, so they had these guys on cherry pickers gluing orange leaves to the tree limbs."

They were finally getting close to the mall. A traffic light turned red before Monica could shoot under it. She stopped the car, took off her sunglasses, and turned to Finney.

"Those leaves put me in a good mood. I like fall, and it was so damn easy to fool me. I drove by again later, but they had already taken them down."

Finney told her how his grandmother would take him to the airport when he was little. They would spend the afternoon there. She'd buy him a comic book at the newsstand, let him play some pinball in the game room, and then they'd eat a sandwich near the departures-and-arrivals board while they watched people come and go.

"I think we were feeding off something those other people had," he said. "They were going somewhere, and we weren't. But it didn't feel that way. It felt like we were right there in the mix, like something exciting was going to happen."

Monica seemed to understand. "You're right. It's not always a bad thing to fool yourself."

Like the suit, Finney's black Suburban was a hand-me-down from Oscar, who randomly withheld money he owed Finney as a "car payment." Finney had met Oscar when he was fourteen and fighting in Junior Golden Gloves. Oscar had donated money to the Boys and Girls Club for gym equipment and sometimes stopped by in his BMW to watch the kids train. He told Finney he fought like Marvin Hagler, power in both hands, and recruited him for a "pro fight." He wanted Finney to beat the shit out of another fourteen-year-old who had found his old man's .45 under the sofa and accidentally shot Oscar's nephew in the leg with it. Oscar was going to take care of the father himself.

He paid Finney a hundred dollars up front and gave him two tickets to the Hawks-Celtics game at the Omni. Finney jumped the kid as he walked home from school; Oscar waited in his car across the street. Finney knocked the kid down, made him cry, but mostly pulled his punches. He went to the game alone, riding MARTA, selling the extra ticket and buying a Hawks sweatshirt and a bag of cotton candy. Dominique Wilkins scored fifty-four points and the older guy sitting beside Finney bought him a beer that he poured into a Coke cup under his seat. After that night, Finney was on board with anything Oscar asked him to do. It was all in motion.

Finney and Monica started at the front of the mall and cruised the rows of cars. It was a sea of red, black, and gray metal, the sun bouncing off the vehicles hotter than when it landed. Finney kept the window down and pressed the security button on his keychain, hoping to set off his car alarm. After they'd covered the Peachtree Road side, they hit the parking deck along Lenox Road. Thirty minutes in, Finney realized he was fucked. It was two o'clock. Finding the phone and making the three o'clock flight wasn't going to happen. It was time to call Oscar and do some lying.

Monica parked in front of Neiman Marcus. "I'd take you to the airport," she said, "but I have to show a house at four. I need to get home and change."

"You tried. I appreciate it."

She grabbed her phone off the middle console. "What's your number?"

He gave it to her, and she punched it in and called his phone. He felt the vibration in his chest pocket, and then she ended the call.

"Call me when you get back," she said.

He stood on the sidewalk outside the department store as she drove away, finally blending into the sea of cars. It felt like the slow fade of a song that he knew he'd never hear again.

The sun was high, the air sticky, but Finney couldn't shed the suit jacket. It felt like a shield he needed at the moment. He called Oscar and told him the burner phone was broken.

"Shit. Where are you?"

"Airport parking lot. I wanted to check it out before I went inside. It's dead."

"You're having a bad day with phones."

"I think the machines are out to get us."

There was a long pause. Finney paced the sidewalk in front of the doors. A pretty woman in a strapless black dress walked up, and he held the door for her and she smiled.

"All bullshit aside," Oscar said, "are you really at the fucking airport?"

"I'm here. South Economy Lot."

Oscar sighed into the phone. "I'm having a hard time believing you right now."

"I don't know what to tell you. I think my record speaks for itself."

"Your record has been shit lately. And now you're talking about going out on your own. Do you think you're gonna compete with me?"

Apparently, Oscar did give a shit. "I didn't say I was going out on my own. I just think it's time to go somewhere different."

"Where the hell are you gonna go?"

"I don't know."

Finney sat on a bench by the mall's doors. He could hear muffled voices through the phone, Oscar and someone else. Oscar was probably sitting on the side of a lounge chair, squeezed into a tight T-shirt, squinting through his aviators with his little mound of dyed hair tucked under a green Masters hat.

It was possible he was already sending someone else to New York. He had plenty of people willing to do this shit. Finney wasn't the first or last to get free tickets and cash. The problem was that, after so many years, Finney had no résumé and no money in the bank to show for anything he'd done. He needed Oscar's ten grand just so he could get the hell away from it all.

Finally, Oscar came back on the line. "I'll get you another

phone and change the flight. There's no way in hell you'll make the three o'clock. I've gotta call New York and get in touch with my guy at the airport. Just sit there and wait for me to call you back. I'll tell you where to pick up the phone."

Finney told him okay, but he felt no sense of relief. He held the breath he'd just taken and tensed his muscles as if he was bracing for something to fall on him. He expected Oscar to end the call, but he didn't.

"What the hell has happened to you?" Oscar said. "You could always take a punch. I mean, your whole fucking family died from one thing or another, and you kept going. And now, just all of a sudden . . ." His voice trailed off, and before Finney could think of anything to say, Oscar was gone.

Finney didn't have friends as much as acquaintances from the things he liked to do—namely drinking, playing basketball, and listening to music. Corey was the one person he knew who he could call and trust. He was his only business connection outside of Oscar's circle. In fact, Corey had only met Oscar once and thought he was "the uncoolest motherfucker on the planet." Finney told Corey he needed a pint of Woodford, a nine millimeter, and a ride to the airport, one stop along the way. He promised him a thousand dollars, and then he went inside the mall and bought a new wheeled duffel.

Corey pulled up in front of Neiman's, the top off his Jeep Wrangler, his short dreads falling out from under his Hawks cap. Finney tossed the duffel into the backseat and climbed in beside Corey, who immediately handed him the paper sack with the Woodford.

"Nice suit," Corey said. "Gucci?"

"Tom Ford."

Corey nodded in approval. "Look at you." He headed for the exit and traffic.

Finney broke the seal on the bourbon and pulled out the stopper. The smell was sweet, like caramel and tobacco. He forced himself to sip, not gulp like a drunk, but he was all too aware that there was no truth to the ceremony.

"All right," Corey said, "where are we stopping?"

Finney pulled out his phone and made sure the ringer was on. "Just head to the airport. I'm waiting to hear back from Oscar."

Corey stopped at a traffic light and glanced over. "You okay?"

Finney took another sip and let it lie on his tongue for an extra beat. "Last job for Oscar today. I'm moving."

Corey appeared skeptical, but let it drop. "I got what you asked for under the seat."

Finney pulled out the Glock and held it in his hand, getting a feel for the balance as if it was a baseball bat, then tucked it away.

"So, what's gonna happen when we stop?"

"Hopefully, I'm just picking up a phone."

"And if you don't?"

"The day might actually get worse."

Finney was glad when Corey turned on the radio. Most of their conversations had been about music anyway. They met when Corey walked into Oscar's recording studio and asked about working there. Oscar wouldn't okay it, so Finney paid Corey out of his own pocket and some skim from the revenue. Corey knew more about the equipment than Finney and helped book people he knew for studio time. Corey also deejayed and rapped, and Finney had helped him record his first mixtape, which had over sixty thousand downloads on DatPiff.

Finney asked Corey when he was planning to record his follow-up.

"I'm already working on it," Corey said. "Hell, I met Jeezy at Lenox last month. He was doing his clothing line release. He knew that song we recorded, the one with the big bounce and the wah-wah."

Finney couldn't even be mad at Oscar for the lost opportunity with the studio. He should have moved on then, when he had a little money in his pocket. That's what Corey had done—moved on, moved forward. A lot of people did that. They got on planes and didn't come back. Finney could have done it too. They had always been right there above his head, reminding him of this.

"I'm going to the studio tomorrow night," Corey said. "You back then?"

Finney had no answer. Oscar's word meant nothing. Now that he thought Finney might be planning to compete against him, there was a chance that he had plans for Finney along the same lines as the tailor.

The interstate was moving well, and Corey punched the gas in the left-hand lane. Oscar finally called. Finney ducked low to buffer the wind noise.

"Where the hell are you? Sounds like an airplane engine."

"I'm just driving around. I've got the window down."

Oscar gave him the details for picking up the new phone. There was an access road off Camp Creek Parkway, near the airport. The road sat between two satellite parking lots. It led to a shut-down construction site. Oscar said the owner had liens up to his ass. Oscar wanted to buy the land and put a hotel on it. Finney was supposed to drive to the site. Oscar was sending someone to meet him with a new phone.

"Who is it?"

"He works for me. Don't worry about it."

"Why the construction site?"

"Every public area has cameras now. This place doesn't have cameras. These are things I have to think about."

Oscar said he'd rebooked him on the 5:45 flight to LaGuardia. There would be no trouble making that one. In fact, traffic was moving so well it made Finney uneasy, as if he was rushing toward some sort of impact. After the phone call, he made himself stop up the bottle of bourbon. He needed to maintain some balance between steady nerves and clear thinking. He tried to focus on the music, the beat coming out of the car speakers, the lyrics winding their way into and around the rhythm.

In order to get to Camp Creek Parkway from I-85, you had to take the airport exit. Camp Creek was the last offshoot before the parking lots, car rental center, and terminal. One minute you were headed toward the terminal, and the next you weren't. The road was lined with satellite airport lots, industrial buildings, and budget hotels. With the top down, Finney could see and feel the planes flying overhead—just like old times.

Corey's GPS found the access road, and he made the turn in between the two satellite lots. Beyond the parking lots was a cluster of pine trees and then the construction site, a big scar of red dirt, partially excavated, with a chain-link fence around it. A white Land Rover was parked at the fence's main gate. Corey slowed the Jeep as they approached it.

Finney motioned for Corey to stop about twenty yards short of the other vehicle. He'd already tucked the nine into the back of his suit pants. "If anything happens, just get the fuck out of here."

Corey set his jaw. "No. I got you, partner."

"I appreciate it. But if this goes bad, it's on me."

Corey's determination seemed to wane. "All right."

Finney got out and walked toward the Land Rover. Dust circled the cuffs of his pants, and sweat ran down his back and puddled around the Glock tucked into his waist. The Land Rover's driver's-side door opened slowly, and Finney stopped. A younger man stepped out, wearing a red snapback with an odd but familiar W on the front. At first, Finney thought it was a Walgreens hat. Then he realized it was the Washington Nationals. They stood staring at each other.

"I got your phone," the guy said.

Another plane flew over, nose tilted upward, engines screaming. They both considered the burly chunk of metal until the noise died down.

"You gonna come get it?"

Finney stood still. "Why don't you just toss it here."

The younger man smiled. "I don't think you trust me."

"Just being careful."

"We're on the same team, though."

Finney pointed to the hat. "I'm a Braves fan."

Even with the hat fixed low on the man's forehead, Finney could read his face. Two-thirds motivation and one-third fear. It was a dangerous mix when Oscar was stirring the drink.

The door to the Land Rover was still open, and the courier reached inside. Finney was startled, realizing the ten or so yards between them didn't mean shit if he came out shooting. He was ready to reach back for the nine, but the guy came out holding a phone in his hand. "Got the contact number programmed in. I guess you know what to do."

Finney slowly let go of his breath. "Yeah, I know what to do."

But the younger man still wasn't ready to give up the

phone. "So you're the man that makes the trips, huh? The bag man wearing the sharp suit."

Finney confirmed that he was the one making the deliveries.

"Oscar's got me doing the same route. On the damn bus."

"Well, today's my last flight. Maybe you can pick up the frequent flier miles."

The guy smirked. "So that's it, huh? You're gonna make me throw it to you?"

"Yeah. I'm gonna make you throw it to me."

The other man stalled for a moment, looked down and shook his head, then pitched the phone underhanded with a high arc. At first, Finney thought he'd done it just to be an asshole. But as he was tracking the phone through the air, he realized the guy was reaching into the car again. Instead of catching the phone, Finney pulled out the Glock.

He got off two shots before the guy started squeezing rounds from a MAC-10, the thrum of the automatic weapon drowning out any lingering airplane noise. Finney hit the Land Rover with his first shot and caught the shooter in the thigh with the second. After that, a spray from the MAC-10 danced across his midsection. There was no pain, yet Finney couldn't control his arm. He tried to raise the Glock to fire again, but he could barely feel his hand. Meanwhile, the MAC had gone silent. Oscar's guy was lying on his side, holding his leg. His jeans were already dark with blood.

Finney felt nothing but immediate exhaustion. His legs turned to liquid. He sat down on the hard ground and moved the Glock to his left hand. Oscar's guy pushed himself up to a sitting position, leaned back against the front tire, and started spraying ammo again. Finney raised the Glock with his less-dominant hand. His first shot was high, the second in the dirt. He finally took his time and zeroed in on the hat. Another burst of fire caught Finney in the collar bone and neck before he could squeeze the trigger, but he kept his focus. He didn't feel anything. He fired the Glock and hit the guy just below his eye. His head bounced back like he'd taken a left hook, then he dropped the MAC and fell forward, the red hat tumbling to the ground.

Finney's shirt was soaked. At first he thought it was sweat. Then he saw the blood. He lay back on the hard dirt. It was warm and smelled like chalk. The sky above him was pale and dirty. He felt a hand on his shoulder. It was Corey. "What do you want me to do?"

Finney couldn't speak. He managed to pull his phone out of the jacket pocket and handed it to Corey. Corey held the phone and took a long look at the blood on Finney's shirt and jacket. "Okay," he said. "You're gonna be all right."

Corey stood up and made the call: two men shot. He gave the address from his GPS. He was still talking when the next plane flew over, this one on approach, wheels down, sinking more than descending, the steel belly right above Finney's face. And that's when it came back to him: Terceira in the Azores. That's where he had planned to go. For years, the postcard had sat on his grandmother's mantel, sent by her brother who'd visited when he was in the air force. The sun-bleached photo captured a volcanic cone sloping down to a green valley and blue ocean. On the back of the card, his uncle mentioned surfing and seeing a bullfight in the street. It had always felt so far away as to be untouchable, far from hospital rooms and prisons and phones that rang with bad news.

And now he was at peace with the fact that he would never go there, that his grandmother never made it either, that his uncle died of lung cancer at Grady Hospital, gasping for breath with an oxygen mask over his face, still scribbling requests for a cigarette on scraps of paper. Terceira didn't save him or anyone else. But it made Finney feel better in that moment. It granted the lumbering metal above his head a quiet music, as if someone was touching the strings of a tiny, delicate instrument. The noise and power didn't rattle him. It felt like an embrace, a welcome home.

THE PRISONER

BY BRANDON MASSEY

Grant Park

On his morning jog through the neighborhood—his first as a free man after eleven years behind bars—Payne saw a Lexus SUV with a broken side window, glass shards littering the pavement like spilled beads.

He slowed for a beat, and in one measured glance he had absorbed all of the details. *Smash-and-grab*, the news called them these days. A crew of teenage boys surely responsible. The Lexus, a Georgia Tech sticker on the bumper, was parked in the driveway of a restored Craftsman bungalow, soft light glowing through the windows at the predawn hour. The no doubt clueless residents were going to be unpleasantly surprised when they came out to go to work. They would feel safe no longer, if they ever had, and why should they? The boys who'd done this were going to strike again. They always did.

Big hands tightening into fists, Payne resumed his pace.

Out of the joint for less than a week, and already he'd been present at the scene of a crime. Would that qualify as recidivism? Did he need to notify his parole officer?

He cracked a smile as the cold October air skirled down Cherokee Avenue, chilling his skin through his sweatshirt and tearing leaves from old elms that towered over equally old homes, Victorians and Craftsmans in various stages of repair. Streetlamps still glowed, and Zoo Atlanta lay to the east, shuttered and dark, but it required little for Payne to imagine all those animals locked in cages, living out the balance of their lives in captivity. He'd been one of them not long ago.

He saw a jogger heading in the opposite direction on the other side of the street. A young blond woman clad in a neon-green jacket and black leggings. She glanced his way but only smiled blandly, unconcerned at the sight of a tall, muscular, bald-headed black man running in her neighborhood. She might have even waved.

Damn, it felt good to be in the outside world again.

He attacked the last leg of his run with renewed vigor. At Sydney Street, he hung a left. He didn't slow until he neared his brother's home.

The Queen Anne Victorian stood at the intersection of Oakland Avenue and Sydney. The house was enormous, but it had seen better days. It was over a hundred years old, and might have continued to deteriorate had his baby brother and his boyfriend not purchased it two years ago and embarked on their restoration project.

It had become Payne's project too. One of the conditions of his stay: he had to earn his keep, and that meant putting his skilled hands to use in a productive endeavor.

His brother Joseph was in the kitchen. The remodeled kitchen was all stainless steel appliances and granite surfaces, with copper pots dangling from a row of hooks. Sitting on a barstool at the island, Joseph sipped coffee and read news on an iPad. He was still in his sleepwear of Morehouse T-shirt and lounge pants.

"Morning," Joseph grumbled. Unlike Payne, he'd never been an early riser. Payne had spent much of their youth dragging Joseph out of bed to ensure he got to school on time.

"Morning, bro. Someone busted out a car window around the corner."

"Really?" Joseph looked up, brows furrowed. "Again?"

"It's happened before?" Payne bit into an apple.

"A month ago. Then it happened again, maybe two weeks after that."

"A crew of local boys learning their trade." Payne chewed slowly, savoring the taste of fresh fruit. He hadn't enjoyed fresh fruit in many years. "Soon, they'll graduate to assault."

"I hope not." Joseph winced. "Where was the car parked?"

Payne gave him a thumbnail description of the residence, and recited the address, make and model of the vehicle, and the license plate number.

"Give me a break." Cal entered the kitchen. "You remember all those details? What are you, like an idiot savant?"

"I notice things." Payne shrugged.

Cal sneered. He was dressed for the season in a crisp orange dress shirt and black slacks. Hustling past Payne in a swirl of cologne, he immediately started organizing items on the counter. He had a serious case of OCD when it came to keeping the house clean.

Cal was an attorney. He owned a tax law firm downtown. Ever since an overzealous prosecutor had worked overtime to send him to prison, Payne hadn't trusted lawyers of any stripe.

"My brother has an eidetic memory," Joseph said. "Always has."

"Doubtful." Cal made a sour expression. "Regardless, I'm not shocked to hear about yet another vehicle break-in. We've got a criminal element preying on this neighborhood."

"All you fine, upwardly mobile folks moving back into the city?" Payne shook his head. "They're crimes of opportunity. Kids have too much time on their hands and not enough guidance."

"I ought to call the mayor." Cal poured orange juice into a tumbler, and used the juice to chase down a set of multicolored pills. He shivered from head to toe, as if suddenly rejuvenated by the ingestion of whatever substances he had taken. "Yes, yes. I'll tell you exactly what we need, my little jailbird friend. We need a more visible police presence to deter these people."

"Kids need their daddies around," Payne said.

"My daddy wasn't there for me emotionally and I didn't turn out to be a thug, so please spare me the simplistic pop psychology." Cal checked his watch. "Damn it all to hell, I'm going to be late. Joey, are you riding in with me, sweetie?"

"Yeah, let me get dressed right quick." Joseph left the kitchen.

As soon as Joseph was out of earshot, Cal gave Payne a narrow-eyed glare. Payne was five inches taller than Cal and had him by probably forty pounds of muscle, but Cal had the confidence that came from inherited wealth and privilege.

"The only reason I'm allowing you to stay here is because your brother vouched for you," Cal said in a low voice. "Don't screw it up, or I'll be on the phone with your parole officer in thirty seconds flat."

"Right," Payne said.

"I expect you'll make some progress on the veranda today." Cal grinned, displaying perfect white teeth, but it was a smile without warmth. "Chop chop, *bro*."

Later that morning, Payne was outside applying a fresh coat of paint to the pine veranda railing when he noticed the kid at the Craftsman bungalow across the street. Brown-skinned, he was maybe sixteen, tall and lanky, dipped in Under Armour gear from crown to sole. He lounged on a swinging bench on the front porch while diddling on a cell phone as large as his head, a basketball wedged between his feet.

Earlier, Payne had watched a well-heeled white couple in their forties leave the house and drive away in their respective electric vehicles. The kid had come out sometime later, yawning and shuffling about in his five-hundred-dollar apparel as if he didn't have a care in the world.

Adopted, Payne thought. *Spoiled too. Why isn't he at school?*

The kid appeared to notice him now too. Payne caught him sneaking looks at him as he ran the paintbrush across the railing.

After Payne finished with the veranda, he set aside the brush and wiped his hands clean on a rag. He grabbed his canteen of ice water and walked across the street, stopping at the flagstone stairway that led to the Craftsman's porch.

The kid barely glanced at him. "Yeah?"

"What's up, young buck? I'm Payne. I'm your new neighbor."

"All right, then." The kid focused back on his phone.

Payne sipped his ice water. "You got a name?"

"Malcolm." Still, the kid didn't make eye contact.

"That's a good name. I've read *The Autography of Malcolm X* at least ten times. All I did in the joint was read, exercise, and work my trade."

That revelation got the boy's attention. He stared at Payne with something approaching genuine interest. "Word?" he said.

Payne nodded. "Eleven years at Hancock State Prison. Got paroled last week."

"Damn," Malcolm said. "What were you in for?"

"Could tell you, but I'd have to kill you." Payne smiled, but the kid's eyes grew large, as if he believed Payne actually might make good on his threat.

"I mean, if it's private or whatever, you ain't gotta tell me," Malcolm said. "I know how it is."

"How old are you? It's Tuesday morning and it's not a holiday. Young buck like you, I figure you should be in school."

"School? Yeah, right." Malcolm chuckled and stretched. He had an impressive wingspan, was probably a terror on the basketball court. "Ain't got time for no school, man. They ain't got nothing to teach me that I ain't already learned in the streets."

"Your folks agree with that?"

"Nah, but whatever. I got big plans." Malcolm grinned. "Hey, you live with those gay dudes, right?"

"I live with my baby brother and his partner."

"Oh, okay. I guess you saw a lot of that in prison, huh?"

"I saw a lot of things in the joint. Know what I saw when I was out running this morning?"

Malcolm shrugged.

"Someone busted out the window of a Lexus truck parked around the corner on Cherokee, right across the street from the park."

"So?" Malcolm muttered, but cast his gaze downward to his phone.

Payne took another sip of his water. A grumbling engine approached, hip-hop music booming like thunderclaps from the speakers. Payne turned to see a black Cadillac Escalade with tinted windows and gleaming chrome rims glide up in front of the house.

The driver's-side window lowered. A pimple-faced kid struggling to cultivate a goatee was behind the wheel. He glared at Payne, an expression that would have been comical had it not been so intense, but Payne merely watched him. There was another teenager in the truck too, talking on a cell phone.

"Time to put in that work, homie." Malcolm rose from the bench. He tucked the basketball underneath his arm and ambled down the steps. He was as tall as Payne, and Payne was six three, but the kid was skinny as a drink of water, as Payne's nana liked to say.

"You shoot rock?" Payne asked. "One of these days, I'll have to drag you up and down the court."

"Keep dreaming, old head," Malcolm said. "We'll do that soon, though."

He climbed into the backseat of the Escalade, and the kids rumbled away down the road.

Payne headed to a FedEx store on Memorial Drive, across the street from Oakland Cemetery. He rode his bicycle there; a used road bike that Joseph had given him. Payne had nearly wiped out the first time he'd climbed on it. There were no bicycles in prison and he was badly out of practice.

Navigating the dense traffic around the neighborhood was a challenge too. Cars moved so fast, much faster than he remembered, and no one seemed to be paying attention to the road—most of the people he spotted behind the wheel were looking at their cell phones. He wondered if they were using self-driving cars already; otherwise their inattention to where they were going made no sense. Twice, he narrowly avoided getting struck by a distracted driver.

At the print shop, he had three hundred copies of his flyer printed: *Payne-Free Handyman Services*. Joseph, a part-time graphic artist, had designed the flyer and offered to make copies too, but Payne had insisted on doing it on his own. A man could accept only so much charity before he lost all his initiative.

A pretty, chocolate-skinned sister with a button nose, copper-brown eyes, and braids showed him how to operate the copy machine. Her nametag read, *Lisa*. Their fingers touched briefly on the machine's touch-screen display, which literally gave Payne a delicious shiver down his back.

Damn, if this woman only knew how long it's been since I touched a female . . .

"What kind of stuff can you fix?" she asked him, studying one of his flyers.

"Just about anything." He added: "Officially, I'm HVAC certified, but I can repair and install all kinds of things."

"Hmm, can I keep one of these? I might need to call you to check out my washing machine. It's been acting up."

The way she looked at him, her gaze locked on his, made him wonder if she had him in mind to fix more than her washing machine. But he was too out of practice with the mating dance to be sure.

"You can call me whenever you want," he said. "I work a lot, but I'll make the time."

She smiled, so he must have said the right thing.

Payne ditched the bike at home to walk the neighborhood by foot and distribute the flyers. Just about everyone's mailbox was affixed to the front of their house, so he settled for slipping his flyers underneath the windshield wipers of parked cars. He had walked perhaps one block when an Atlanta Police Department cruiser pulled up beside him.

Tension coiled like an angry snake in his gut. He was prepared for this, but the predictability of it all . . . well, some things never changed.

"Excuse me, sir," the police officer said through the lowered window. "You live around here?"

Stopping midstride, Payne pressed his lips together. *Be cool.* "Yes, officer." Payne crisply offered his address.

"What're you passing out there? Advertisements?"

"I run a business. I provide handyman services. Would you like a flyer?"

The cop grunted. "Are you licensed?"

"I'm HVAC certified, sir."

"Don't be a smart-ass. You got a license to be distributing business advertisements?"

"I didn't realize a license was necessary to advertise a local business."

"I don't like your attitude." The cop then barked into his walkie-talkie, got out of the car. He swaggered to the sidewalk. He was nearly as big as Payne, and he had the badge and the gun.

Payne had fought a corrections officer once, a notorious sadist determined to break Payne's even-tempered demeanor. It was the last time the officer had attempted to assault a prisoner.

As the cop advanced, Payne braced himself for anything.

"Hey, Tommy, this gentleman, he's okay," someone said.

A stoop-shouldered, white-haired guy approached, trailed by an English bulldog on a red leash. The man wore a checkered shirt, baggy jeans held up by suspenders, and dusty work boots. A set of bifocals dangled from a loop around his neck.

The cop halted. "You know this guy, Judge Mackey?"

Payne blinked at the older man. *Judge?*

"He lives on Sydney," the old man said. "I see him outside working all the time. He's okay."

"Fine." The cop nodded stiffly, withdrew to his cruiser. "Have a nice day, gentlemen."

As the officer headed off, Payne released a deep breath. "Thanks for that." He offered his hand to the older man. "I'm Payne."

"Name's Dave Mackey." The man's grip was dry and firm—he had some of the biggest hands Payne had ever seen, like shovel blades. He slipped on his bifocals, and his blue-eyed gaze sharpened. "Tommy's a good kid, but he can be a little too eager."

The bulldog waddled up to Payne and sniffed his paint-splattered boots. He grunted, as if offering his approval.

"Quincy says you're okay too." Dave grinned. "Listen, can you help me with something? Won't take but a few minutes. I could use a fella with a strong back."

Dave lived with his dog and his wife of fifty-three years in a stately Victorian on Cherokee Avenue, directly across the street from Grant Park, on a steeply sloped plot of land. With its perch atop the hill and picturesque view of the park, the residence dominated part of the historic district's most prized real estate.

A red Ford F-150 pickup was parked in the driveway; about a dozen bags of pine bark mulch were stacked in the truck's flatbed.

Payne noticed that a wooden carport stood at the head of the driveway too. A vehicle was parked underneath, completely concealed by an olive-green cover. Whatever was there, Payne figured it was valuable.

"Listen—usually, I'd do this myself," Dave lowered the truck's gate, "but my arthritis is acting like a mean bastard today."

Payne unloaded the mulch and placed the bags at spots throughout the front and side yard, as Dave instructed. Dave thanked him and said he could stop there, but Payne requested his shovel.

"My nana used to say, if you're gonna leave a job unfinished, you might as well shouldn't have started it," Payne said.

He split open each bag with the shovel and carefully spread the mulch in the designated areas around the elm trees, porch, and shrubbery. It took nearly an hour to complete the job, but to Payne, the time passed quickly. One of his favorite activities during his incarceration was to pull the plum shifts on the road detail crew, breathing fresh air and savoring the sunshine on his face and feeling, if only for a short while, like a free man.

"This looks great," Dave said, fists on his waist as he surveyed the yard. "How much do I owe you?"

"You got me out of a tight spot with that policeman. I'd say we're square."

"Fair enough." Dave nodded. "You drink beer? I got some cold Bud in the fridge."

"That sounds good."

Beer cans in hand, the two men settled on Adirondack chairs that had been arranged on the veranda. Quincy made himself comfortable between Dave's feet.

For a long moment, the men sat quietly, while the sounds of the neighborhood went on around them. Cars whizzing to and fro; the snapping of a nail gun as someone worked on a house; an ambulance warbling in the distance. The American flag in the front yard rippled in the autumn breeze.

"What brought you to this neck of the woods?" Dave finally asked. "You haven't lived here long. What's it been, a week?"

"You don't miss a thing, do you?" Payne took a sip of beer. He almost coughed at the bitterness of the brew; it was his first drink in eleven years. "Yeah, a little over a week."

"I've been walking these old sidewalks around here every

day for four decades. I don't need to watch the news to know what's going on. You live with the dinks."

"The what?"

"Dinks. Means dual income, no kids."

"Oh, yeah. Right."

"Our neighborhood's full of them. They're renovating all the old homes. I'm glad to see it, for the most part. Some of these houses had gone to shit. Only thing I don't like is my property taxes have hit the ceiling, but, well, that's the price of progress, I guess."

"My brother offered me a place to stay," Payne said. "Meanwhile, I'm helping them renovate their house. I'm also working on starting my own thing too—I've always been good with my hands."

"There's always work for a man good with his hands." Dave took a sip of his beer, burped. "You got any training?"

"HVAC is my specialty, but I'm versatile."

A sudden coughing fit wracked Dave. It was the deep, bone-rattling cough of a long-time smoker. As the man bent forward, hacking, Payne noticed the gold necklace dangling from his neck: from it hung a pendant shaped like a judge's gavel.

I can't believe it, barely a week out of the joint and I'm drinking beer at a judge's house, Payne thought, and almost felt dizzy at the idea.

When the coughing episode finally passed, Dave wiped his lips with a checkered handkerchief. "Listen, I oughta have you take a look at my furnace," he said. "I got a guy who comes out twice a year, in spring for the AC and in fall for the furnace, and he always finds some new way to charge me more money. I've been telling Edna we've got to find someone else before the guy eats up my whole pension check."

"Well, I'm your man," Payne said, and handed him a flyer.

Dave skimmed the paper, nodded. "I'll give you a call, then. I'll pass the word around to my neighbors too. My word carries some weight here."

"I'd appreciate that, sir."

Lisa, the cute lady from the print shop, called Payne a week later. She lived with her mother in a town house on Boulevard. Their washing machine had gone on the fritz and required a new fuse. Payne ran out to Home Depot, came back, and repaired the appliance in less than an hour.

"It's so nice to know a man who can fix things," she said as he was wrapping up. "My daddy was like that. Anytime something in the house was broken, he found a way to put it back together."

"I'm glad I could help you." He tried to keep from appraising her figure, which was even more comely outside of her work uniform. He decided to take a chance. "Do you like coffee?"

"I do." She smiled. "Why?"

"There's a coffee shop around the corner. I figure sometime soon, you and I can meet there and get to know each other a little better."

"I'd like that."

Payne could barely suppress his grin as he pedaled his bicycle back home. Joseph was already there. He had the flatscreen television in the living room tuned to the evening news.

"There was an armed robbery in the neighborhood last night," Joseph said. "Over on Milledge, three guys in Halloween masks held up a woman at gunpoint. They snatched her purse and pistol-whipped her."

"Shit," Payne said.

* * *

Two days later, on a Saturday afternoon that felt like summer, Payne was on a ladder, cleaning leaves out of the gutters on their house, when he saw Malcolm wander outdoors. For a teenager who'd dropped out of school, he was rarely home—though Payne had a good theory about what the kid spent his time doing all day.

"Yo, young buck!" Payne shouted. "You up for learning how to shoot that rock?"

"Whatever, dude," Malcolm called back, but he picked up his basketball and sauntered across the street. "Where you wanna go?"

They found an outdoor basketball court at a nearby school. Payne had worried that it might be crowded, but there was no one there. Did teenagers play outside anymore?

"Let's do this." Malcolm peeled off his jacket. He wore a Warriors throwback jersey underneath, his bare, noodle-thin arms exposed.

"You need to hit the gym, son." Payne stripped down to his own T-shirt. He flexed his thick, muscled arms.

"You been hittin' them prison weights," Malcolm said. "Don't matter, though, I'm still gonna school you."

They played a game of twenty-one. He had assumed the kid was good, but he was better than Payne had thought, with a vicious crossover move and a silky jumper that he could rain down from damn near twenty-five feet. He beat Payne in the first game, twenty-one to eight, and he was barely sweating.

Payne bent over at midcourt, breathing hard.

"You need some oxygen?" Malcolm grinned.

Payne straightened. "Let's go again."

The next game was tighter. Payne had determined Malcolm's pattern and how to cut it off. And Malcolm couldn't stop him from muscling close to the rim. Payne won by nine.

"Tiebreaker, man," Malcolm said, face flushed.

"Tell me what you know about the car break-ins," Payne said. "And the stick-up of that white woman the other night."

"You think I had something to do with that?" Malcolm scowled. "You a snitch or something?"

"Just concerned. Mostly about you. Your future."

"What the fuck do you care about my future? You ain't my daddy." Malcolm flung the ball at Payne, who caught it. "Play the game, old man."

The last game was closely contested. Malcolm unveiled some new tricks; Payne switched his strategy too. They grunted and cursed, sneakers slapping against pavement, while the October sun baked the sweat on their skin and the occasional breeze sent dead leaves swirling across the court.

Payne won the game by one point, on a twenty-foot bank shot.

"Fuck!" Nostrils flaring, Malcolm threw the ball against a fence, veins standing out on his neck, and in that one instant, Payne got a glimpse at the kind of errant violence of which the boy was capable.

Payne retrieved the ball. He wiped perspiration from his brow with the tail of his shirt, flipped the ball back to the kid.

"You know, you could be All-State," Payne said. "If you were in school."

"Man, whatever. Don't try to pump up my ego after you won and shit."

"Just stating the truth. I was All-State in '98."

"Damn, no wonder." Malcolm shook his head. "You didn't play in college?"

"Played a year at Georgia Tech before I got kicked out."

"Kicked out for what?"

"Being dumb, but thinking I was smarter than everyone." Payne pulled on his sweatshirt. "I wasted my potential. It's taken me almost twenty years to get back on the right track."

Malcolm laughed. "Right track? You ain't got shit. You ride around town on a damn bike and live with them gay dudes."

Payne merely smiled. "All a matter of perception, young buck. What's your story?"

"Hell you mean?" Malcolm lobbed a shot at the basket. "I ain't got no story."

"You're adopted. Your folks give you a wide berth since you've apparently dropped out of school, and they aren't sweating you about it too much."

"What the fuck they gonna do?" Malcolm cracked a smile. "They can't make me do shit. We ain't blood."

"How old were you when they adopted you?"

"Shit, like just a baby, man." Malcolm deftly dribbled the ball between his legs. "I don't even remember my birth mom or nothing."

"Or your father."

"Fuck you think?" Malcolm glared at him, shot the ball. "I ain't got no real family."

"I'm sorry, Malcolm," Payne said. "But it sounds like your folks have been taking good care of you. That's got to count for something."

Malcolm shrugged. "What about you, old head? What's *your* story?"

Contemplating his words, Payne looked past the kid and off into the distance. In a grassy field beside the school, a little boy and his father were flying a kite, bright red streamers fluttering against pure blue sky. "I took some people's lives," he said quietly.

"Oh shit." Malcolm stopped middribble. "You popped more than one?"

"Four. My sentence was for the one the state could prove to a jury."

Malcolm sat on top of the basketball as if all the strength had drained out of his legs. Thin arms crossed over his knees, he looked up at Payne, and Payne imagined how this boy might have been at a much younger age, before life had clouded his vision. He regretted that he'd told him the truth.

But as his nana had liked to say, you can't unring the bell.

"They owed me money," Payne said. "Back in those days, the way I rolled . . . well, that was unforgivable."

Malcolm had lowered his gaze to the asphalt. Payne started walking back home. After a moment's hesitation, Malcolm got up and followed.

On the night of Halloween, while neighborhood kids were trick-or-treating, Payne was in the cellar of Dave's house servicing the furnace. Dave stood nearby and watched him; his wife Edna was upstairs passing out candy to the visiting children.

Before taking him into the basement, Dave had revealed the vehicle that he kept covered and stored underneath his carport. It was a 1965 Corvette Stingray coupe, skyblue and in stellar condition. He drove it only a couple times a month, and only on Sundays.

The finished basement was as meticulously maintained as the rest of the house, and a virtual museum to Dave's longtime interest in classic Corvettes. Miniature models of the sports car stood in display cases, and photos of his annual visits to the Corvette plant in Bowling Green, Kentucky, adorned the brick walls.

Although the Victorian was generations old, a new furnace had been installed fifteen years ago, much to Payne's relief. He had a lot of experience working on natural gas systems such as this one. After shutting off the furnace, he removed the combustion chamber door and burner cover.

"Looks to be in fine condition," Payne said. "I'll check out the flames and then clean the burners."

"Saw you hanging out with that teenage kid a few days back." Dave sipped beer from a can in an Atlanta Braves koozie. "Looked like you two were chattin' it up real good."

"Man, you really don't miss any details, do you?"

"You know what they say, the king has a thousand eyes." Dave grinned.

The subtle shift in the man's tone made Payne pause in his labors. He lowered his hand to the toolbox, wrapped his fingers around the Phillips screwdriver.

"I want to know what you've been talking to my boy about." Dave still held the beer, but his other hand had slid into the pocket of his denim overalls. "He's beginning to show some reluctance to carry out his responsibilities."

"What's going on here?" Payne asked. "I just came by to work on your furnace, man."

"Do you think I don't know your history?" Dave's ice-blue eyes, nested within the bifocals, were slitted like a snake's. "I'm seventy-eight-years old and ten years retired from the bench, but I haven't lost a step, friend. I pulled your file the first day I saw you."

"The cop who questioned me . . ."

"Works for me, of course. Malcolm works for me. I'm bringing him along slow, letting him and the boys work their way up the chain, doing small muscle jobs for me here and there. Till you showed up trying to play daddy. I can be okay with that, but on one condition."

Payne tensed, grip still on the screwdriver. "What's that?"

"You've gotta work for me too." Dave chuckled. "Hey, in a sense, you already are, right? But I want to bring you into my business."

"I thought your business was sitting on the bench passing judgment, probably putting away kids like Malcolm for life."

"I'm a distributor at heart. I get medicines of choice into the hands of a select clientele of upscale individuals, like many of our fine residents here in Grant Park. Hydrocodone, Valium, Ritalin. Other things. Whatever the customers want. Sometimes to keep the operation running smoothly, I need to send, shall we say, *stronger* messages to various parties at different points in the chain."

"You want me for enforcement."

"Like I said before, there's always work for a man good with his hands. You're skilled with a knife from what I hear, not afraid to get dirty." Dave grinned, a joyless expression. "You want to hang out with the kid, you work for me. Actually, that'll be a bonus, 'cause you'll work for me whether you want to or not. I've got your parole officer on speed dial, friend."

Still a prisoner, Payne thought. *What kind of fool was I to think I could be set free from the past?*

Dave started coughing, that old smoker's cough, and as the spasm wracked his frame, Payne lunged at him, raising the screwdriver high. Dave's eyes widened, and he started to withdraw his hand from his pocket, but Payne brought the screwdriver down with tremendous force, square into the man's sternum, cracking the plate of bone and puncturing his heart. Dave reflexively squeezed the trigger of the snub-nosed .38 revolver that was half out of his pocket. The gun's report was like a bomb blast in the enclosed space, and the hollow-point bullet blew through Payne's upper thigh, causing him to lose his balance and fall on top of the dying old man.

Shit, shit, shit. The word looped through Payne's mind in a mad cadence. *Shit.*

He heard rapid footfalls thumping across the ceiling. Beneath him, Dave was gasping, his glasses askew on his face. Payne ripped the necklace from around his neck and slowly rose to his feet. Numbness spread through his wounded leg, and a bloodstain oozed across his jeans. He felt no pain yet, but that would come soon enough.

Dave had breathed his last breath. He lay in a growing pool of crimson, the screwdriver sticking like an exclamation point out of his chest.

It was the fifth time Payne had killed a man—but it was the first time he'd felt good about it.

Clutching the necklace in his fist, Payne staggered to the narrow staircase. He was halfway up the stairs when the door at the top flew open.

Edna was up there, dressed for the holiday in an orange and black dress. "What's going on down there?" she asked. "Is Dave okay?"

Payne nudged her aside and got out of there. Darkness had settled over the city, the neighborhood lit with glowing jack-o'-lanterns. One leg dragging, blood dripping from the cuff of his jeans, he staggered along the sidewalks. Kids in Halloween costumes saw him struggling past and screamed in mock terror, assuming he was putting on an act for the holiday, and someone snapped a photo of him with a cell phone.

He collapsed in the front yard of Malcolm's house, fingers digging into the cold grass. He struggled to sit up, but the wound was worse than he had thought. The bullet must have damaged his femoral artery.

"Old head?" Malcolm's voice, sharp with concern. The kid bent over him, tears glistening in his eyes. "What the fuck happened?"

"Free," Payne whispered, and pressed the necklace into Malcolm's palm. "You're . . . free . . . now . . . but . . . I . . . never . . . was . . ."

The boy looked at the cold necklace in his hand, and through his tears he could make out the unmistakable pendant, the judge's gavel. A stone loosened in his heart. He held the cooling hand of the man who lay on the ground, and did not let go until the paramedics arrived.

KILL JOY

BY SHERI JOSEPH

East Atlanta

When I pulled into my driveway near midnight, just off my shift at the Earl, a person was standing at the mailbox. Creeped me out. The street was a sleepy one usually, composed of tidy, two-bedroom brick ranches built in the fifties. Most of the neighbors were elderly. Crime reports, which clustered around streets farther south or closer to the Village, had lately spiked with muggings, carjackings, a pattern of ambushes as people arrived home. But on our street, nothing like that, nothing worse than a stolen lawn mower now and then, the stray kick-in when people were away. If a decoration disappeared off a porch or mail went missing, it was probably only Miss Joy.

The carport security lights came on as I parked and looked back. The person, who seemed alone and not large or furtive, remained in place. I didn't see a waiting vehicle, as in the other ambushes reported on the listserv. Getting out with caution, I heard a hoarsely feminine sobbing, a gasping for breath. "Help me," she wailed, but didn't step into the driveway, as if an invisible fence blocked the property line. "Call the police. There's a man. He's at my house. He's gonna kill me!"

"Okay," I called back, moving up the walk as fast as I could, just wanting to get inside. Had to be Miss Joy, though she didn't ordinarily speak, not in sentences with words in them. Next door, her house lay in darkness, no car in her drive, no person visible. "I'll call them. Right away."

"Promise!" she shouted. "Oh, please." So many words, arranged in civilized patterns, with real fear in her voice—why shouldn't there be a man? Had she run up to me, I might have considered bringing her inside for her safety.

Fern, asleep in front of the TV, woke when I hit the mute button. On the phone with the 911 operator, I repeated my neighbor's story, though by the time I reached a person I was wondering why I bothered. "I'm sure she's off her medication," I said. "Y'all know her. Joy Markham. You're over here arresting her every other week. She's probably hallucinating."

Fern rubbed the heels of her hands into her eyes. "Demons! Maybe she got one in a trap." She giggled, then shouted toward the receiver in my hand, "Tell 'em to bring a straightjacket!"

To the operator I said, "She asked me to call, so it's possible she's looking for a ride to the psych ward. She doesn't usually like the police."

"A man!" Fern said once I'd hung up, thrilled with anything Miss Joy did. Fern was one of those slim, boobless girls who could rock a super-short haircut, big round eyes and delicate skin always dewy and flushed as if she were near tears. But Fern was not a crier. "Maybe he'll knock her in the head and make her sane."

I'd felt slightly less freaked out by Miss Joy ever since Fern moved in. She made monitoring the whole crazy situation next door a little more like entertainment. I peered out through the tiniest crack I could make in the blind. At first I didn't see her anywhere and expected her warped, haggard face to pop into the window. Ten minutes later when I looked again, I thought I spotted her trudging up her own driveway in her usual flatfooted waddle, head down, as if only returning from her day's wanderings.

"I think she went home. Guess he wasn't too scary."

On certain days I loved my neighborhood, only a few miles from downtown but practically in a forest. Every yard had trees of some sort, dogwoods and crepe myrtle, the backyards laced together over their fences in towering mature oak, sweetgum, maple, pine, made denser with an overgrowth of honeysuckle and English ivy. After dark we'd be serenaded by choruses of owls; by day we might see wild turkeys or deer in threes or fours just trotting by. My house had a screened porch that looked out on the dense green of the backyard, where I liked to sip coffee in the morning while huge woodpeckers swooped like pterodactyls from trunk to trunk and quick, shy forest hawks darted through the understory, whipping up a chitter of squirrels. I could walk to East Atlanta Village, a faintly divey bohemian punk-hipster crossroad with good bars and coffee shops and burger joints, like the one that now employed me, even a crack-in-the-wall bookstore. For some reason, perhaps the smallness of the houses, or the perception of crime, the property values had never taken off the way they had in nearby neighborhoods like Ormewood Park or Kirkwood, which was how I could afford to buy there in the first place.

Of course that was before Dekalb County shut down five elementary schools at once and I lost my job teaching third grade, started cobbling together temp jobs and then waiting tables just to pay the mortgage and utilities. Fern saved me, frankly, by moving in, paying half. I hated the idea of a roommate, and Fern in particular was a little rough for my tastes, turning my lovely screened porch into an ashtray for two packs a day, before I even got around to considering how she made a living, which was, no kidding, as a lingerie model. And not the Victoria's Secret kind—I mean Naughty Girls on Cheshire Bridge Road, where her usual shift started at eleven a.m. Who is that guy, exactly, who needs to jerk off to lingerie on his lunch hour? You'd think having the body of a late-blooming fourteen-year-old might prove an impediment to that line of work. But no, quite the niche market.

We'd been friends as kids, that way-back kind of friendship that sinks in deep enough to shock you when you grow up and find out how little you have in common. But Fern had good qualities: she was impossible to irritate, and in a related way, since I found it hard to be in a bad mood around someone I couldn't irritate, she had a talent for reminding me to have fun sometimes. So the whole roommate adventure had been less bad, so far, than expected. I'd warned her in advance about Miss Joy—the reason I couldn't sell my house, the reason I was stuck here forever—kind of hoping to scare her off even though I needed her. But my stories only got her more interested.

At first, Joy Markham had been only the middle-aged woman next door whose name I didn't know, who, in rare sightings, would not return a wave or a greeting. Head down, scowling, she shuffled up the street to a bus stop; sometime later, hours or days, she shuffled back home. I saw her so rarely that I often wondered if she'd gone away and left the place empty. The first sign of something amiss was the radio. It seemed to play at top volume in an open window facing my house, and it would play for sixteen to twenty hours straight, then go silent for six to ten hours, then start up again. Not wanting trouble, I said nothing, did nothing; the spells always ended after a couple weeks. Their regularity led me to assume she must be a drug addict, the noise related to her high. Various guys went in and out at these times, drug-addict pals, or maybe, I thought, my hydrant-shaped, middle-aged neighbor was a crack whore?

Then, in the silent hours past midnight, she would come outside and make gruff barking sounds, louder than seemed human. The first time I connected that sound with a shadowy human form, I thought it must be a man wandering about under my bedroom window. Her vocalizations were accompanied by a vicious metallic banging that for a long time I couldn't place, until I figured out she was slamming her wrought-iron security door with great force against its frame.

This cacophony, I later decided, could only be meant to scare away the demons.

Her yelling shifted into daylight hours, acquiring sounds like words, sometimes a cracked tune like singing, a preacherly gospel cadence. Who was she yelling at? Whoever it was, she was furious, calling out sin. If you weren't accustomed to finding the language in it, it called to mind the recordings played at haunted houses: the pitch-shifting caterwaul of many voices, all monstrous. She took a great interest in raking her yard, and then she often moved into my sight line from a window, so that I could observe her twitching as if being bombarded by small birds, hollering back at voices only she could hear. Her attire on a good day was a crimson velvet housecoat and mule slippers; on a bad, it was a filmy nightgown, or a robe hanging open over bra and panties, or the gold-lamé halter she generally reserved for catching a bus—her going-out clothes—and accessorized with a waist-length orange wig falling precariously askew.

Raking and hollering, she never picked up a leaf, only moved them into patterns: demon traps, I called them. She tied bedsheets onto the low branches of her trees, covered her windows in tinfoil. Her tone was generally angry, her words too garbled to decipher, but on certain days she was plainly afraid. Once she raked for nearly an hour while wearing a hooded sweatshirt backward, the hood up over her face. Often she went to catch a bus, wearing the halter if not three outfits and two different shoes; she'd return a day later pushing a grocery cart stolen from the Kroger and filled with all the porch decorations and mail she had collected along her route—thankfully, she seemed to prefer ransacking houses on streets other than her own. Trudging past my house to the corner bus stop, she kept herself quiet and orderly, but still, some drivers learned to not stop for her, and then we'd all hear about it, her howls of fury carrying for blocks.

These spells, as regular as the radio, tended to conclude with the arrival of a cop or two, then many cops, then a dramatic screaming arrest. We in the neighborhood rarely knew where she was taken or why, the hospital or jail, for treatment or punishment, as she was prone to all manner of petty crime. Once or twice she'd been gone for months, but it was usually only weeks or, precisely, seventy-two hours: the time span of the psychiatric hold a neighbor could put into effect by taking an entire day to swear an affidavit under oath at the courthouse.

I had called the cops once, and social services many times, and other neighbors must have done the same. We didn't really confer. When she was bad, we all hid indoors, let her scream alone. In its more verbal phases, her shouting seemed directed at those of us who had called the cops, who were, apparently, trying to steal her house. "You got ten days to get out of this neighborhood!" she would screech at no one in particular. Lucky for me, she most often ignored the neighbors she shared a property line with and aimed for more distant offenders. "I know what you done! You run a whorehouse! You have sex with dogs!" On some days, she owned all our houses. We were all squatters on her property. "Call the cops on me!" she would snarl. "My house!" When particular neighbors incurred her wrath—like the elderly shut-ins across the street— she draped a heavy black blanket over their mailbox. Poor Mr. Norris, who hadn't been seen outdoors in three years, would hobble on a cane down his driveway to remove it and return it to her yard.

"Well, of course," Fern said. "That mailbox was talking to her. The blanket keeps it quiet."

Usually Miss Joy ignored Fern as she did me. Once, sitting on her front step as Fern arrived home, she had called over asking for a light for her cigarette, pleasant enough until Fern claimed she had no matches, no lighter, and so sorry, no stove either.

"Right," Fern said to me, "like I'm giving the crazy lady *fire*."

After her next arrest, which she seemed to blame on us, she left us gifts. Fern and I watched her place the first package in the mailbox, then spent half a day prodding each other like frightened children to go look. Finally we went together, slinking up quick with gloves and a bag to scoop it into— good thinking, since at first glance what sat where our mail should appeared to be a petrified hunk of vomit. Back in the house, where we could deposit it on the washing machine and gingerly investigate, we determined it to be a piece of fried chicken from the Kroger deli.

"She thinks we look hungry?" Fern said.

"Well, you told her we don't have a stove."

The next day, she left a straw purse stuffed with a damp washcloth, a plaid shirt, and a cigarette butt. "That's because you wouldn't give her fire," I told Fern.

Lately she'd been working on a neighborhood art instal-
lation, composed of all the junk in her house. Its key com-
ponents were moldy shoes, besides other people's once-cute
porch decorations and their years-old stolen mail. She cre-
ated meaningful-looking arrangements on certain lawns. Her
yard equipment—two rakes and a shovel—she arranged in
a line end to end, curb to curb, across the street in front of
her house, redoing her work often since kindly joggers and
bikers and dog-walkers who passed by were always pausing,
perplexed, to move it out of the road.

And like I said, Miss Joy really only became entertaining
to me once I had Fern to share her with. On my own, she
was worrying. *Harmless,* I called her, a so-far-accurate term,
but hers was such an angry affliction, always expanding itself
into new and unpredictable activities. Seemingly superstitious
about property lines, she would not enter other yards, but she
didn't mind throwing trash into them, mine included, and I
had no faith that on some night a demon wouldn't tell her
she'd best set a house or two on fire.

On top of my general fear of *What next?* I was stuck, slowly
being sucked into debt, foreclosure on the horizon. I needed
a real job and seemed out of options in Atlanta. My brother,
who had all kinds of connections in Philly, was forever sending me leads on jobs there, one so good I applied and had
been called for an interview. But I did the math, and I simply
couldn't afford to move when I couldn't sell my house. As long
as Miss Joy lived next door, I could assume I'd never be able
to. I couldn't even rent it, since rentals were not in demand
in East Atlanta, and if someone came by chance to look at it,
Miss Joy was bound to be out there making haunted house
sounds or broadcasting accusations of inappropriate relations
with house pets.

Every time seven cop cars converged on her house and carried her away screaming, I would think, *Quick, now put the house on the market.* But there was so much involved in selling a house, and no telling when she'd return.

Fern and I liked a bar in the Village called Mary's, good karaoke every Tuesday. "Lesbians love me," Fern liked to say, though it was pretty much all gay men in there. She once asked me to get up and sing "Total Eclipse of the Heart" with her as a duet—which happened, because I was super drunk. I didn't remember it and hoped no one else did either. Fern's usual was "Jolene."

"If we're going out, you need to dress to impress," she said, while pulling the world's tiniest, trashiest dresses out of her closet—formerly my closet, of my spare bedroom, cleaned out for her with some difficulty—throwing them at me.

"Mary's is not *out*," I argued. "There's not a straight man in the place."

Fern opined otherwise, which is how we came to be perched on barstools wearing a couple of sausage casings, hers silver and mine gold. Many very hot, shiny men told us we were hot. Four drinks in, I was sobbing into my hands, because I hated waiting tables with a passion, because I was going to lose my house. Why had I bought a house in the first place? I was too young to own property. I'd gotten some inheritance money when my dad passed and thought it would be the sort of smart investment he'd approve of. Ha. I should have waited for a husband. I hadn't known this before, but men were freaked out by a woman who owned a house.

"I bet I can get you in at Naughty Girls," Fern said. Taking my gasp of dismay for doubt, she added, "No worries about your weight! A lot of guys go for a little extra, and you've got some seriously excellent tits, sister." I remained half-convinced the place was a strip club, though she insisted it was borderline legit, a deadly dull little room in which, by modeling, she helped awkward gentlemen pick out extremely expensive underwear for their girlfriends.

"I'm a teacher!" I declared. "I teach *children*. We learn things like . . . how to be good citizens." This still felt somehow true, though I hadn't been a teacher for a while and my future prospects in the city were zero. "I'm a role model!" I downed the rest of my cosmo. For some reason I was grinning like a deranged clown, sole weapon in my battle against hysteria.

Fern shook her head. "Didn't you always hate it, though? Embrace your freedom to be badass!" She leaned her forehead against mine. "You know, I'm considering giving up some inhibitions for Lent. I think you should too."

Me and Fern, we knew how to make a scene at Mary's. She especially enjoyed giving the cold shoulder to women trying to buy her drinks while she tended to me, petting me in that way she did only in public, for effect. Lesbians didn't register my existence, no matter what dress I wore. Fern had a line forming.

To be clear, I wasn't fully one of them, wanting her—my imagination lacked that limberness—but her attention was seductive. In moments like now I craved her energy, willed it to cross over through our skulls so I could yell, *Fuck it all!* and leap onto the stage, belt out some angry solo—no "Jolene" for me. Maybe "Cherry Bomb."

We ran out of money and left before midnight. It wasn't drunk driving, Fern contended, if it was less than a mile, but as I slowed to turn into the driveway, a dark shape appeared at the left fender, a flash of gold in the headlights. Fern screamed.

"Shit, you almost hit her!"

"What? Who?"

"I don't know." She peered behind us. "I think it's Miss Joy."

As we parked and got out of the car under the security lights, I could see her lumpy shape pacing in the dark at the end of the drive. I was near enough to sober to feel relief that she was upright and moving. "The man!" she moaned. "He's going to kill me! He's over there, the murderer! Help me! Please help!"

It was the same voice as the last such incident a few weeks before, and again hardly sounded like her, with its coherent words and higher pitch—some shifted phase of her illness, I presumed. Maybe an alternate personality. Over the years there had been a couple times she'd approached me with an almost bubbly friendliness, an in-her-right-mindness that was so extreme it seemed like a joke. "Hey there, honey," she'd greeted from her porch one day, waving. "I'm Joy! How are you doing? It's good to see you! I *worry* about you!"

"Okay, we'll get some help," I called out to her now, locking the car and rushing up the walk. Fern trailed behind, peering out toward the mailbox where Miss Joy sobbed, then over to the dark house next door.

I was picking up the phone as she came in behind me. "Don't call!" she hissed. "She didn't say police. She wants *our* help. So let's go. I want to see that hellhole."

"No. You can't be serious."

Once, after a dozen cops had finally coaxed Miss Joy out from behind her ironwork door, Fern had pressed one for the scoop. With me they were never very forthcoming with the charges, but Fern had a knack for men with a little authority, and this one mentioned bad checks as a possibility, then added: "Y'all don't even want to know what's in that house."

He was right. I didn't.

"Besides," Fern said now, "I want to try out my new friend." From her silver handbag, the same she'd hung from the back of her barstool at Mary's, she extracted an enormous black-barreled revolver, a Colt Python—not that I knew guns, but I knew this one. "Can you believe it? The gun from *Heathers!*" It was our favorite childhood movie.

"Shit, Fern!" For a few weeks she'd been arguing we needed a gun, for the crime and all, saying that she could buy one from a client. But really she was less concerned with self-defense than with the accessory for her image. A gun offered the perfect hilarious ending to most of her workplace stories, which were rarely about being menaced—a bouncer kept the creeps in line—and more about whiny clients who complained without tipping enough, or her boss who wouldn't give her prime hours or keep the bathroom clean. *Can't you picture it? Wouldn't he just piss his pants?* I'd told her I wasn't sure I wanted a gun in the house, end of that discussion.

"Relax," she said, "it's not loaded. I still have to get bullets, if you'll *let* me. And learn how to shoot, I guess." She struck a pose, aiming at the TV, the vase of daylilies on the dining table. Dropping it into her coat pocket, she went to the kitchen for the two longest knives in the block, one of which she handed to me. From the front closet, she pulled out the tool box. "Pocket the knife and hold this," she instructed, giving me the hammer, while she hefted a pipe wrench. "Use the claw end. Go for his eyes."

"Whose eyes?"

"The man's!" she cried in fearful delight. "We're gonna go get that guy! We'll be that crazy bitch's new best friends."

I was drunk—that's my excuse, to this day—but also, once provisioned with Fern's weapons, it seemed I had signed on for her evening's adventure. And why not? If I refused, she'd go alone, return with a story she'd be telling for years that I could have been a part of. I hardly had time to feel afraid, to wonder if there really might be a man, or what other monsters could be waiting in that house, before I was following her toward it, spike heels sinking into the lawn across the line I'd never crossed.

"No!" came Miss Joy's raspy voice from the end of her driveway. "Don't go in there. He'll kill you."

"Oh, Miss Joy, it's okay," Fern said warmly, going to her, taking her by the shoulders and scooting her toward her door. "We're armed. We're trained man-killers, so we'll just go in there and get him for you."

"No, no, no." Miss Joy braced back, stiff with horror—probably as much from Fern grabbing her as anything else—and refused to move. Fern went on ahead, and I after, and then Miss Joy followed us at a distance, repeating in a small, wounded voice, "Gonna kill me, gonna kill me."

Fern swung open the iron door, kicked something aside to step in, flicked a light switch that did nothing. But there was power: farther into the house, a shadeless lamp burned on the floor, beside what looked like a mattress. The smell was oppressive and hard to place, dank and swampy, old food and unwashed skin mixed in. Joy, huffing for breath, was pushing in behind me, making me jump inside quickly so she wouldn't touch me.

Piles of junk everywhere. Cockroaches. Smears of writing on the walls, what was left of the walls, in bloodred and shit brown, curving in snatches with a biblical flavor around massive holes, some patched with duct tape and tinfoil and posters of soft-eyed Jesus. *The demons must live in those walls,* I thought.

"Hello," Fern called, her pipe wrench at the ready in her fist. "Where are you, Mister Man?"

The answering silence made the house feel empty. I relaxed just enough to follow Fern deeper in, toward the light. "Be gone, Lucifer," she whispered to me in a witchy voice, pointing out the wall above the lamp where something like those words had been scrawled. Beneath them, a pink flowered quilt draped the mattress, a pair of dingy throw pillows embroidered with the American flag. Together we peered into the room's junk-shop accumulation of treasures: an iron Scottie dog on a stack of molded newspaper, a rusted Weedwacker, colored glass bottles full of sticks, a small forest of alarm monitoring signs, a wooden placard that read, *Home Sweet Home*. Seizing me by the arm, Fern hissed, "I need a souvenir!"

Before I could get out the word *No*, a crash sounded from the room ahead. She flinched to face it with her wrench hefted. "Who's there?"

No response. She tiptoed toward a doorway, silence a feat on three-inch heels—the kitchen, faint light shining on a faucet—and I meant to follow, should have. But fear locked me in place, while some spectral me, unaware of my immobility, went on with her to encounter the hissing thing in the kitchen: not a cat, not a snake, but—she swore—a raccoon, or a small bear, a bear-raccoon that reared up on its hindquarters big as a child.

And just then, as I felt how far from me she'd gone, there came at my back a roar of sound. It reverberated through my body—familiar, very male, a silverback gorilla sound, the precise sound from under my window. Instantly, I understood there had always been a man over here, a murderous man who terrified Miss Joy flat out of her mind. I whirled around, hammer out, having formed no intention nor gathered the requisite power, and the flat side of it smacked into Miss Joy's head with a meaty thunk. She gave a cry and went down. For seconds I barely noticed, still peering in terror past the heap of her for the man who wasn't there, who had been only her.

"Damn, girl," Fern said, stepping up beside me. She hooked her arm through mine, breathing hard. "Well, that's one way to get her out of here."

If there were windows in this room, they were pasted over in tinfoil and newspaper. The lamp lit Miss Joy only dimly, and I noted tension in her shoulders as if she were trying to rise, some movement in her mouth. I couldn't tell if there was blood. Fern stepped up and nudged her gently with the toe of her mint-green stiletto. A moan rose from her, climbed steadily in pitch and volume to become a shriek. She rolled to her back in a shimmery flash of metal—she was wearing the gold-lamé halter. It matched my dress, I thought, just as Fern reared back and struck her with the wrench.

I screamed, more surprised than anything, not entirely sure of what had happened, where or how the wrench had connected. Fern bent close, peered down critically, and swung again, hitting Miss Joy unmistakably in the head. "Fern! What the fuck!" Too dark to see much, brains or blood, but the woman lay silent and still. Past the simple numb shock, I felt a strange and tremendous rush of gratitude for Fern.

"I had to do that," she said, panting, but in a voice matter-of-fact, reasonable.

Because I had assaulted Miss Joy. "An accident . . ." I started to say—it had been, it was true. It had been true and it no longer was. In an abstract tone that approached Fern's calm, I said, "She attacked me. It was self-defense."

Fern cupped her wrench elbow in the other hand, considering, using the bottom of the tool to scratch her chin.

"Neighbors would buy it," I said. "Cops too."

Fern circled the body. "Or we were never here. It was the man. She was screaming about a man gonna kill her, and then he really did."

I wasn't thinking clearly enough to find the holes in this. But a story that left us out of it, that let us go home and go to bed and be uninvolved in whatever was decided, had tremendous appeal just then. We slipped out fast, checking the neighborhood for lights or spies as we left. But we knew these houses, knew the occupants kept to themselves and would all be in bed at this hour. We crept back next door with our profusion of weapons. Washing quickly, changing clothes, we checked each other for blood and found none. Fern went out into the backyard to hide the hammer and wrench while I called 911.

When the operator came on, I asked for the police, then repeated a version of the same call I'd made a few weeks before: my mentally ill neighbor says there's a man. "I don't know if y'all sent someone out last time," I added, "because I was pretty sure she was hallucinating. She probably is again. But she seems really scared, and my roommate thought she saw a man over there earlier. I'd feel better if someone would check it out and make sure she's okay."

Fern was smoking on the back porch, lit with white Christmas lights that draped the eaves. She aimed her pack toward me as I came out the door, and I took one, though I'd never smoked a cigarette in my life. "Now you can sell your house," she said, lighting it for me as I took a seat on the flowered cushion beside her. "Though it seems a shame to. Such a sweet little neighborhood."

I wanted to go to bed, to be asleep when the sirens came,

but Fern said no, they'd want to talk to us. We peeked at the blue lights through the blinds, then the red, our signal to go outside. We watched from the porch for a while, keeping polite distance until a cop stepped our way. "Was there really a man?" Fern asked him, as if only confused by the ambulance.

"We don't know."

We answered his questions: What time had we seen her, and had we noticed anyone else on the property, any strange people around lately? Fern mentioned seeing a man earlier that evening, before we went out, no one she could describe, just someone taller than Miss Joy. Later she had heard arguing. "But Miss Joy argues with herself," I explained. "She's yelling all the time at someone in the neighborhood or someone in her head, so it's hard to know."

"Yeah," the cop said grimly, "we know. We've been to the house before."

The ambulance, pulling out of the drive, turned on its sirens. My heart had not been racing too badly until then. "Is she hurt?"

"Hit in the head, looks like. Hard to say how bad."

Which meant she wasn't dead. I knew better than to look at Fern but couldn't help it. She stared fixedly at the cop with her giant baby eyes. "There was really a man? Oh shit, we should have called sooner. She said he was trying to murder her. You should check with the other neighbors. Maybe she tried to get help from them before she came to us. We really thought she was just off her medication."

"Oh my God," I said. "Poor Miss Joy."

Every night for weeks, we waited for the cops to knock at the door. When they did, it was to arrest Fern: for threatening a client with her *Heathers* gun and stealing his cash. I spent the last of my money getting her bailed out, then lost my job at the Earl with all the back-and-forth to the courthouse. Armed robbery seemed a crazy charge under the circumstances but that's what it was, bullets or no, mandatory ten years, until Fern cried a few tears and pleaded on a lesser charge, for two. The lawyer thought she could be out in one. I took over her slot at Naughty Girls: no denying it was good money, though I'd never make as much in tips as she had.

By then, Miss Joy was home. Her shamble had become slightly lopsided, her vocalizations somewhat subdued. Her mood had shifted on its spectrum closer to fearful, so that her former territorial snarl at the UPS driver was more likely to be a shrieked, "He's got a bomb, he's got a bomb!" But she was unkillable, she owned her house outright, she received a monthly Social Security check that kept the lights on and food in her stolen shopping carts, five or eight of them parked in her yard until a truck arrived to load them up and return them.

For me she reserved the core of her rage. "Murderer!" she shouted every day as I dragged home from the lunch shift. "You murdered me! You run a whorehouse! You have sex with dogs!"

ONE-EYED WOMAN

BY GILLIAN ROYES

Virginia-Highland

She worked the iron around the faded orange flowers in the middle of the doily, trying to avoid the cheap bedspread beneath. The childhood gift from her mother was now spotted with age, but she held to the ritual of washing it before leaving one house and pressing it at the next.

Setting the iron beside her boxes to cool, she put the doily on the bedside table with the lamp on top. There was nothing attractive about the room, shown to her earlier that evening by the old woman's nephew, a bulky man who'd tiptoed delicately down the corridor ahead of her.

"I'm sure you're anxious to see it," he'd whispered as he led her to the caregiver's room. That's what he'd called it, *the caregiver's room.* The smallest of the three bedrooms, at the back of the house.

A smell of mothballs had assaulted her from the doorway. The short, square woman had walked in, back erect, instantly disliking the drapes and bedspread. The room's only window looked onto the neighbor's wall and, as soon as the taxi driver had deposited her boxes and left, she'd pulled the curtains, creating a lavender tomb.

Dollops of rain had hit the window a few minutes later, turning the room a deeper shade of purple. *Apropos,* she'd thought.

She'd been hoping it would hold off. At least for today.

Humming the birthday song that morning, she'd fried an egg in her apartment kitchen and eaten it standing at the window, looking at the looming clouds with the wisp of a hope that someone, a cousin, her brother, someone would remember her.

"It's my birthday," she'd announced that afternoon to the taxi driver after he'd piled her boxes and suitcases into his SUV.

"'Appy buthday," he'd grunted as he wiped his forehead with a handkerchief. Then they fell into silence.

Birthdays hadn't always treated Veronica Williamson well. On the day she was born her face had been squeezed by the doctor's forceps, leaving her with sunken cheeks and a boxer's nose. A plastic surgeon hadn't been able to help; the thoughtless nickname of *Mash-face* in school hadn't either. The damage to the child's face had changed the trajectory of her life from what it would have otherwise been, leaving her shy and solitary, her only comfort being that her light complexion and family status placed her high on the ladder of Jamaican society. She'd come to believe that class always trumped looks, the belief of a heart that had also been damaged.

The nephew came to the door just when she started unpacking. "I took Aunt Jessie her tea, so she's fine for the night. Can I get you some supper?"

As soon as they sat down in the dining room, the questions started: "Where in Jamaica are you from? My wife and I went there once."

"Kingston," she answered and took a silent sip of soup. She didn't want to appear too ravenous.

"We went to Kingston—to visit the Bob Marley Museum. We didn't like it much." He swept his hand over the table, frowning, suddenly irritated. "All the rich people living up in the hills and the poor crowded together in ghettoes."

Veronica nodded, recalling the view from her home's veranda looking down on the harbor and the poor.

"What did your family do there?" he asked.

She sat up and ran a hand over her neat, gray hair. "My father was a solicitor, with one of the largest practices in Kingston. My mother didn't work."

He picked up his toast. "You said you went to college there."

"Yes, the University of the West Indies, MA in history."

"Great." His eyes flickered around, unsure of what to light on next.

She could tell by the lowering of the eyebrows, the narrowing of the eyes, that he was puzzled about her descent from graduate school to caregiver, but he knew not to ask. She'd liked him from their first meeting at the Starbucks in Little Five Points and spotted the wedding ring when he put out his hand. There was something genteel about him—an architect, he'd said he was, a man with breeding. He'd tried not to stare at her nose.

"When did you come to the States?" he asked while he washed up the dishes, his back to her.

"Thirteen years ago."

He'd asked fewer questions during the brief interview, waving a cup of chai tea while he talked about his aunt, an invalid who was childless and widowed. Her last live-in had just returned to Guatemala and he'd had no luck finding a substitute.

The ad in the *Journal-Constitution* had been equally brief: *Virginia-Highlands. Live-in companion needed for elderly woman. Room and board and stipend.*

"A hospice nurse comes in three days a week to bathe Auntie, and we have a lady who cooks and cleans every day except weekends," he'd told her in the coffee shop. "We just need a responsible person there—in case of anything."

"I have lots of experience," she'd assured him. "I took care of my mother before she died. I had to be up with her at night and go to work the next day." They'd chuckled as if it were a joke, and he'd seemed relieved when she accepted the position. Later she'd thought him a very nice man—but too trusting. He should have asked for references. Anyone could put a pillow over an invalid's face or disappear with the valuables.

He was more measured this evening, taking his time washing up. "Are you a . . . a citizen?"

The corners of her lips twitched. Ah, there it was. He'd forgotten to ask if she was legal during the interview and his wife had reminded him after.

"I'm a permanent resident," she answered. "I have a green card." His big shoulders relaxed. She wouldn't mention her birthday; he'd try to find out how old she was.

Before he left, he handed her a sheet with instructions for his aunt's care from morning to night, starting with, *Change diaper*. Below that every meal, every medication, every bath was listed. There was nothing about talking or reading, nothing about being a companion.

"Should I supervise the woman who comes in the day?" she inquired.

"Yes, please, and pitch in when necessary, if you don't mind. You can call us in an emergency."

As he escaped through the front door, the new caregiver wondered if pitching in meant changing diapers. Shuddering, she returned to her room, tiptoeing past the ninety-seven-year-old.

"I know you'll both become friends," he'd commented at the end of the interview, and she'd smiled and said nothing.

There was little chance of becoming friends with his aunt. It would have been out of character for Veronica, who'd never trusted women and only occasionally men. It wasn't that she was mean-spirited. Just the opposite. She'd worked for thirty-five years with a Jamaican nonprofit that housed and fed the poor. But when it came to intimate relationships, she was most comfortable in the well of her own thoughts, preferring a safe distance between herself and others.

Returning to her unpacking, Veronica placed her cosmetics bag on the dresser. She couldn't leave it in the bathroom since there was only one. The house was smaller than she'd been expecting, but it didn't matter, because she'd just escaped eviction from her former apartment, the best birthday gift she could have given herself. Even better, she'd escaped to live in the city, and not just any part of the city, but in Virginia-Highlands. Trendy, gentrified, quietly classy, the neighborhood had enthralled her from the first day she'd seen it a few years earlier. The boutiques and restaurants at the intersection of Virginia and Highland, the tall old trees, the updated bungalows with their compact gardens had made her hanker to live there, to live among people who didn't spit and throw litter out the car window, who didn't shout curses in the middle of the night, who knew how to behave.

She slid the closet door back and hung up the black Alfani, pausing for a second to straighten its plastic bag. Her mother would have loved this suit. She'd always loved beautiful clothes. There'd been that day—she'd been around thirteen—when her mother had tried on a black cocktail dress.

"Like it, ma'am?" the hovering dressmaker had asked.

Her mother, never a diplomat, had been looking in the mirror. "I hope they don't mistake me for a maid," she'd said, laughing, ignoring the wounded seamstress's face.

The cream Chanel was hung next in the closet, followed by a dozen more designer suits and dresses. The underwear came next, Veronica layering them carefully in the drawers, then her jewelry box, which went on the dresser in front of the photographs. After sliding the empty suitcases under the bed, she attended to her boxes (sent from Jamaica by a cousin several years before), most still sealed with the original tape. She opened the smallest of the boxes, the one with her family photos, another ritual never neglected. Removing the bubble wrap from the first, she placed it on the dresser. She was sitting on her father's knee, his handsome brown face looking into the camera as if he were posing alone. It was followed by a photo of her holding hands with her older brother Ralph, her parents' favorite and now a neurologist. With her sleeve, she wiped the glass over another: she was a baby in the arms of Nanny Brown. Tall and black in a starched white uniform, the woman's prim smile hid the tongue that was forever quick to judge and slow to forgive.

"Bitch," Veronica muttered as she set the picture beside the others.

Her heart pumped with guilty pleasure at the comment. Normally tight-lipped, comfortable with deception, she'd been having a recent urge to speak hard truths. Not unlike the crude remarks she'd abhorred in her recent neighborhoods—ugly names that had started leaping from her lips like unruly children. She'd murmured the word *slut* in reference to a neighbor the week before, loud enough to be heard and cursed out, and a creditor with an Indian accent she'd called a *coolie*. She was starting to get accustomed to her new habit, even a little proud. At seventy, she reasoned, she'd earned the right.

A cry came from the room next door—or was it her imag-

ination? Rubbing a stab of arthritis in her knee, Veronica tiptoed to the old lady's door. Only a soft wheezing emerged from
the darkness and she returned to her room.

Ripping open another of her boxes, she removed a photo
album. About to place it in its designated drawer, she sat on
the bed and opened it to the pictures of her European trip,
the high point of what had been up to then a monotonous
life. Financed by her inheritance after her mother's death, the
trip thirteen years before had taken her first to London where
she'd stayed with Ralph and his British wife. She'd moved on
after two weeks, taking the Chunnel train to France. As she
turned the pages to the Eiffel Tower, followed by the Colos-
seum and the Acropolis, she remembered how wildly courageous it had felt to travel alone, to be free. She touched a
snapshot of Christos, a shoemaker in Athens who'd made love
to her twice, who knew just enough English to say she looked
Greek.

The skyscrapers of New York sprang from the next page,
sprang with the same energy that had rippled up from its sidewalks into her feet. How she'd loved the city when she arrived from Heathrow! No one had stared, no one had judged.
They were too busy living their lives. She'd planned to spend
a week there before returning to Jamaica but kept extending
her stay, living first in the Waldorf Astoria (a rash decision,
even she had to admit), then in a small hotel in Brooklyn,
visiting museums and parks, once the site of the World Trade
Center attack.

One morning she'd awakened to a thought. With her parents gone and the family home sold, her job handed over to
her assistant, she had nothing to go back to in Jamaica. There
were few jobs to be had, especially at her age, and even if she
found work, there'd be no safety net when she retired. After

her money was gone, where would she be without her parents to fall back on? Everyone in New York seemed to be working, and in retirement they had an infrastructure: Social Security and Medicare. The brash courage she'd had in Europe would pull her through. She would stay in America—on her visitor's visa.

The idea was naïve rather than courageous, made by a person with little experience operating outside of her island bubble, no one to advise her that she was about to step on to a path that would spiral—ever so slowly and ever so surely—downward.

With her inheritance dwindling, Veronica's decision to work had started her descent. At the suggestion of a Trinidadian dry-cleaning clerk, a younger, single man who flirted with her, she'd started giving evening classes to West Indian children—quiet, sporadic work that didn't feel illegal. Her clients were blue collar, the apartments smelling of garlic and curry, but she'd swallowed her pride and arrived punctually at their doors.

Shortly before her six-month visa was to expire, an African woman on a bus had asked her where Flatbush Avenue was. "My husband need a coat," the woman had explained, indicating the much older man beside her. An unfortunate arranged marriage, Veronica had decided—or maybe a convenient one. That night another idea had blossomed and she'd invited her dry-cleaning friend to dinner. When he appeared in the restaurant, his shiny suit and pointed-toed shoes had alarmed her but she'd soldiered on with her mission.

"My visa is running out," she'd announced while he was attacking a chicken bone.

"So you going illegal?" the man had countered. "You sure you want to do that? I is a citizen, but I know how it go. This ain't no easy country and you all by yourself. People who grow up soft like you don't know how to survive here. Next thing, they throw you in jail and deport you." He'd shaken his head. "You come like a one-eye man in a four-eye country."

She'd screwed up her courage, her stomach already in a knot. "That's why I want to get a green card. I was wondering— would you consider . . . I could marry you."

"What kind of money you talking?" he'd asked eventually, examining his long pinky nail. Two thousand dollars later she'd moved into his filthy apartment, spending her first week cleaning, relieved he was rarely home.

In for penny, in for pound, she'd told herself. Wearing the Chanel suit for the city hall ceremony, she'd promised to love, honor, and cherish Allan for as long as they both should live. She told her brother she'd married on an impulse. It had felt like lying to her parents, disagreeable but necessary. There were no photographs of the wedding, the celibate marriage, or the husband who'd disgusted her.

"My mother want me to come down to Atlanta," he'd told her after he lost his job. "She have a friend can give me a work." With the last interview yet to come, Veronica had gone south with him on a Greyhound bus, vowing to shake off his poverty as soon as she had her card.

Betty, Allan's mother, only a few years older than Veronica, hadn't seemed perturbed that her son had married for money. It was she who'd suggested that her daughter-in-law apply to Macy's.

"Like how you dignified," she'd told her. "You going to look good in black." Macy's had been delighted to hire Veronica, now the owner of a work permit. She was *just the kind of person we like in the Macy's family*, according to the HR woman.

The last immigration interview had gone well, Veronica telling the Atlanta officer it was love at first sight. A few months and a green card later, she'd moved into her own apartment, having decided to stay in Atlanta because it was cheaper than New York, the weather warmer—and she had a job. The album started filling again with photographs she'd taken from her new Nissan: the CNN building, the Coca-Cola Museum, Martin Luther King Jr.'s birthplace, some sent to her brother to let him know she was fine, despite her divorce.

Pulling a nightgown out of a drawer, Veronica rubbed the scar on her spine where she'd had back surgery two years before. She'd been forced to quit her job to have it, the HR woman telling her, sorry, she was really only a part-time worker. After her recovery, it had been nearly impossible to get work. Macy's wasn't hiring; the public schools didn't want her. The only job she'd found was sorting clothes in a thrift store, but her back had started acting up again and she'd had to leave.

The words of a colleague at Macy's came back as Veronica headed for the bathroom. "Backache is just about stress," the makeup artist had said.

There'd been stress all right, beginning with the medical bills from the surgery, even with Medicare. She'd added them to the credit card invoices that listed the temptations America had thrown at her. The creditors' calls were the most stressful, though. Arrogant young people who addressed her on the phone as if she were a criminal, especially the IRS man who sounded like he was wearing a suit but was probably in shirtsleeves in a cubicle. They had no feelings, saying they'd take her to court. She, whose father had been a lawyer!

Ralph had advised her to invest her inheritance: "You don't want to end up in the poor house."

His wife had added with her all-knowing smile, "And you wouldn't want to depend on anyone, would you?"

Financial advice was now too little, too late for a woman who'd spent almost six decades living rent-free in her family home, one maid to cook her meals and another to launder her clothes.

"Why waste your money on an apartment when we have lots of space?" her father had argued, a lawyer used to winning.

Her low salary had been spent on books, her car, and a few trips to relatives in Canada and Miami. She'd seen no reason to save, having been well trained by parents who'd embedded the message that women didn't need to handle the finances. That was the man's job.

"How come you never married?" her mother had asked when Veronica was about to turn fifty. They'd been drinking tea on the veranda and her mother had lowered her voice after the maid left.

"I never wanted to get married," she'd retorted. "And no one asked me."

She was lying on both counts. Other women's engagement rings had released bile in her stomach; wedding receptions made her feel sick. Two men had actually proposed to her but she'd rejected them both. One had been too dark, the other unable to pronounce an *H* (her parents would have been horrified). She'd never invited them home and had told herself they'd only proposed because of her class and color.

Veronica clicked on the bathroom light and placed her cosmetics bag on the top of the toilet tank. The room was a cramped, dark closet and there were signs of mold around the tub, the house cleaner obviously unsupervised. Leaning into the mirror above the sink, the aging woman stroked the dark spots on her cheeks. She'd have to wear a hat when she went outside.

After her ablutions, she returned to her room and rubbed ointment into her joints. Tomorrow she'd go for a walk, she decided as she turned off the lamp, take a look at the azaleas and dogwoods in bloom, and if she could get away on Sunday, she'd go to the church on the corner that she'd seen from the taxi.

She was sure of one outing: as soon as the day worker came on Monday, she'd find a library to check the online dating site where she had her profile. She'd posted a better photograph of herself recently, one with her head tilted up, a glamour shot she'd had done in a mall. Someone might have written her by now. The world was full of desperate people. There might yet be an old man somewhere who needed taking care of—who might leave her a house and some cash when he died. She'd tell him she loved him and clamp her lips shut to keep the insults inside. Oh well, if wishes were horses, all beggars would ride, her father used to say.

She wriggled around on the mattress, trying to get comfortable with the truth. The vultures would find her again, they always did. They'd demand their pound of flesh, their $183,000. It helped that her cell phone had been cancelled but they'd still find her, and when they did, she'd tell them the truth.

I don't have a dollar to my name, she'd say, *do with me what you will.* Maybe that would hold them off. One never heard of debtors going to jail in America; the country seemed to thrive on debt.

"There's always bankruptcy," one creditor had advised. "If you filed as a—"

"Are you out of your mind?" she'd interjected. *Bankrupt?* If her brother ever heard of it, if family friends back home ever knew!

Acid spurted into the woman's throat and she swallowed hard once, twice, pushing down the inevitable truth, threatening since that first interview with the nephew. One day, one day not too far in the future, the old lady was going to die—and then where would she be? She'd be homeless, that's where, her Social Security check unable to cover a cheap apartment in the suburbs. Bankruptcy wouldn't matter. All her suits would have to go to a consignment shop, her jewelry to a pawnbroker, and her books to a secondhand bookstore. There'd be nothing left of her. Nothing.

Her heart pounded with the image of her hand searching the treasure trove of medication in the old lady's room, pushing a bottle of sleeping tablets deep into her Aigner boots. Just in case.

"God help me," she whispered to the ceiling, more intention than actual prayer. *I will survive. I will not end up in the gutter. I am strong.*

She took a deep, shaky breath to calm herself. Yes, she'd imagine instead the family's beach house in Ocho Rios, where she'd spent all her summers growing up. She could hear the waves rolling in and out, feel the sand under her bare feet and the sun hot on her arms. Her brother was calling her from the water. Her parents and their friends were sitting in lounge chairs on the veranda, chatting and laughing. A maid was handing them drinks. She was warm and safe.

I'm still warm and safe, she reminded herself, taking another breath. *I'm living in Virginia-Highlands, and I have a roof over my head and food in the kitchen.*

She rolled onto her side, shrugging off the threatening shroud with one last intention-prayer. Sleep came in fits and starts, the dreams tiring. Toward morning she found herself in the maze at Hope Gardens in Kingston and she was little again, running between the box hedges, trying to find a way out.

She was still asleep when a voice pierced through her fog—a shrill, ghostly voice—

"*Girl!*" the voice called again, more insistent now.

The immigrant's eyes popped open. She struggled to sit up in the purple gloom, the nylon bedspread sliding to one side.

"Yes ma'am," she heard herself answer—the truth at last.

PART II

Kin Folks & Skin Folks

SELAH

BY ANTHONY GROOMS

Inman Park

I can hear sounds I've never heard before. The creaking of the floorboards, the footsteps on the stairs, the aching grind of the door hinge—these are common music in this century-old house. The sudden ping of acorns striking the roof, the groan of the giant water oaks and the fluttering shadows they cast from the streetlight playing through the rooms, the scramble of the roof rats in the attic, the possum's hissing growl as she makes her midnight track—these noises I delight in; the more vigorous, the greater my delight. But it is the voice. The sweet, babbling voice of the child that gives me all the more pleasure. What is she saying? *Nevermore* or *Evermore?* You don't hear it?—yes, you hear it too. Long—long—long—many minutes, many hours, many days, you and I shall hear it. *Evermore!* Her little voice gives all the more certainty that I *am* the instrument of the Most High and the vengeances I exact are pure and justified. *Selah.*

Was it only a week ago? Six? No. Seven days. Perhaps only five, the first cool evening of autumn after the long, too long, Indian summer. I am a gentle man by all accounts, and so when I stepped out of the front of the house and saw a pair of pine beetles crouching to spring across the threshold, I stomped my feet, rather than crushing them, and sent them scurrying into the beehive of dried leaves that had accumulated on the porch. I was gleeful in spite of the dull, dark, damp, and soundless day. The low-hanging clouds seemed to lift rather than oppress my spirits. I felt the kind of giddiness one gets from a toke—just a toke, mind you—of weed, as that's all I manage these days. Skipping over the rotten plank on the steps, and through the iron gate—just the gate, the fence having long rusted away—and into Druid Street, named for the oaks which tunnel over it; the street's name has nothing to do with priests!—I heard a squirrel bark. I recall that barking and the scratching the rodent made as it ran around eaves of the turret with its one vacant eye-like window. One would think a witch lives there, but no, it is only a nest to rodents. Night and day, I've heard their kits peeping. My philosophy is to live and let live, so a squirrel in the attic is nothing to me. I do not fight against nature. But people: that's a different story. Though I should say, not all people.

Forty, fifty years ago, my neighbors were wonderful people. Just like me. It was when the neighborhood was in decline—decline!—according to the tour guides who glide through on their Segways—*simply robotics*—simple robots! *Declined!* they say, from its Gilded Age glory to a hippieville—the grand Greek revivals and Queen Annes given over to tenements and flophouses—and to hippies—they say. Now, it has been rescued. Rescued! This is the language they use. On the brochures. On the websites. The gentrifiers! I've heard them cluck. Cluck. Cluck. At my house. It needs painting, they say. The windows need repair. It could be lovely, if only . . . Ha! Remodelers. Relandscapers. New Yorkers and Californians! Saws and leaf blowers all day long. And their self-congratulatory tour of homes and festivals. So-called arts festivals—T-shirts and earrings! What do they know of art? They've Home Depot-ed everything—everything except the sidewalks! The hundred-year-old tiles, beautifully buckled by water oak roots, cracked, crushed, missing. That's art! May they break their damn ankles on it. *Selah.*

But that day, nothing bothered me. I strode up Euclid Avenue, past the colorful Queen Annes and Craftsman bungalows, reveling in the change of season. The cool air. The billow of storm clouds glowing in sunset. Bats, like phantoms, looping through the sky and the barn owl's who-whooing. I passed the woods at Springvale Park, where the owls live and where the Wiccans still hold their lunar rites among the silver-barked beeches. On a spur of the moment, I decided to go to the Porter. I liked sitting in the very back of the narrow dungeon of a club and drinking an ale. Perhaps I'd even eat a brat and sauerkraut.

Then I noticed the child. I was passing the hill at the Sibley Park, an ostentatious collection of contraptions of Scandinavian design meant to entertain the spawn of said gentrifiers—oh, such precious urchins! God forbid they play on a swing—when the ephemeral look of the girl startled me. I peered hard, but no, she was a child of this world, six or seven in age, naked except for a ragged, oversized T-shirt that draped her like a tunic.

I see the homeless all the time. In the old days—those hippieville days—they squatted in the old mansions, abandoned by commerce and condemned by the state. Now they haunt the periphery of the district. They wander Ponce, and camp at Little Five Points, but would be hustled along by the IPP if they ventured into this purlieu! Private police. The "I-pee-pee," I call them.

"Where is your mama, little girl?" I asked, my tone conveying my caring nature. I was concerned that a chill would catch her. Already, her bare arms were pimpled with goose bumps. "Where do you live?" She was of indeterminate race—

light-skinned black? Mediterranean? A mix of some kind. A tangle of sandy hair matted her head. I came closer, resisting the urge to reach out. As I said, I am a compassionate man. In a sudden burst, she fled, running like a Hiawatha to the playhouse—a structure for the gentrified children to "play" house—ha! "The melancholy House of Usher"—as if any one of them expected to clean and cook as adults.

I followed the child, not chasing, but approaching cautiously. Two souls crossed in front of me, walking the path toward the train station—a double murder from two decades ago. Inside the square little playhouse, among a scatter of toy pots and sand buckets, was the girl holding tightly to another figure—girlish too, and only slightly larger. The larger, older one was perhaps in her midtwenties, her youth though was blanched, and her face, yellow and negroid, was blooming with purple and pink bruises. A cut on the lip.

We stared a moment and when my breath came back to me, I whispered, "Are you all right?"

The older one—the woman—drew herself smaller, wrapping herself around the child. They were cold. I had only a light jacket, and immediately stripped it off and held it out to her. With a quivering hand, she took it, and nodded slightly to show gratitude, and true to her maternity, she fitted it on the child, whose frame it swallowed up.

If ever there was a need for the police, I thought, it was now. I broached the subject carefully, as I myself have a well-cultivated distrust of the law. The woman's reaction was blank, but the bruises spoke loudly. I stepped from the playhouse, took a deep breath, and surveyed the park as it fell into a miasmic darkness, a thin fog seeping from the ground. Streetlamps, ringed with prismatic halos, illuminated the marble steps of long ago–razed mansions which led up the hill to nowhere. I flipped open the phone and dialed 9-1-1. And waited.

After several rings, far more than any dying soul would have lasted through, a voice asked me to leave a message. I am as patient as I am compassionate, but I have little patience for such sloppiness. I resolved at that moment that I would be the hero; I would help the poor woman; I! Not the Atlanta police, and certainly not the I-pee-pee. They were but functionaries, paid help. They helped without compassion, but I am called to it by the Highest Power, the power of God, or the power of gods. Whichever. *Selah.*

I raced down the hill toward the street, toward home. The damp grass clumped between the sole of my sandals and my toes. Some hand, grasping my ankle, nearly tripped me up. But soon I was on the sidewalk, walking swiftly home, my mind listing, relisting what I must do to save the child, the mother. Suddenly a light, blue and holy, burst around me. I tasted the contents of my stomach at the back of my throat. Such excitement is not good for the heart. Then out of the light came a figure, burly and haloed. My knees weakened.

"Hey, pard-na! Where you going so fast?"

Hardly an epiphanic salutation! It was a damn cop. True to calling, they come when you least need them.

"Officer," I intoned, appropriately obsequious. It is the best strategy, especially around the black ones, and this one was not only burly but as black as a moonless night. And yet, in the foggy streetlamp, he glowed somehow, the bulge of eyes and round jowls, a monstrous chest under his shirt and his massive arms, swollen in his sleeves which acted upon the veins like a tourniquet. Anabolic steroids—mum's the word; dumb's the word. "I was just running to call you for assistance," I explained, and he, fiddling with gadgets pinned here and thither on his person, talked in a gibberish of codes to which a crackled and popping voice replied.

Whatever they had to settle was settled, and reluctantly the cop, hefting his big frame up the hill, followed me. He shone his flashlight inside the playhouse like he was chasing down a fly. Finally it rested on the Pietà, cowering in the corner by the play cook stove. Through blunt and gruff questioning, he ascertained the obvious: they were homeless. If they ever had a home, they had been driven out of it.

"What do you want to do?" he asked the mother, and to her credit, she didn't answer him. He turned the question to me: "What do you want to do?"

"What *can* I do?"

"Do you want to go to the Pine Street shelter, ma'am?" he blurted.

Her response shocked me. No. She wouldn't. She'd been there. She said that it wasn't safe. It was crowded and filthy and she would rather make her bed where she was.

The forecast called for cold and the child's nose was snotty.

"If she don't want to go," the cop said, "I could arrest her for trespassing—in jail, she be out of the cold."

The cruelty of his suggestion, his arrogance, nearly sent my hand against his fat head. I looked to the sky. A half-moon slid behind the skyline, diffusely ablaze as if shining behind theatrical scrim. It was God speaking and I knew the mission. "I will take her!"

"Take her where?" the buffarilla asked. Did he suspect misconduct from me?

"To shelter! I will find succor for them or succor them myself."

The cop pursed his lips and asked the woman if she wanted to go with me. I'll have you know, she hesitated. Help on the way, and she hesitated! Then he said she'd have to come with him. Was it such a Morton's fork? Jail or me? The gods led her to the right choice, and quickly. She took the child in her arms and followed me home through the roaming mists.

Before there was city here—either gilded ghetto or hippieville—this was a battleground of the War Between the States. Thousands of boys lined up, blasting musket balls in one another's faces. Look out any moonlit night into the mists that gather in the hollows of Freedom Park, or the grove at Delta, and you will see them. Regiments and squadrons at a time. They are not so invisible. And why should it be strange? Lives have been lived in this place since the time of the unfortunate Creeks, some of whom clung to these very oaks to save themselves from the Trail of Tears. You scoff? Your arrogance will be the end of you. Life piles on life. Hurt on hurt. That is why I, by the grace of the Almighty, am merciful.

Several times during the short walk, the woman trailing me disappeared in the fog. I waited until she was in sight, only to lose her again. There is the tale of the apparition that trails and vanishes, and reappears on one's own back. Thinking this, I was beginning to feel some regret about my bravado, as I watched them descend, ragamuffin and ragamitten, from Euclid Avenue down the hill on Druid Street.

"You live here?" the little mother asked. It was the first time she seemed to have looked at me, her rheumy eyes catching the porch light. "It's such a big house."

"But?" An impatient flash heated my face. Next she would say it needed paint or repair.

"You live here all by yourself?" There was a pleading in her tone that I caught but did not fully understand.

"Wait here. I'll run into the yard and get the car."

"But we're tired. We tired and hungry, sir."

"I'll fix you a sandwich. Peanut butter? Egg salad?"

"Maybe we could just rest awhile. Just a couple of days."

My imagination sprang. What an idea! A lovely young Negress in the house. To cook and clean and who knows what. She was quite a little spinner. The gentrifiers would talk and talk about that one. And the child? As light-skinned as the child was, we'd be thought to be a little family. How we could roam the neighborhood, the graying, balding, long-haired Ichabod and his darling little girls!

Just then an owl hooted and a door slammed. I jolted out of my reverie. "Impossible!" I went into the yard and brought around the Beetle.

Peachtree, Peachtree. Everything is Peachtree. That's tourist talk. Beware the Druids. The Decaturs and DeKalbs. The Morelands and Memorials. The Capitols, the Hardees, the Aarons, the Williamses. They writhe like a tangle of snakes. And we traveled them all. She and the child, scrunched together on the back bench, the springs of the passenger seat having cut through and made it uncomfortable if not dangerous to sit there. We went first to one shelter for women and children, and then another, only to be told that like old cemeteries, there was no room in the tombs. City ordinances, all of that. Or too late to check in, as if exigencies punched a clock. The brute husband plans to slap the wife around at two in order that she may be checked in by three thirty! The gods are gracious, but they do not chime to a human clock. With each failure, we were directed to the next. And the next. Until we had made a circuit of the eastern neighborhoods from Edgewood to Glenwood. Then I was instructed by a burly black devil hiding behind a clerical collar to go deeper into the southwest. Even deeper into the poor Negro habitats. Deep into Summerhill, into Mechanicsville and Peoplestown, where a wholly different set of souls abide.

Once I got a call from South-View Cemetery. Generally I am not compelled to answer the land line. Solicitors, you know. But for some reason the receiver seemed to beckon; it trembled in the cradle. Hesitantly I answered, and a chill crawled from my coccyx to the nape of my neck, and then spread like a contagious itch across my scalp. "It is your auntie," the voice said. It was Auntie's voice and yet it was not so.

"Auntie," I said, "where are you?"

"I am in South-View. South-View Cemetery. I am waiting for you. Waiting."

My dear auntie who raised me—and how I treated her, abandoned her. Had I the presence of mind, I would have asked why she was at a colored cemetery. In life, she would have never associated with the colored, except Louisa, her maid. She refused to go to the tea room at Rich's after integration. She voted for Lester Maddox. When she died I inherited the house—just as the neighborhood "declined" into hippieville—and at her funeral, there were only me and Louisa. Now she calls from South-View—the rooms of Tartarus are heated by ironies. *Selah.*

But I am determined not to be among the damned. I pressed on, shelter after shelter, and no room at the inn. The night grew old. The poor child nodded, whimpered, shivered, though I blasted the car's heater. The mother, clutching the child, cringed and said nothing; I spoke, not loquaciously, but with good cheer and encouragement.

At last, we drove up to a little soul-saving station on a short, poorly lit street with overgrown and abandoned lots. Pope Street or Hope Street. It could even have been Dope

Street, it seemed so much on the edge of nowhere. The square, whitewashed building with its slanted steeple nonetheless buoyed our expectations of succor. I helped the darling mother and child from the cramped backseat, though reluctant she was to take my hand for fear of losing grip of her daughter. I offered to carry the girl. I am good with children. They might be brash with others, but they are quiet around me. We walked the muddy path to the building, guided only by the dim bug light next to the door. There was a sign, written in red block letters against the whitewash: *LIGHTHOUSE OF DELIVERANCE*. A large, very black—purplish black— negroid woman—no girl, she—all woman—peeped through the inner door, leaving the security door locked. *What breasts! What breasts!* I thought. You scoff! It is a compliment that even in that hour of exasperation, I took heed of the well-formed breasts, and the curve of ample hips. I am a man, not a priest, though priestly is my nature.

"Can I help you?" Her voice was gruff.

I have come to blow your house down, I wanted to answer, but turned my tongue to better purpose. "We seek shelter!"

She studied the three of us, her mouth turning down as she looked me over.

Quickly, I clarified: "For the woman and child, not for me."

I saw the moment of decision, when the suspicion dropped from her face and the vixen unlocked the security door. My little woman practically sang out a sigh of relief. The child, sensing her relaxation, chirped and gurgled. Was it *Nevermore* or *Evermore*? In we went through a narrow, stale hallway. It might as well have been lit by gaslight. On the walls were portraits of the Living Christ, as blond as a movie star. His eyes followed me. We were taken to a card table that served as a desk, and our Hottentot Venus sat and began to ask questions for her forms. Bureaucracy haunts every kindness. The room behind her, I could see, served as a sanctuary, though it was sparse and void of any of the ornamentation that God expects in a place of worship. The few pews had been dragged to the periphery of the room, and on the floor, about three feet apart, lay three rows of twin-sized mattresses, ten or so in a row. Each mattress was bare, but covered with a blanket, and on each—all of them, except for one—reposed a soul. This was the shelter I had driven so long to find.

The innkeeper, such as she was, gave me the evil eye. She turned her lips down smugly. "Not good enough?" she challenged.

Any room in my own house would be a palace by comparison. I'd take the little charges home rather than have them spend ten minutes in such a kennel. I'd house them in Auntie's grand old boudoir, full of cobwebs and dust bunnies. How she would spin in her grave at that. Round and round she'd go. Where she'd stop the devil knows. They could become my wards, my little family. Papa, mama, and baby. The thought enticed and gratified me.

"It's good," the mother replied. The child babbled like a happy brook.

Yes, I then thought, *happiness for them. A great sacrifice for me. But for the greater happiness, a just and small sacrifice.* Seeing I had done all I could do, all that was expected of me, I smiled, reached to pat the little cherub on the head. She shrank back, but I touched the scruffy little naps anyhow. I drew in deeply, the close air catching in my throat, and turned to leave.

Then the big one stopped me. Her voice boomed. I turned to see her thick lips moving in slow, bumbling motion. "You be paying?"

"Pardon?"

"You be paying?"

"Paying?"

"Twenty dollars a night."

"I thought this was a charitable enterprise."

She rolled her neck. It was as if her head danced on her shoulders, and when it settled, she smirked and conveyed both incredulity and menace. I stepped back to the table, my hand itching to slap the baboon. No doubt she saw it in my eye, and slid her chair back with a squelch, ready to meet the challenge. Oh, but she couldn't have known what scrap I'd give her. It was the child then, touching me lightly on the arm, who drew my attention. Her eyes, wide and watery, pleading. Her mouth quivered. And my heart broke open.

I found my wallet, slipped out a twenty, and flipped it like an ace of spades onto the table. I had another twenty and flipped it out too. "Two nights," I said.

That took the smirk from the vixen's face. And when I looked at the child, I nearly burst into tears to see her happiness, her once-tired face suddenly bright. The mother closed her eyes and formed a silent *thank you* with her lips. That portrait of the Living Jesus turned His head away in shame, and the sun portals of heaven opened and rained light down on me.

"You got ID?" the wench asked.

"ID?" the mother whispered.

The thing rolled her eyes at me. "She needs to show ID."

I saw distress cloud my little mother's face.

"What does she need ID for?"

"It's for her own safety."

"Her own safety?"

"In case she comes and goes."

"I won't go," the poor mother managed. "I'll stay right here. I won't be going out."

"Dem's the rules."

"Dem's stupid rules," I mocked. "Obviously she has no ID. She's homeless. Look at her. She's been beaten, thrown out, abandoned."

The head was dancing again and the big woman stood. "You might not like da rules, but deese is da rules. No ID, no bed."

"Whose rules?"

"My rules."

I changed tack. Obsequious now. "Sorry, so sorry. Listen." I took out my wallet and put a twenty-dollar bill on top of the other two. "I'll pay extra. What do you want, twenty? Thirty? How dare you scoff!"

She put her hands on her hips, inhaled, and the big chest filled out. Now she had the upper hand. A pine knot of a horn swelled above her left brow. The shadow of a tail flicked behind her. I saw then that I played against a devil, but devils can be tamed.

"I don't want yo' money. I was doing y'all a favor, till you come in here all . . ."

"All what?"

"All too-good." Glee cackled in her voice and her lips trembled to play it down. "Y'all need to go on to Pine Street. Pine Street will take her in."

"Better to go to hell," the mother said.

"You can do that too," said the bitch.

Outside, standing before the rusty Beetle, the mother turned to me. Standing close, whatever kept us distant melted for the moment. "Thank you," she said, "but I'd rather just sleep outside." She clutched the now-weeping child, whom she had held the whole time.

But I couldn't allow it. I drove to the Pine Street shelter. Hardly had the engine shut off when hands were helping the mother out of the car. Resignedly, she passed the child over to one of the young souls, and she was led away, living, into the tomb. The steel door clanked as it shut behind her. Gloom pervaded me. An iciness, a sinking, a sickening of the heart, an unredeemable dreariness of thought—my mind was in a swirl. I fought to satisfy myself that my little family would have shelter, incommodious though it was. Shelter and twenty dollars, and I would never see mother or child again.

But as the gods would have it, I would see that anthropoid bitch again. Ha! I am nothing if not a centurion in an army of good. She would pay for her falsity, for none are more false than those who pretend to do good. I waited for her, waited for her through the blackest hour of the night passing into the dreariness of dawn. And there she came. On all fours, as it were. I bagged her head. Oh, how she did fight! Kicking and scratching, and screaming such vexations that my ears hurt. In that neighborhood, such commotion draws no attention. Good twine held her and I stuffed her under the hood of the Beetle. Ho-HA! The little car shook with her struggling in the trunk. It took effort, but the strength of the gods were, as they are always, with me.

Kill you? Now *I* scoff! I have told you how I am a merciful man. But no. You shall keep company with the rats and the squirrels and all the dark shadows that creep and crawl in this old turret. That is how I am directed. The sweet little voice always in my ear. What does she say? You heard it rightly. *Evermore*, is what she says. *Selah.*

CARAMEL

BY TAYARI JONES

Cascade Heights

O n the day before Thanksgiving, Angie bought a skimpy strand of lights and strung it over the front door, asking why everything had to be so goddamn pitiful all the goddamn time. In my opinion, the lights with the lazy on-and-off only made the place more dreary and actually gave me a headache.

Last week a fight broke out in the lobby, so I grabbed a magazine and sheltered myself behind the desk. When I came up for air, the lights weren't working anymore and I just let them hang there, dead. No one complained. This job isn't a Secret Santa type of establishment. When Angie brought up the possibility, I cut her off: "The secret is that there's no Santa." Like everyone who doesn't have family, I hate Christmas like the devil hates holy water on the rocks.

All this took place at the LPF, a motel right off I-285, between Campbellton Road and the airport. When I was coming up it was called the Mark 6, but now it has new management, a new name, and a new sign out front with *LPF* tricked out in cursive like a rich lady's monogram. It's an inside joke that there are three types of hotels—tourist hotels, business hotels, and LPFs—which stands for *Local People Fucking*. The LPF isn't an hourly place because the blue laws in the state of Georgia don't permit that, just like they don't permit you to buy alcohol on Sundays, though they can't stop you from drinking it on the Lord's day. Underneath the monogram, the sign promises $49 *a night* because we know that nobody will stay here longer than a couple hours and that makes it a fair deal for everyone. It's a good business. I should know. The same room can be rented out three times in one day, adding up to $150 a night, same as the Peachtree Plaza downtown.

I've been here too long. For two years I've sat behind bulletproof glass, handling stolen credit cards and sticky dollar bills. But I always say working behind the counter of an LPF sure beats working on your back in one of the grimy rooms.

Not that I'm judging the horizontal occupation. Angie, the one with all the holiday spirit, earns her money like that and we are best friends. She and I were Mutt and Jeff when we were little and stayed with the same foster mother way out in Jonesboro. She gave me a nickname, Bluebuttons, because of my winter coat. We lost touch after my mother Regina got her act together, sprung me from the suburbs, and carried me back to our small cozy apartment where the sheets were always clean.

Fifteen years later, Angie tripped into the "lobby" of the LPF, pulled in by a white dude who swore up and down that America could be great again. Her back was to me as he handed over a pair of limp twenties and a ten. All I could see was her wig, a riot of curls the color of strawberry jelly. As he led her to the staircase, I saw her profile and recognized her instantly. The hair was new, but her face was the same as the little girl who let me share the bottom bunk because the other one smelled like pee.

"Angie?" I blurted.

"Of course it's me. Who else could it be?"

After that, my old friend became a regular and I tried to keep room 106 free for her.

We never really talk about what she does for a living. She calls the guys her *boyfriends,* and I go along with that, even when I see money exchange hands right there in the lobby. Being a friend means not asking too many questions. For her part, Angie never asks what became of Regina.

On Christmas Eve I got the night off, but I really didn't have anywhere to go. Holidays in general are a drag, but Christmas is the worst. It's like the world prints up your account statement and you see exactly how fucked up and lonely your life is. To raise my spirits, Angie invited me to room 106. The room was a little musty, but she tidied it up, making the bed and filling up the ice bucket. On the little particleboard dresser was a fifth of booze. Somehow, a giant pear floated in the belly of the bottle. As I unwrapped the thin plastic cups I found on the back of the toilet, I wondered how the hell the pear made it through the narrow glass bottleneck.

"My boyfriend gave me this for Christmas," she said, pouring me a slug. It tasted like someone took a can of fruit cocktail and set it on fire.

"It looks expensive," I replied, because it did, and because I knew this would make her smile.

"I wish he had just given me the money," Angie said, only pretending to complain. She tuned to V-103. Donny Hathaway sang out "This Christmas" in a very tiny voice. Angie twirled in the middle of the room wearing a green-sequined tube dress; the Santa cap pinned to her pink wig bobbed to the beat. "C'mon, Bluebuttons," she said, "dance."

There are two kinds of people: the ones who get drunk and want to dance and the ones who get drunk and want to cry. I fall into the second category.

"Oh sweet black baby Jesus," Angie said, "what's wrong?"

And just like that I let it all out, filling her in on everything that had happened since I left foster care holding my mother's hand. Regina had died three Christmas Eves ago. It hadn't come as a surprise exactly—anyone using that much heroin wasn't going to live forever—though I had expected her to last until Christmas Day. But no. On Christmas fucking Eve she took a hot shot somewhere near Bankhead Highway and died with the needle dangling from her arm. If it wasn't for the Medical Alert bracelet I'd given her, they would probably never have identified her.

"Blue," Angie said, "I liked your mother. She was pretty. That's what I remember."

"But wait," I responded, trying to lighten the mood, "there's more." I stood up and snatched open the worn blackout drapes. The view was of a clogged stretch of the perimeter highway lined with billboards, though I only cared about the one sporting the welcoming face of Lerome Johnson. Reverend Romie, the pastor of Rebirth Baptist Church, posed with his wife, both of them looking like real estate agents. Romie wasn't up there with Creflo Dollar and the late, great Eddie Long, but he was yapping at their heels. His parishioners couldn't buy him a private jet like Creflo's people, but Romie had a TV contract and there was coin enough in the collection plate at Rebirth Baptist to pay for a pair of Benzes. His wife was never seen after Labor Day without some kind of fur, even if it was just a fox collar on a wool suit.

Angie looked out the window. "Don't tell me ol' Romie is in this story. Seems like all roads in Atlanta lead back to Romie Johnson or Tyler Perry."

"You know black people are serious about their pastors."

"Romie wasn't always a preacher," Angie said, pouring herself some more brandy. "Before he got saved, he was a pimp. You don't believe me? He has this sermon about it. Look it up on YouTube. I heard it has over six million views."

"I've seen it. Doesn't he say his wife showed him the way?"

"She must have some good you-know-what." Angie helped herself to another splash of brandy. "But I can't lie, I do love me a singing preacher."

"You think he looks like me?" I asked her. "Maybe around the eyes?"

Angie squinted at me and I sat perfectly still. I could smell her pear-fire breaths.

I turned so she could check out my profile. "Not my nose, but the shape of my chin?"

"Sweet baby Jesus!" Angie hooted. "Please don't sit up here and tell me the Right Reverend is your real daddy! You thinking too small. If you talking crazy, tell people you are the lost bastard baby of President Obama's first cousin!"

"Angie. For real. My mama told me. She said they went to Washington High together and he carried her to his senior prom. She was just a freshman, but my grandmother let her go anyway. They went together two years, but when she got pregnant, he vanished."

"Trifling ass," Angie said with real sympathy.

"I just wish I could have five minutes alone with him. Five minutes."

"You sure he's the one?"

"Yes. My mother told me his name a long time ago. Used to say he was coming to get us and take us to Detroit."

That had been Regina's story and she'd stuck to it up until she first saw him on TV. This was about five years ago, and she was pretty far gone. My grandma warned me not to let her in the house, but how could I shut the door on my own mama? I gave her what money I had, mostly change I needed for the laundromat. She took it, shamefaced, then she sat on the couch, pretending like she had come over to say hi and watch some TV. This is how I knew she loved me: she cared about my feelings.

With nervous hands, she flipped through the channels and asked me about school. I told her I made straight A's which wasn't true, but she grinned, showing her teeth, dark and crooked. Still, there was real joy in her face. When you love a drug addict, you take what you can get. And that smile was all I got.

"Well I'll be a motherfucker," she said.

I looked at the TV and saw a large, well-groomed man speaking from the pulpit as the choir rocked behind him. She turned up the volume and closed her eyes as she took in that sweet singing voice. "Honey," Mama said, "that right there is your daddy."

"Well," Angie said now, "if you want him, you know where to find him every Sunday."

This, I knew. I had warmed the pew at Rebirth Baptist six Sundays in row, and on the jumbotron I watched the Good Reverend, glorious in purple robes, sharing the Good News in song. His voice was a rich baritone that filled me with longing. "He puts on a good show," I admitted. "I'll give him that much."

"So what you want with Romie? You want back–child support? All your pain and suffering? You should get double for that bitch of a foster mother we had." She lifted her cup and drank a long hot swallow to her own wisdom.

"No," I said, "I don't want money. I mean, if he gave it, I would take it. But really, I want to show him these pictures of my mother." On the bedspread I laid out two photos. On the first, you could see how beautiful my mother was when I was little. She was seventeen years old, thick-legged with bright eyes. As I rode her hip, we wore homemade floral dresses cut from the same fabric. The other picture told a different story. "This is her close to the end. On Thanksgiving. She looks like she's already dead."

Angie held the picture of my mother's ravaged face carefully, like she didn't want to cause more pain. "You can't tell nobody this, Blue. Romie didn't get where he is today by being a gentleman. You think you'd be the first person from his past to pop up with your hand sticking out?"

"*What?*"

"I know him. I know Romie. He's one of my boyfriends. He's a lot of people's boyfriend. It's not like I'm special, but he does call me by my name."

"You bring him here?" I said, looking around room 106 like I was going to discover something meaningful

Angie smirked. "Girl, the Right Reverend can't be seen in the LPF unless he claims to be trying to convert the wicked."

I sat back on the bed feeling stupid. "You must meet him at the W Hotel. Or the Biltmore."

"No hotels. He can't risk it. We go to his house."

"*We* who? You and him *we*, or *we* like he lets you bring somebody with you?"

"Oh no," Angie said, looking at me. "No ma'am, no way. You're not going to make me lose the best boyfriend I have. It's nice over at his house. He lets you take a bath in the whirlpool tub. Tip, everything. The only thing he asks is that you can keep a secret."

"One time when I was little," I told Angie, "my mother took me to Rich's downtown to ride the Pink Pig. That's the last time I can remember being happy on Christmas. Back then she used to sign a couple of my birthday presents *Daddy*. She thought he was coming back. When she realized he was gone for good, that's when she hit the streets."

Angie and I were so close that our heads rested on the same pillow. "Why don't you just leave it alone? Remember your mama and Rich's and whatever shiny memories you have. Keep the first picture and throw the other one away. You're not going to get nothing out of Romie. Trust me, I know him."

"I just want to show him the photos."

"Why?"

"I want him to live with it for the rest of his life, just like I have to live with it."

"Let it go, Bluebuttons. That's survival rule #415. Look at me. You got a sad story. I got a sad story. My mama finally got me out of foster care and took me to live with her and my nasty dog of a stepfather. She never did a thing to help me. But do I play that same home movie over in my head on loop?" Angie turned over on her side, facing the window. The talking and the blues gave weight to the air in the room.

At the edge of my line of vision, Romie Johnson smiled on his billboard. *All are welcome*, he promised, as the soft face of his wife seemed to agree.

"Angie, if you could meet your real father, wouldn't you do it?" Now I turned on my side too, and fitted my body around hers the way we did when we were two little thrown-away children. Christmas Eve at the LPF. It was depressing as hell.

"Bluebettons," Angie whispered, "I have a date with Romie just before the new year."

The Right Reverend Dr. Lerome "Romie" Johnson lives two turns off Cascade Road, and so do I. The difference is that I live in the West End where the primary business establishments are strip clubs, churches, and beauty supply shops. The only modern convenience is the chrome-and-glass Krispy Kreme said to be owned by Hank Aaron. The reverend, on the other hand, lives ten miles west down this same road, but down there subdivisions sit back from the street, protected by wrought-iron gates, softened with twists and curlicues. This is something that never ceases to amaze me about Atlanta: whatever you can think of, there is a black person doing it—probably up and down Cascade Road. Crackheads, CEOs, and everything in between.

When Angie and I arrived at the gates of Guilford Forest, the guard waved us though like he was expecting us. We looked like two girls home from college in our V-neck sweaters and tight jeans. Safe in my purse were the two pictures of my mother. I opened the bag to take a look, hoping the nice photo would be on top, but instead Regina's dead eyes stared back at me.

Angie said, "Before we go in, tell me one more time what you think this is going to accomplish."

"I just want him to know what he did to her. She would have gone to college if it wasn't for him." And if it wasn't for me, growing inside her.

"Remember," Angie said, "when this goes down, I don't know nothing. I'm going to act shocked as hell. I might call you a bitch or something, so don't take it personal." Then, before she could ring the bell, the Right Reverend threw open the door and stood in the glow of a gorgeous chandelier the size of a Volkswagen. Behind him a Christmas tree stretched up all three stories; glass ornaments cast rainbows across the room.

After he took a quick look inside our handbags, finding no weapons or cell phones, his face opened into a smile. "Angie," he said, patting her on the ass. "Looking good."

"You ain't too bad yourself," she countered with a wink.

"Who you got with you? Damn, she's fine. Is she for me or Deacon Shipp?"

"She's all yours," Angie said.

I took a cautious step forward. As he looked me over, I took stock of him as well. According to the Internet, he was forty-eight years old, but he managed to look older and younger at the same time. His attire was what they call *business casual*, but his bald head gleamed like it had been waxed and his salt-and-pepper facial hair was groomed more carefully than my weave. I took my time on his face, searching for some resemblance. I settled on his eyes, round like mine, and his lips, fuller on the bottom than the top, just like mine.

"Come say hello to Romie," he said, opening his arms, though he was distracted by a noise on the stairs behind me. I turned to see a man dressed in a tracksuit and an Obama hat, looking like somebody's uncle. "Sorry to be late, ladies. I was waiting for my medicine to kick in. Ooh," he added, staring at me, "is that for yours truly? 'Bout time I had me something nice."

"Naw, Branford," the reverend said. "Yours is in the kitchen. This is for me." He turned and motioned toward the Scarlett O'Hara staircase. "Shall we go upstairs? I'm sorry to be abrupt but Mrs. Johnson will be back in two hours and I don't like to rush." He raised his eyebrows and wet his lips. Somewhere in the belly of the huge house, I could hear Angie giggling. Her voice was light, like that of a little girl.

The reverend took me by the hand and led me to a white-carpeted bedroom. The furniture was old-fashioned, maybe antique. Cherrywood everything.

He held my small cold hand in his large hot one. "Are you nervous? Do you watch me on TV?"

"Sometimes," I whispered. I couldn't take my eyes off the large four-poster bed in the center of room.

"Well, don't be scared. I'll be gentle. At first." Then he chuckled and sat on the side of the bed, began unbuttoning his shirt, and motioned for me to do the same. When I couldn't convince my body to move, he stood up, caught me around the waist, and tossed me playfully onto the bed. "You want me to undress you?"

Thrashing like a bug on its back, I struggled up off the soft mattress. I reached for my purse on the nightstand, removing the pretty picture and holding it up to his puzzled face.

"Who's that?" he asked.

"My mother, Regina Owens."

He frowned. "Is that supposed to ring a bell?" He took another look, muttering her name slowly like the syllables tasted good in his mouth.

"She lived over by Washington High? She said you took her to the prom."

Now his face changed from curious to suspicious. "Is this some kind of hustle? You and Angie running some kind of con?"

"No, it's not like that."

"Well, what's it like? Do we have to stroll down memory lane before you give me what I paid for? See, this is why I don't like girls who work without a pimp. No one to complain to when service is bad."

"I'm not a ho," I said.

"You're one today." Gracefully for a man so large, he was suddenly on his feet and standing between me and the door. His cologne smelled like matches. "Now get out of those clothes and give me what I paid for."

"You're my father," I said in a rush, like it was a magic password. And it worked. He sat back on the bed.

"Get the hell out of here. Show me that picture again."

I gave him the pretty one.

"What did you say her name was again?"

"Regina."

"Oh yeah," he said, absently scratching his hairy chest. "I knew her back before I was saved. Back when I was still living a life of sin. But we called her Caramel."

I shook my head. "You got her mixed up with somebody else. My mother was in high school when she knew you. She wanted to go to Spelman College."

He looked at the picture again and barked out a laugh. "That's Caramel all right. She was mine for just a little while, that's why I can't hardly remember. How's she doing these days?"

Now was the time to hand him the second picture, yet I hesitated. When I'd taken the photo, Regina asked me to delete it, to wait until she could fix herself up, though I knew that she would never be fixed. She had tried to cover her face with her hands, which were dotted with sores, but she was too slow.

My fingers on the photo hesitated. I took in the reverend, fatted like a calf and prosperous as Abraham. I couldn't stand the idea of him seeing her ashen, slack-faced, and toothless, all the while mumbling her name. Regina's ruined face was her own private business. I zipped the purse shut on my mother's suffering.

"She passed," I told him.

"Did she find the Lord before she went?"

"She found the needle."

He looked at the crystal clock beside the bed. "Look, young lady. I'm not your daddy." He lay back on a stack of six or seven lacy pillows. "I never dipped in the kitty. Not even to break them in; I let Branford take care of all of that." He smiled at the memory.

I plucked the pretty picture from his hand and slipped it into my jeans pocket. I thought about what Angie had said about leaving things alone and I figured that maybe she was right—but it was too late now. My sad story had just gotten sadder.

"Come on, sweetheart," the reverend said. "How long have you been in the family business? Come show ol' Romie how your mama trained you up."

"Can you tell me anything else about her? What she was like?" My voice was soft like a sleepy child's.

He flashed what I knew was his pimp smile, the one he'd flashed at my mother so many years ago. It was a smile that said, *I'll take care of you*, while at the same time saying, *Don't make me angry*, and, *Nobody loves you but me*. He held out his hand and gripped me tight on my arm, jerking me down onto his bare chest, his arms closing around me like a gate.

"Don't be scared, little girl," he breathed hot and wet into my ear. "I'm not your father but I can be your daddy."

COMET

BY DAVID JAMES POISSANT

Stone Mountain

The morning is cold and dark, and my father has brought me to the mountain to see the comet. This is February 1986, a Sunday. This is Georgia. People have gathered at the base of Stone Mountain, jacketed and hatted, mittened and earmuffed. They stand in line for bathrooms, for concessions, for tickets to the cable car. The cable car isn't a car, but a big blue box that pulls people through the air on wires and up the mountain's side. The cable car travels in minutes a distance that will take us an hour to cover on foot. My father doesn't have money for the ride. He tells me it's an honor to walk, that I won't get this chance again for seventy-six years. By then, he says, my kneecaps will be gravel and he'll be dead, so we might as well make the most of it. My father calls himself a *realist*, which I've learned means a person who sometimes doesn't know what's not okay to say in front of your ten-year-old son.

"C'mon, buddy," he says, and I trot to keep up.

My father is not like other fathers, not like the fathers of my friends or the fathers who come to school on Dad Day and talk about their jobs. Those fathers are doctors and plumbers and lawyers. My father has no job. Other fathers dress in suits. They wear watches and ties. They carry briefcases with silver dials that spin and click when they lock. My father wears jean shorts and tank tops. He wears an Atlanta Braves baseball cap. He smokes, which Miss Gillespie says will give him lung cancer. My father says I'm too young to worry about cancer and that I can tell Miss Gillespie to mind her own *goddamned* business, which I can't because that word's not allowed in fourth grade.

Everyone at the bottom of the mountain has come prepared. They carry thermoses and water bottles. Binoculars hang from their necks. Telescopes hang in bags from their shoulders. Nothing hangs from us and we have nothing to drink. My Hawks sweatshirt is the kangaroo kind, and I hide my hands in the pouch to keep warm. I wish I had a hat. I wish I had gloves. When the sun rises, we'll be warm, but the goal is to get up the mountain before the sun is up, to see the comet in the jet-black sky.

Miss Gillespie says we're a lucky generation, that we're young enough to see Halley's twice if we don't die from lung cancer first. (Miss Gillespie is also a realist.) Her mother died over winter break, which is why she's all the time talking about death. My mother died two and a half years ago when a man ran his car into her car. She was wearing a seat belt, only sometimes seat belts don't save lives. Sometimes the other car's just going too fast. The man driving the other car died on impact. *On impact* was how the officer put it to my father on the phone. I know because I picked up the upstairs phone to listen in. I don't do that anymore.

My mother did not die on impact. At the hospital, a man in a white coat told us she'd pull through before he told us she hadn't.

Not long after this, my father started smoking. Then came the first tattoo. Later came the layoffs at work, the second tattoo, and the man in the jean jacket. Then came the women.

Each woman hangs around a week, maybe two, then

we never see her again. My father thinks I don't know what they're in his room doing, but I know. Aunt Susan calls them the *Rockettes*. As in, she'll call the house and ask, "Are the Rockettes in town?" and I'm supposed to tell her whether a woman's staying with us that week or not. Some weeks, I tell Aunt Susan the truth. Some weeks, I don't. Aunt Susan was Mom's sister, so she takes her job seriously. Her job, as she sees it, is to see that I don't turn into my dad.

Starting up the mountain, my father takes my hand, then drops it. Sometimes he forgets I'm ten, that I can make my own cereal, tie my own shoes, wait for the bus on our street by myself. Mornings, he'll pour us bowls of Lucky Charms. He'll put in more milk than I like, then ask, at the end, why I don't drink the milk, which by then is electric blue because of all the marshmallows and the food coloring, which Miss Gillespie says causes cancer too, but which I don't tell my father about because I like to keep my mornings quiet. So I'll drink the milk, and my father's arms will be huge with tattoos—dragons, knives, a snake encircling a skull—and my father will stub out his cigarette in an ashtray already full, and I'll try not to cough so he won't feel bad for how much the smoke burns my throat, my eyes, and I'll ask him to maybe next time let me pour the milk, knowing next time he'll forget. Mom never forgot.

We walk, and I'm cold. The mountain is quiet and dark, and the people on it walk in dark and quiet ways. It's like we're on our way to church, but it's too early for church, for church bells or for birds, plus Dad and I haven't been to church since Mom died. There's no moon in the sky, which Miss Gillespie calls the *new moon*, which I say makes no sense. My father says the new moon will make it easier to see the comet. I tell him he should have brought a flashlight. There are few lights on the mountain. My shins hit rocks. My sneakers catch on roots. He tells me to pick up my feet when I walk, another expression I say makes no sense.

I look up, and Halley's is a smudge, a thumbprint caught in wet paint. I think this, then feel smart for thinking it. *Figurative language*, Miss Gillespie calls it. It's a metaphor, or else it's a simile. I can't remember which uses *like* or *as*.

It's not a school night. Even if it were, my father would have brought me here. He says school is for people who think the answers to life's questions can be found in books. When I ask him where he finds the answers to life's questions, he takes me in his arms and says, "You."

The trail narrows, and we migrate in a herd. It's not our first time up the mountain, Dad and me. When you live in Atlanta, the mountain is a tradition, a landmark.

Stone Mountain, if you don't know it, is a big, big rock. It's rounded on top like the dome of an egg, and there's a picture carved into its side. In the picture, Jefferson Davis, Stonewall Jackson, and Robert E. Lee ride into battle. The carving's bigger than Mount Rushmore. Most people don't know that. Most people don't know it's the biggest carving in the world. Some people don't like the mountain on account of its history, how before it was a park the mountain was owned by a man in the Klan. It's here the KKK burned their first cross. My father says that was a long time ago. Miss Gillespie says 1915 was practically yesterday. She says people who forget the past are doomed to repeat it. She says the park and its laser light show celebrate hate.

Except, if the mountain is a place of hate, it's also a place families gather in love.

Stone Mountain, for me, is more than its light show or the cure for a long summer day. It's the place my father proposed to my mom. It's where I'm told I took my first steps. It's where my mother brought us to watch fireworks the night before she died.

Stone Mountain is the place my father takes me to fish and swim. I'll swim, and my father will sit on a towel and smoke. He rolls his own cigarettes. He thinks I don't notice when he pulls from the second baggie, the one the tobacco's not in. And maybe a year ago I didn't notice. Or maybe a year ago he wasn't yet smoking weed and the man in the jean jacket wasn't always at our door.

We climb. On the trail, a girl whimpers. She wears one shoe. Her mother throws up her arms, cursing. A minute later, we pass a dad, red-faced and sweating. "Trevor," he yells, "you just *went* to the bathroom!" The boy named Trevor lowers himself to the ground and cries into his mittens. My father puts his hand on my back and pushes me past Trevor, past the girl, up the mountain, and ahead of him.

One good thing about my father is that, though he yells, he almost never yells at me. He used to. Before Mom died, Dad had a temper. I'd forget to wash my dinner plate or make my bed, and he would be in my room, screaming. After the accident, Dad was different. These days, dinner comes in Styrofoam containers, and neither of us make our beds. These days, Dad saves his shouting for the things he says matter, like who should be president or what gets taught in school. Instead of shouts, I get smoke and dust, ash in the ashtrays and garbage begging to be carried out. Twice a month, Aunt Susan drives down from Nashville with a bottle of Windex and a mop. She makes me shower, even if I showered the night before, then watches while I brush my teeth. The weekends Aunt Susan's here, Dad doesn't bring women home.

Halfway up the mountain stands a shelter with picnic tables and benches, a lamppost, boulders smoothed by centuries of butts. My father finds a boulder, and we sit. This morning, he's not dressed the way he's usually dressed. He wears jeans and cowboy boots, a green jacket with brass buttons and what he calls *fruit salad* on the front. He looks like a soldier from a war from before I was born. I don't know who the jacket belonged to, whether it was handed down or whether my father found it at Goodwill.

From his jacket pocket, he removes his rolling papers and tobacco pouch. At home, he lets me roll cigarettes for him, or at least lick the paper, but not here, not when other grownups are around. Dad says I roll a *mean cigarillo*. By *mean*, he means *good*. Miss Gillespie calls this a *Janus word*, how a word can mean its opposite, the way in Hawaii they say *Aloha* both coming and going.

Dad licks his cigarette. I ask if I can hold the lighter. He looks around, gives the Zippo wheel a spin, and the dark between our faces turns to flame. He hands me the lighter, which I hold while he touches one end of the cigarette to the wick.

"Nice work," he says, and I flip the lighter closed.

A woman on a bench watches us. She gives me a look. It's a look I'm used to getting these past couple of years, a look that asks, *Honey, are you okay?* And I want to tell her to go away. I want to tell the woman on the bench to leave us alone, that yes, my father smokes too much, that he curses, but he doesn't curse at me, that yes, his teeth are yellow, his hair greasy beneath his baseball cap, that his clothes are dirty, yes, but that he always makes sure I'm clean and have clean clothes. That while he may look like the father in movies with bad fathers in them, my father hugs me, feeds me, listens, never hits. That he lets me play his records. That he takes me to the zoo to see Willie B. That at night he reads me the funny pages, and when I ask, he tells me stories about Mom. And so what if he reads with a cigarette in his hand. So what if there's a halo of white around his nose. So what if some nights his eyes go watery, and he'll rise, midsentence, and walk out of the room. Or if some nights he'll keep me out too late. Or if last winter I got sick because Dad forgot a bill and for a week we had no heat.

But mostly I want to tell the woman on the bench that this is my father. I am his son. Where she sees danger, worry, I see *love*.

Of course, I can't say any of this, so I stick out my tongue.

The woman's eyes widen. If I thought I could give her the finger without my father noticing, I would.

Then the woman is up and coming toward us. She's standing at our feet. She's tall. Her jacket is blue and puffy. On the front, in block letters, the jacket's stamped, *Land's End*.

"Sir," she says, addressing my father.

My father takes his time addressing her. He sucks on his cigarette, exhales, and sets the cigarette, still smoldering, on the rock beside him. He runs his palms the length of his pant legs, then looks up.

"Sir," the woman in the Land's End jacket says, "is this your son?"

My father looks me up and down like he can't make up his mind. "I reckon I'll claim him," he says.

The woman isn't sure what to make of this. She's lost the swagger she walked over with. Her hands leave her hips and cross her chest, and standing like that, she looks like the man in the jean jacket, how he stands in our doorway, arms crossed, and shouts. *My boy's home*, my father will say, and most nights this stops the shouting. One night, the man in the jean jacket did not stop shouting. The next day, when I got home from school, my father's arm was in a sling.

"Your son—" the woman says, and it's like she's so angry she can't find the words. I've seen this too. I see it every other weekend when my aunt walks through the door. It's the face of my mother, except that the face is otherworldly in its anger, furious in a way my mother never was in life. Each time I see it, I wish my aunt didn't look so much like Mom.

The woman in the Land's End jacket is all but shaking. "Your son stuck his"—and here her voice drops to a whisper—"he stuck his *tongue* out at me."

My father's eyebrows lift in what looks like genuine befuddlement. "Well," he says to the woman, "what on earth did you do to deserve that?"

At this, the woman's eyes roll in their sockets. Her arms uncross then recross her chest. My father plucks his cigarette from the rock beside him and brings it to his lips.

"You, sir," the woman says, "you ought to have your son taken away from you."

"I'm going to stop you right there," my father says. He stands, and he and the woman are eye and eye. And my father doesn't have to say anything more. The woman's eyes narrow, but soon she about-faces and marches back to her bench where she takes the hand of a boy about my age. The boy wears a jacket that matches his mom's, and his hair is hairsprayed into place. His pant cuffs are tucked into his socks, and his Nikes look new.

I watch the mother pull the boy up the mountain away from us, and I wonder, not for the first time since the accident, what it would be like to be a boy like that, to have a mother like that. My mother would have been a mother like that.

The women Dad brings home are nothing like my mom. They wear too much makeup or no makeup at all. They use words I've only ever heard men say. Some of the women are nice to me. One took me out for ice cream. She bought me chocolate, which I don't like, but I ate the ice cream anyway. I didn't want to hurt her feelings. Her name was Claire, and my father talked about her like she might be my new mom. She had a pretty smile and smelled like maple syrup. She didn't stick around for long. The nice ones never do.

My father sits. He puts his cigarette out on the rock. "The heck was that?" he says, but I can see he's trying not to smile. "You can't make faces at people, buddy. You know that. Not at grown-ups, anyway. Save your faces for school. And, I don't know, respect your elders."

Sometimes when my father's parenting, he says things he thinks he's supposed to say, echoing truths I'm not sure he believes.

"Sorry," I say.

"Don't be sorry. Just, you know, be nice."

My father stands, and in the lamplight he casts a massive shadow. He is not massive. He used to be bigger, like my uncles, like me. *Husky*, my mother called it, that word parents use for *fat* when they're trying not to hurt your self-esteem. But my father's no longer husky. He's thin. He's, like, really, really thin these past few months.

"You know," he says, "I didn't think to bring binoculars."

"That's okay," I say. And it is, it's okay, though this is an exchange we have a lot, my father forgetting something important—essential, even—the kind of thing a normal parent would never forget, and me assuring him that I don't want a normal parent, I want him.

Up the mountain, walking, walking. The higher we climb, the steeper the trail gets, and wider too. The people spread out, and there is room enough to stretch my arms, though I keep my hands snug in the pocket of my shirt.

My father whistles. He's an expert whistler. He loves music, the radio dial at home frozen to 96 Rock. There's no song he can't whistle, but he'll whistle without music too, making a melody up as he goes. I like when he does this, and he does it now. A few heads turn, but that's never stopped my father. He fills up the mountainside with song.

We're close to the top when he asks to stop again and rest. I know what it is he's wanting, so I walk far enough away that he can do what he needs to do.

I stand beside a pine tree. I pull off black shingles of bark. I catch a branch and pull the needles from it, green and whisker-thin. On a rock, my father sprinkles powder on the back of his hand. He lowers his head. When his hand leaves his face, the powder's gone. I don't know the name for this, I only know it's what makes my father thin. And I know enough not to ask. Not my father, and not Miss Gillespie or Aunt Susan, who don't need another reason to be hard on him.

My aunt likes to scold my father about money. "That settlement could have lasted you ten years," Aunt Susan said late one night. She and my father sat at the table in the kitchen she'd just cleaned. They thought I was asleep, but children are never asleep when parents think they are. In this way, from the quiet of our beds, we learn our parents' lives.

"Ten years," Aunt Susan said, "and it's lasted you two."

My father didn't say a word. He's grateful to her, for what she does for us, for me.

"Some people," he'll tell me, "you just have to let them talk."

I imagine my father would let Aunt Susan say anything to him. The man in the jean jacket too. He gets to say whatever he wants. But that's something else. My father calls it *re-*

spect, but I know my father. When the man in the jean jacket speaks, my father is afraid.

That night, though, the night in the kitchen, the night my aunt went on about the money that came to us after the accident, she said too much. "You know," she said, "my sister would be ashamed of you, of what you're doing to her son." My father didn't say a word. There was only the squeak of his chair on linoleum, the front door chain pulled free. The door opened and shut. I thought he had walked outside, but then he was there at the foot of my bed. I shut my eyes. Outside, my aunt's car started. When I opened my eyes, my father had left the room. In the morning, he told me that my uncle had the flu, that she had to get back to Nashville to make him soup and sing to him, the way she had the winter before when I'd been sick. We watched each other, then, across the breakfast table. We both knew I'd been awake, but it was as though we'd agreed, right there, over our bowls of Lucky Charms with too much milk, to pretend otherwise. "The flu," I said, a Janus word for why my aunt had gone.

When the limb in my hand is free of its needles, I return to my father. I chew on a single green pine needle. It tastes the way Christmas smells.

Dad stands. His head tips back. He watches the night awhile, black sky, no moon, white comet, bright stars. "I thought it would be bigger," he says.

I nod. I'd thought so too. Then my father is kneeling. His face is close to mine, so close our noses almost touch, and I see he's been crying. Tears don't run down his face. It's more like he'd tipped his head back to keep the tears in. His eyes swim in bright water.

"You know I love you, right?" my father says. "That I'll always love you?"

But before I can answer, he has my hand. He's pulling me, dragging me, walking fast, too fast, up the mountain. I pick my feet up, and I'm jogging, running, and then I'm flying. My father is big again, and strong. He lifts me onto his shoulders, the way he hasn't done in years, and my hands leave my pockets, I reach out my arms, and soar.

But only for a minute. And then we reach the top.

Hundreds have gathered, women and men and children in the dark. They stand in groups and watch the sky. Telescopes are everywhere on tripods short and tall. Above us, Halley's Comet is fuzzy, as though no matter how close we get, the comet will remain a thumbprint caught in paint, a cosmic smudge. Miss Gillespie says this is because every comet has a *coma*, a halo of gas and dust that makes it hard to see.

My father and I stand beside the mountaintop control tower, a small gray building two people, maybe three, could fit inside. From here, the big blue gondola goes up and down. The box arrives, swaying. Ten people in hats and jackets step off, and ten people take their places. My father pulls back the sleeve of his jacket. He's wearing a watch I've never seen.

"C'mon," he says, "we've got some time."

So we walk into the crowd. And we spend an hour that way. We borrow binoculars and look through other families' telescopes. We see the woman in the blue jacket and her son, and when my father's not looking, I stick my tongue out again. My father smokes three cigarettes, and I play tag with a girl in pink gloves.

And then my father motions for me to join him, and we sit. The rock is cold, and I can feel the granite through my pants.

"What do you think, buddy?" he says. "Cool asteroid?"

I nod. I don't correct him, though I know from school that

comets aren't asteroids. A comet is an iceberg caught in space. Halley's is ice and rock and dust squeezed in God's fist and let go, an intergalactic fastball doomed to forever circle our sun. The halo around Halley's is sixty thousand miles wide and its tail is six million miles long. It travels at speeds of forty miles a second, which Miss Gillespie says is faster than the human mind can comprehend. But I can comprehend it. How some things take less than a second. How a life can go out like a light.

And I'm thinking how I should maybe be nicer to Miss Gillespie, how on Monday I should take her hand and tell her that I know how she feels, that my mother's dead too. Maybe she won't believe me, or maybe the second I say it, she'll know. Maybe there's a current that runs between people who share the same vast grief.

My hands are back in my pockets, and my father pulls me close to keep me warm. He checks his watch again, and then he's standing.

"What now?" I say, but he doesn't have words for what comes next. We walk in the direction of the control tower. In the distance, a glow, and I know the sun will soon be up. Around us, people are collapsing tripods and packing up their things. One family has put down a blanket and eats breakfast on the rock.

We join the line for the cable car. "We don't have tickets," I say, but my father won't look at me. The box arrives. Ten people step off, ten more step on, and the box rides cables down the mountainside. The line moves forward. I count, and my father and I are *nine* and *ten*. I wait for the next ride.

The cable car returns, and it's a long time emptying because one of the passengers doesn't want to get off. I wonder what this means, whether I'll ride down with my father or wait for the next car. But I don't have to wonder long. My father hugs me. "Son," he says, but the rest is lost to wind and sunrise, to the groan of the swaying cable car, and to my father's eyes, which are wide and wet and hungry and wild, like no eyes I hope to see again.

He turns me away from the cable car and points. And there is my mother. She holds one hand to her mouth. With her other hand she waves, and I lose my balance. I have to sit. When I turn, my father is in the cable car and the door is closed. His back is to me. And maybe I only imagine it, but I swear, the man in the jean jacket is there beside him, a hand on his shoulder, and they're all wrapped up, enclosed in a cloud of something like light. Then the car pulls away.

I stand. I want to cry out, but there is a hand at my back. I turn, and it is not my mother beside me. It is my aunt. She stands very still, and I cry into her coat.

Then she walks me away from the cables, past the control tower, past children playing and parents shedding coats, to an outcropping of rock where my uncle is setting up a telescope that I will peer through, looking to see what's been, and what's to come.

COME YE, DISCONSOLATE

BY DANIEL BLACK

Mechanicsville

Paused at the corner of McDaniel and Abernathy streets one hot, muggy summer night, I encountered the hypnotizing melody of a songbird. It was a sweet, soothing tune, a child's lullaby—light and majestic, smooth and easy like a trickling brook. My windows were down because the AC was out. That, plus a grueling day at the post office, left me longing for an amaretto sour and a cold shower. When I heard the voice, I searched desperately, left and right, but saw only a church—the Perfect Church—on one corner and a hoodied young man on the other. He was rail-thin and tall, like a young oak sapling. His hoodie matched the nighttime sky and draped his shoulders like an oversized curtain. I knew he was dealing; I saw the look in his beady eyes. He couldn't have been more than twenty, but his aura showed older, as if somehow he'd grown tired of living. Every few seconds he glanced about, anxious, it seemed, for something he couldn't find. When our eyes met, we seemed to study each other's desperation, wondering what had forced our meeting in the wee hours of the morning. His brows rose suddenly, though slightly, inquiring of my need. I blinked and turned away. He did likewise, but kept his hands in his pouch. That's where Death lay, I supposed, waiting to devour the last remnants of a dejected people. I shook my head, but didn't judge the youngster. I'd been lost most of my life too.

Some had hoped this part of town might evolve into a thriving minimetropolis, being only minutes from downtown, but it never happened. It was a war zone, really. Old, dilapidated shotgun shacks still characterized the neighborhood, and the one new apartment complex, built alongside train tracks on McDaniel, was so gated as to feel militaristic. I lived in one of the newly built town homes farther down Abernathy, which used to be Gordon Road, walking distance from the Braves' stadium. Months after settling in, I considered flipping the property, but then heard rumor the city meant to demolish the stadium and rebuild it—twenty miles north. Damn.

My wife, a second grade teacher, was never seen after sundown. She hated our neighborhood, she said, overrun with goons and crackheads, and she hated she'd ever married me. She simply couldn't believe I'd brought her *here*, she emphasized, flailing frustrated arms in every direction. If she needed something from the car at night, she either begged me to retrieve it or simply waited until morning. When news broadcasts reported a murder or theft in our area—Mechanicsville— she'd murmur, "I must be the biggest fool in America. Mama warned me against this."

Last thing I needed that scorching summer night was her negative belligerence, so I lingered at the light as the distant melody pacified my fatigue. Trying to catch every note, I listened closely, narrowing eyes as if somehow that might intensify my hearing. The voice was so beautiful I almost cried. Straining frantically, I turned my left ear to the wind, hoping to catch more clearly a melody I'd heard only once before. When the light turned green, I didn't go. No cars lingered behind me, so I sat spellbound, determined to discover the source of the sound. Suddenly, with squinted eyes, I saw her. She sat in an abandoned lot with her back against a deteriorated brick structure that should've been demolished. Her face was turned away from me as if she were watching something pass by, so I guessed she didn't see me. She was nearer than I'd supposed, singing a faint, sweet soprano that reignited something within me. Only by reading her lips did I discern the lyrics: *I sing because I'm happy, I sing because I'm free . . .*

Her slender eyes glistened topaz beneath a full moon. She knew something; she understood something; she believed something. Confidence shone all about her. Her head shook like one who finally comprehended a difficult thing. I couldn't move. A tan SUV approached from the rear, blaring its horn. In a flash, it pulled around me and sped away. I engaged my hazards and continued listening and reading her lips: *His eye is on the sparrow, and I know he watches me . . .*

She repeated the final line as her voice tumbled into an alto abyss. I had closed my eyes, but now I opened them and stared out into the night. She was looking at me. It wasn't a gaze of shame or desperation, but of curiosity, wonder, and hope. She wasn't despondent as I thought she would be, as I assumed she *should* be. Rather, her eyes, questioning and wandering, assaulted me. They asked who *I* was, why *I* had stopped, what *I* wanted. I had no answers. I think I was offended. Who was she to question *me*? I was the privileged one. I lived in a *legitimate* home, with real, store-bought food and paid utilities. What did she have?

After turning off my hazards, I crept away. The woman's stealth and poise had unsettled me, while her voice, like falling rain, drummed steadily in my head. *Why should I feel discouraged?* she'd asked, as though once guilty of ingratitude. I chuckled. She had every right to be discouraged, it seemed to me. The lot in which she dwelled held trash, broken bottles, discarded tires, and dirty weeds. A scenic foretelling of the apocalypse. A breeding ground for disease and dismay. The fragile shack at her back threatened to collapse at any moment. There were no windows, no doors, no soul. Just a brick shell abandoned like a forlorn lover. But more than that, it bore a painful emptiness I couldn't forget. The burnt-out structure exuded disgrace and shame, as if naked and on display. Perhaps it would be rebuilt one day and acquire newfound meaning and purpose. One day.

This seemed the hope of Mechanicsville itself. Poor, silent residents shuffled about, waiting for someone to recognize their humanity. Or for the world to end. Most looked sullen and gloomy, shrouded with grief. Unemployment had done its work, and crack was more accessible than food. The closest grocer, miles down Abernathy, was too far to walk to and yet too close for a cab—if a cab would ever come. Even the mailman sensed danger, slinging letters and notices onto front steps instead of placing them into proper boxes. I'd noticed him looking over his shoulder every few minutes, as if running from something unseen. Still, as with the hoodied boy, I didn't blame him either.

Yet the singing woman wasn't like the others. Streetlight had illuminated a baby-smooth complexion and dark, glowing skin. There were no wrinkles, no crow's-feet, no signs of aging. Only worn, tired eyes. She looked to be in her forties but she was probably older. Her mouth twisted and trembled as she sang, as though tasting each note on her tongue. She was petite—frail, really—with small breasts that hardly bulged. Yet she reeked of femininity, bearing hoop earrings and a ragged head wrap like rural women of Africa. Something about her demeanor suggested dignity, even nobility, and that's what disturbed me most. I'd wanted to think of her as impoverished, as pitifully indigent, yet her spirit wouldn't allow this.

It insisted that I see her, that I honor her, that I recognize her survival.

So did her voice. It wasn't of this world. It shimmied bold like morning dew and echoed in my head with the clear, precise pitch of a thrush bird. There was no rasp, no guttural growl, no shrill, harsh tone. Only elegance and grace. It sounded trained and polished, as if she'd studied vocal technique, although I knew she hadn't. Her runs, unlike those of many singers, were controlled and tempered, rippling through the air like eternal life, dancing in the ether like newborn freedom. I'd never been so taken. Halfway home, I thought to return to the desolate corner and hear more from this poor cherub, but instead I pulled into my driveway, silenced the car, and closed my eyes. There it was again, her voice, tumbling through my consciousness. It evoked tears I hadn't felt in years. So much pain unspoken, so much hurt ignored. But now her voice massaged my weary soul and unleashed immeasurable anxiety. *Why should my heart be lonely, and long for heaven and home?* I hadn't cried like that since I was a kid. About anything. My wife said I'd become someone—no, she said *something*—unrecognizable, unfeeling, uncaring. But it wasn't true. I simply didn't share my heart with her because what I felt was no one's business—including hers.

Still, I took a chance and told her about the singing woman. She said, "That's nice!" smiling the smile of tolerance. I escaped to the den and played Nancy Wilson's "Guess Who I Saw Today?" The song made me pensive, reflective, and that's what I wanted—to relive the encounter and be consumed, once again, in the homeless woman's mercy. I poured a cocktail and reclined in the leather rocker. I'd thought I'd wanted a divorce last year, and had even asked for it, but after weeks of tortuous therapy, I acquiesced and stayed. Patricia was a decent woman. She had no drive, though, no ambition outside of me, which of course I despised, but who else would tolerate, without complaint, a middle-aged, half-bald man of moderate income, one who had brought her to hell and decided to stay? It just wasn't worth the fight, I decided. We knew how to be miserable together. No need learning a new thing.

I heard the woman's voice in my sleep. At first I thought I was dreaming, then I sat up as the strain intensified: *When Jesus is my portion, a constant friend is he! His eye is on the sparrow, and I know he watches me!*

Outside my bedroom window, branches waved in rhythm to the song. As rain fell, I wondered if the woman was still on the corner, still singing contentment in the midst of a storm. If so, her faith certainly exceeded mine. She seemed able to see beyond the obvious, to find beauty in any situation. I'd never learned that. Things had to make direct sense to me. Gleaning goodness from tragedy, for example, meant simply lying about pain. Faith meant hope, and I simply didn't have it. I believed in being positive, but I also believed in being truthful. And the truth was rarely beautiful to me. I asked God about it—the decision to let pain run rampant—but He ignored me, so we went our separate ways.

Yet something about the woman's voice restored my hope. I can't explain it, but something shifted within me. Notes lingered in my mind like thoughts revisited: tranquil, serene, unblemished. The way I once imagined God. Years ago, a flock of birds descended in Grant Park, pecking at new spring seeds. I sat on a bench reading Marilynne Robinson's *Gilead*, when suddenly the birds rose as if spooked. I looked up. It wasn't the black mass that startled me, but the harmony of their chirping. Each strain bore a different sound, but the melody wasn't discordant. It was beautiful, complex, intricate—without human equivalent. They swooped through the air in waves, tweeting a song so precisely I marveled. I'd never heard the chorus of angels before. I wasn't sure I believed in it, but now I did. Those hundreds of birds sang for me alone. They reassembled what a lifetime of hurt had dismantled. I stood and closed my eyes. Each choral part rang in perfect balance, and I wondered if this might be the sound of hope. That's why the woman's voice astonished me—it sounded like those birds. It sounded like hope. And I never wanted it to end.

I rose quietly in the dark and stood before the window. Rain drenched the glass, and thunder rumbled in the distance.

I grabbed my robe and car keys. I would go get her, invite her home, bring her to a warm, dry place. My wife wouldn't understand, but it would be okay. Eventually. She'd hear her sing and perhaps they'd become friends. Or, like me, she'd reconsider life as she once knew it. Whatever happened, it would be better than knowing I could've saved a songbird and didn't. She couldn't bear exposure to the elements for long. She had no health care, surely, no one to see about her in a time of need. And she couldn't die. Not now. The world needed her. *I* needed her.

Torrential rain calmed as I reached the corner of Abernathy and McDaniel. I lowered my window and there she was—wet and shivering like a stray dog. I stalled at the stoplight once again and beheld other young men lurking in the dark. There were more now, scampering like frantic ants, waiting for the arrival of the despairing. I sighed and huffed. Where were their families? Didn't someone dream these boys' futures? Wasn't there a grandmother or uncle or distant cousin who believed they might be something one day? What does it mean to a child that no one imagines his tomorrow? I considered taking them home too, teaching them the ways of men, but I couldn't do that. Seeds had been planted within them that I didn't want to harvest. So I, too, forfeited the cost of their survival. I wasn't any more committed than anyone else. So what could I expect? We'd given them no hope, so they had none.

Truthfully, I cared only about the lady with God's voice. No one else. She'd reminded me of the hidden possibilities of life. I discovered that, unlike what my wife believed, my heart wasn't dead. It was alive and eager to feel again. Not since our wedding night had I been so invigorated. Who knew that someone in the ghetto, someone unknown and inconsequential, had the power to set me free?

I activated my hazards and waited. It was just after three a.m. Wind blew hard enough to bend the tops of trees and swirl trash in miniature whirlwinds. The woman winced and bound her lips tightly. I wanted to park and offer her a jacket or an umbrella, but I didn't want to chase her away. So, for the moment, I did nothing—except hope that she might sing. And she did: "*Come, ye disconsolate, wherever ye languish . . .*"

It was a bold invitation, a sudden intrusion into the atmosphere, an insistence that life prevail where death once reigned. She didn't look at me. Not at first. Her voice simply plowed through the denouement of a storm: "*Come to the mercy seat, fervently kneel . . .*"

Then, like a broken stem, her head fell back as she belted, "*Here bring your wounded hearts! Here tell your anguish! Earth has no sorrow that heaven cannot heal . . .*"

She repeated the last two lines with trills so smooth and exact that my hands lifted in praise. *That's the power of the Holy Ghost*, my grandmother would've said. *It moves without permission. It heals the brokenhearted. It just won't leave you alone.* I was glad. I didn't want to be left alone. I wanted to be lost in the woman's arms, to feel her touch, to be consumed in her restorative power.

She knew I was listening. She had to know. My car flashed in the intersection like a Christmas tree. Far as I was concerned, we were the only people on earth. She gazed into the cloudy sky, but never stopped singing. Every distress, every burden, every disappointment dissolved in my heart. Her voice was a gift to a dying world. Without it, she was nothing; with it, she was divine. Slowly, she rose and stretched her hands toward me. Something electric penetrated the air. My consciousness clouded. I felt faint. What was she doing?

I sat at the intersection, fully mesmerized. No one in their right mind would've been where I was at that time of morning. Not unless they needed something desperately. Not unless they sought peace they could not find.

Tears came again as her energy anointed me. Our eyes beheld nothing but each other; our needs danced between us, exposed. Slowly, step by step, she moved toward me. Her battered, soaked dress clung to her thin, wispy frame. She looked different now, marching in the spirit with outstretched hands, giving me something I could not articulate. She waltzed until reaching the corner, then stood still a moment, all the while repeating, *"Earth has no sorrow that heaven cannot heal."* Then, suddenly, she retraced her steps, moving backward in the same time sequence. Her form faded into the dark, as her voice waned to a whisper. Her lips continued trembling but all sound ceased. Only whiffs of wind murmured in the night, repeating the song's refrain in circular bursts of cool, moistened air.

I shivered. There was only one thing to do, one risk to take if I were to access her fullest offering. It's why I was there; it's why we had crossed paths. I turned off the hazards and pulled into the lot where she dwelled. Our gaze remained constant. We exchanged something—life force, healing, love—that we both had presumably forsaken. Her head swayed slightly as if the refrain repeated in her mind. *Earth has no sorrow that heaven cannot heal.* I believed her. I needed to believe her.

I got out of the car. My head said this was not right. That I was in violation of something sacred. But my heart urged me on, pleading with me to trust what I knew, what I felt. I obeyed. Her smile eased my nerves, and her beckoning right hand summoned me onward until I stood right before her. She extended small, feeble palms, and I lay thick, heavy ones upon them. Storm clouds passed through slate-gray skies. With the slightest tug, she lured me next to her, thigh to thigh, and pressed my head onto her shoulder. A strange aroma welcomed me, like the scent of healing, so I sighed, dropped all inhibitions, and melted into the womb of a songbird.

Soon, a murder of miniature birds descended, pecking frantically for food they could not find. In one dark swoop, they rose, just like years before, chirping the same harmonious tune that reminded me of a chorus of angels. There was no violation here. I was where I was supposed to be. This was right. It had to be right.

Once again I cried. I cried for a wife I didn't love anymore. I cried for the life I had settled for. I cried for boys with futures unimagined. I cried for a son conceived, but returned. I cried for a people alive but not thriving. I cried for my mother whose trust of my father killed her. I cried for a father too broken to care. And all the while, the songbird massaged my hand and purred, "*Earth has no sorrow that heaven cannot heal . . .*"

She took my pain away. She told me everything I had ever done—not in words, but in melodic forgiveness. I felt whole again; I felt renewed. I was changed.

I asked her name, but she shook her head and whispered lovingly, "Just go home." So that's what I did. When Patricia asked where I'd been, I told her the truth. The full truth. She asked if I loved the woman, and I said no. I didn't even know her; I just loved her voice. Of course Patricia didn't believe me.

"You're such a liar," she mumbled, staring over my shoulder at the life she could've had. "All you had to do was tell me, and you weren't man enough to do that. You're such a fuckin' liar."

I tried to convince her there was nothing between the woman and me, but I failed. We argued for hours, calling each other names we'd promised never to use, and by sunrise we both knew it was over.

"Just admit you're in love with her. Can you at least do that?"

We'd been silent several minutes. I'd thought the exchange concluded, but obviously not.

"Patricia, I don't even *know* the woman! I heard her voice and it did something to me. That's all."

Patricia's eyes showed a vulnerability of sorrow and regret. She'd always been strong and self-assured but now she looked sullen and defeated. What more could I say?

She covered her face and wept with grief. I stood before her, alone, like a disobedient child awaiting reprimand. When I reached to comfort her, she jerked away.

"I'm done," she said finally, frowning at the magnitude of my error. She went to the bathroom and slammed the door behind her. I wanted to say so many other things. Like, *I love you*. Or, *I need you*. But it was useless now. Perhaps if she'd heard the woman's voice, she might've understood. Or if I could've taken her to the vacant lot, she too would've been transformed. But as it was, Patricia wanted no part of that life. And hence no part of mine.

Patricia has been gone four years now. Every Christmas she sends a card. The return address and her new last name let me know she has found someone else. I don't blame her. How could I? Still, all these years later, I hear the woman's voice in my head. Every now and then, I drive past the corner of McDaniel and Abernathy with hopeful eyes, but I've never seen her again. Her life's mantra rings in my ear whenever I consider my many losses: *Earth has no sorrow that heaven cannot heal.*

If only this were true for us all.

PART III

NOSE WIDE OPEN

THE BUBBLE

BY JENNIFER HARLOW

Peachtree City

Despite the strange wet, hot, stifling air of an atypical Georgia spring night, Emma shivered as she drove her golf cart to her best friend Maddie's house on Lake Peachtree. Not that it was much of a lake that night. For years the residents who'd paid a million dollars for lakefront property had been stuck staring out at a mud pit or dying grasslands as the county and city battled over who would pay the millions for the repairs to the dam and the dredging that was needed. For decades the shining symbol of Peachtree City's beauty, grace, and opulence hid a problem. Under that calm water families picnicked near and canoed over was a mess of neglect, poor planning, and denial no one wanted to take the blame for.

But at long last, the next morning, the status quo would return to Peachtree City. The fixed lake would return to its natural glory and all would be right in the bubble once more. Which was why if Emma and Maddie were actually going through with their plan, it had to be *this* night.

Emma passed an elderly couple also on their golf cart, and all parties nodded and smiled. It's just what you did in the town. Emma once visited New York City with her family for a week and was shocked at how nobody there smiled at one another. They never asked how their days were or even held doors. A person would probably be arrested for not holding the door in Peachtree City. The cops were so bored they jumped on any infraction, including crimes against civility.

Even that night, even with what they were planning, Emma glanced around the dark forest nervously for any signs of the ATVs the police drove along the forested paths. Curfew was fifteen minutes before, and the police had been out in force during the whole of spring break. Not that her parents would care or even know if she were arrested for any crime. Emma's mother was passed out on her usual cocktail of wine and Ativan after a busy day of exercising, gossiping, and attending her pottery class in Newnan, while her father was, as always, on a business trip. Maddie's parents were divorced—her father lived in Atlanta, but her mother and stepfather were on a cruise around the Mediterranean to recover from their couples' trip to a golf resort in California. Maddie didn't mind. Her sister supposed to be watching her spent all her time in Little Five Points with her boyfriend, helping him set up his craft beer business. For the whole of spring break, Maddie had the house to herself. A fifteen-year-old's paradise. Emma and their friends spent most days and nights since middle school there getting stoned, watching Netflix, fooling around, and raiding the wine rack. But that night, like the rest of the week, was just for the two of them. The ultimate thrill. An act to bond them for life. Emma shivered again.

She turned off the cart path onto Maddie's quiet street, past the Lexuses and SUVs tucked away behind their gates. Most houses were dark inside. It was ten o'clock. The city died around nine. Shops closed and adults lay in their beds watching television after putting the children down. The adults always commented about what a great place it was to live, how it was named one of the top one hundred cities in America by several magazines, how safe it was to raise children. It truly was a bubble, an oasis in the urban sprawl. Great for some, death for teenagers, especially ones without driver's licenses. The golf cart paths only went around the city, and there are only so many trips to the shopping center, The Avenue, a teen could make. There were only so many shows to binge watch or parties to attend with the same people they'd all known since kindergarten, talking about the same gossip. Maddie often commented it was as if their life forces were slowly being drained by the boredom, the sameness. How *something* had to be done to save their minds and spirits. And it would be done that night.

"I was beginning to think you weren't coming," Maddie said after opening her front door.

She was a beautiful girl, they both were, but it was Maddie who made heads turn, especially since she added purple and pink in her long shiny brown hair. That night her long limbs and thin frame were dressed in all black, as was Emma per Maddie's strict instructions. All part of the plan.

"Sorry. Mom took forever to pass out," Emma said, walking inside the three-story Georgian with all her bags.

"You got everything?" Maddie asked.

Emma set down the bags on the marble vestibule floor right below the crystal chandelier. "Yeah. They had everything at, like, Kmart."

"Eww, you went to Kmart?" Maddie asked with a sneer as she checked the bags. "Did you have to take, like, seven showers after?"

"Totally."

"And you paid in cash, right?"

"Of course!"

"Good." Maddie picked up some of the bags. "Then let's get this shit to the boathouse already. He just e-mailed the

Craigslist account. He'll be here in ten," she said in sing-song.

Ten, Emma thought, another chill running down her spine. If Maddie noticed the quick expression of sheer terror on her best friend's face, she didn't let on. Or she didn't care. Maddie never seemed to care. Since they were children, Emma always wished she could be as self-assured, as strong, as cool and collected as Maddie, but felt she never came close. Well, that night, she'd finally prove herself to Maddie, prove she was worthy of being the best friend, the sometimes lover, and true BAE to a goddess like Madeline Whitlock. Emma picked up the rest of the bags and trailed behind her goddess.

The rare times her parents were home, Maddie commandeered the boathouse for her social gatherings. Before her grandmother died, the Whitlocks converted it into a small apartment. The only thing that kept Maddie from making it her private residence full time was the size. It was barely bigger than her mother's master bedroom. That night it appeared larger than normal, with only a couch and chair in the living room. Earlier in the day the girls had moved everything into the bedroom so they could lay the plastic sheeting on the floor. Maddie even made sure they bought plastic covers for the chair and couch.

She thinks of everything, Emma thought with awe. Emma's father often chided her about forgetting the basics, like not wiping off the counter right after use and rolling the toothpaste incorrectly, never mind about her grades. Maddie of course got all A's while Emma worked hard for her B's. One day her father's constant berating, his constant pressure proved too much for Emma, and she actually broke down crying in class after getting a C on a calculus test. But Maddie knew how to make it all better. She made sure Mrs. Adler found the texts on Mr. Adler's phone from his mistress. For months Mr. Adler was too busy trying to keep his marriage from falling apart to pay any attention to Emma. No matter how many second or eightieth thoughts Emma had that night, they didn't matter. She owed Maddie for that act alone.

"Want something to drink?" Maddie asked as she poured two tumblers of whiskey.

"Should we be drinking? Don't we, like, need our brains at maximum?"

Maddie sauntered over to Emma as she so often did, as if she owned the room and the rest of the world, and handed the glass to Emma. "One won't hurt. We need to toast, anyway." She held up her glass and Emma did the same. "To us. The baddest, hottest bitches in the PTC. And to the experience of a lifetime."

Both chugged their alcohol, but only Emma shuddered. She hated whiskey. "What if he doesn't, like, show up or something?" she asked, silently praying for that exact thing.

Maddie chuckled. "Yeah, right. Like, who doesn't show for a threesome with two gorgeous teenage girls?"

"What if he tells someone where he's going? You told him not to, but what if he does?"

"Emma, he's like, *thirty*. He's hardly going to tell anyone he's about to commit statch. Plus, he promised to bring us cocaine. He'd be in like way more trouble than us if he did tell anyone. It's all fleek, I promise."

When Maddie said it, Emma believed it. A week of planning. Of conspiring. Of researching, of setting up false Craigslist and Facebook accounts, of trolling for the perfect guy, of talking out every angle and contingency. And Maddie listened. She actually listened to Emma's suggestions and seemed impressed. It had been the best week of Emma's life.

Just her and Maddie in their own private bubble. She just never thought it would get this far.

Emma had to look away from Maddie's studying gaze.

"What?" Maddie asked. "You want to wuss out, don't you?"

"No! No, I don't! I just . . ."

Maddie took a step toward Emma, even throwing her arms over Emma's shoulders. "I know you're nervous. I am too. This is, like, a huge deal. But we can do this. We *need* to do this. Not only will it totally bond us for life, we're doing the world a massive favor."

"We are?"

"Uh, totally. This guy was like trolling the Internet for little girls! When we told him we were only seventeen, he totally didn't care! He's probably molested tons of girls. We're like avenging them. We're heroes."

"I guess."

"You can do this," Maddie said with a sweet smile before lightly kissing Emma's lips. "I'll bet you even enjoy it."

"And if we get caught? The police—"

"We are not going to get caught," Maddie interrupted with utter certainty. "We're like totally smarter than the police. We've got everything covered. No one's even probably going to like report this guy missing. And if by some chance we do get caught, then your dad will get us off. We'll just say we were two stupid girls who got in over their heads and when this big, black, ghetto asshole tried to rape us, we defended ourselves. Who do you think the jury will believe? Plus, they'd probably even, like, make a *Lifetime* movie about it. Gigi Hadid can play me and Victoria Justice can totally play you. But we're not going to get caught." She pecked Emma's lips again. "You trust me, right?"

"More than anyone and anything," Emma said.

"And I trust you. That's what this is about, right? Bonding for life. No matter how far away life takes us, we'll always have this. Tonight. Like a tattoo you can't laser off. And there's no one else I'd rather be tied to for life than my best friend. And like, of course you're nervous. So am I. This is like a huge deal. But I was right about you punching your V card with Braeden, and like that night I'll be right here with you. I *so* won't let anything happen to you. Just like . . . enjoy this transcendent experience." Maddie took Emma's hand, entwining their fingers together. "With me." She leaned in once more and tenderly kissed Emma. As always the act made Emma's body sing, just as it left her desolate when Maddie ended the kiss. "We can do this. Now come on, we gotta get ready."

The chills, the doubt all but faded away with Maddie's words. With that last kiss. Emma smiled and nodded. She may have been nervous, she may have been sick to her very core, but there was no way she wouldn't go through with it. She just had to try and enjoy the experience like Maddie said. She'd enjoyed the planning. The talking to various men online trying to lure in the perfect guy, or *avatar of transcendence* as Maddie called him. Because that's why Maddie wanted to do this. To transcend their boring, predictable lives. To prove they were more than what their parents, their friends, the school said they should or could be. It was to save their spirits. From a life of mediocrity and sameness. Emma almost believed her friend when she gave that little speech the day before. Almost. Still, Emma stood in that boathouse grinding up her mother's tranquilizers and mixing them in a glass as Maddie set the stage.

"You know, it's too bad we can't fuck him before we do it," Maddie said as she hid the baseball bat behind the bar. "He kind of looks like Kanye. And I've never had a black guy."

"African American," Emma corrected automatically.

Maddie rolled her blue eyes. "Whatever, PC Principal." Her phone chirped and she removed it from her black hoodie. "Oh shit! He's here! He's here!" Maddie cried out as if she'd just woken up on Christmas morning to find a new puppy. "OMG, this is like totally happening!"

Bile rose up in Emma's mouth.

"He just e-mailed he's parked down the street just like I told him to do. See? All going like steampunk. Okay, you finish taking care of things here. I'll go get him." Maddie began walking toward the door. "Tonight is gonna be fucking epic!"

When the door shut, Emma could finally let herself crumple onto the plastic-covered couch. She let out shaking, weighted breaths as the adrenaline coursed through her every cell. *I can do this*, she thought as she rocked back and forth a little. *Nothing* mattered but Maddie. After a few seconds for herself, Emma forced herself to stand and return to the bar for the final preparations. They could leave nothing to chance. Their very lives depended on the details. She slipped on her new gloves and checked that everything was in its proper hiding place. She was just tucking the knife in the side of the couch when the door opened again.

When *he* stepped in.

Maddie was right—what else was new—he did resemble Kanye West, at least around the eyes. He certainly didn't look like a child molester. In fact, he looked like a nice man. Early thirties, over six feet, full lips, muscular under his Atlanta Braves T-shirt and blue jeans, with braids down to his shoulders. He was just . . . a guy.

"Victoria, he's here," Maddie said in singsong as she walked in behind the guy. "Jordan, this is Victoria."

"What's up?" Jordan said with a nod.

"Nice to . . . meet you," Emma muttered as she turned her eyes to the ground. She just wouldn't look at him unless she had to. It would help.

"Told you she was prettier than the chick in the pictures we sent you. Victoria, Jordan was a little pissed we didn't send him our real pics. I just hope you're as big as the dick shots you sent us," Maddie said with a smirk. "But we'll, like, find out soon enough. Vicki, get Jordan a drink, huh? He has to catch up."

"Uh, right," Emma said as she rose from the couch. "What would you like?"

"Rum and Coke?"

"Okay." With her gaze still down to the floor, Emma moved toward the bar again. She mixed the drink with the tranquilizers as Maddie maneuvered Jordan to the couch. *Just don't look at him.*

"What's with the plastic shit everywhere?" Jordan asked.

"We're like painting the whole place tomorrow," Maddie said without missing a beat. "I thought it needed a change. I'm totes bored with it."

"Why? This is nice. Didn't know people even had boathouses and shit."

Emma returned to the couch, her trembling hand holding out the laced drink to Jordan. "H-here," she whispered.

"You okay?" Jordan asked.

"She's fine," Maddie said. "Her hands are just a little fucked up. That's why she's wearing the gloves. Plus, we already had two of those while we were waiting for you. You gotta catch up."

Emma sat in the armchair beside the couch, her whole body a coil that not even her jittering leg could help loosen.

Jordan drank his alcohol but grimaced after one sip. "This tastes weird," he said.

Maddie took the glass and pretended to take a sip. "Tastes fine to me. Maybe you're just like not used to imported rum. My stepdad has the stuff shipped in from, like Cuba or somewhere. That's like fifty bucks of rum. You totally gotta finish it." She handed it back to Jordan. "We're pretty fucked up already. I mean, just look at her," she said, gesturing to Emma. "It's not rape if we're all fucked up, right, Victoria? Her dad's a lawyer, she'd know."

"Yeah, th-that's right," Emma replied quietly.

"So finish it or leave," Maddie said.

Jordan glanced at Maddie, then Emma, then back to Maddie, who just raised an eyebrow. Emma silently prayed he'd get up and walk out. *Just walk out. Please . . .*

But of course he didn't. He downed the drink in one gulp. "Shit," he muttered.

"Vicki, get him another." Like an automaton, Emma stood up, took the glass from Jordan, and returned to the bar in a daze. This time the drink was straight rum and coke. With that big a dose of Ativan combined with the alcohol, he'd be woozy in minutes. Plenty of time for Maddie to play with her food. "So, did you bring the coke like we asked?"

Jordan pulled a tiny baggie out of his pocket. "Yeah."

Maddie took it from him. "Hope it didn't, like, cost you too much. I'll totally pay you back before you leave. You ever done it before?"

"Once or twice. It ain't my favorite," Jordan answered.

"We've never done it before. We're totally about the new experiences, right, Victoria?"

"R-right," Emma replied. She handed Jordan his glass and sat down in the lounge chair again.

"Like you being here. We've had threesomes before, but never with someone over twenty or—"

"Black?" Jordan cut in.

"Yeah. B-but not because we're like racist or anything," Emma said. "We just, there aren't that many African Americans in Peachtree City."

"Yeah, it's like literally 90 percent white," Maddie said, rolling her eyes. "It totally sucks. That's why I totally can't wait to move to New York City. This town is so fucking boring, you know? Nothing ever changes. Nothing ever happens."

"I don't know. Seems pretty nice, quiet, you know what I'm saying?" Jordan said, drinking his alcohol without protest this time. "You guys got the golf carts and shit. That's cool."

Maddie smirked. "Try living here. You want anything remotely interesting to happen, you totally have to make it happen yourself. Like we did tonight," she said with a seductive smirk. "Insanity is like doing the same thing over and over again and expecting a different result, right? No wonder most people around here are on antidepressants. You can't grow, you can't transcend without like trying new things, you know?" She shifted in the couch to face Jordan, even putting her hand on his thigh. "What about you? Is tonight a new experience for you? Being with two girls at the same time?"

"Uh, yeah," he responded nervously, sipping his drink.

"Well, don't worry. *We've* done this before."

"Are you two together or bi or . . ."

"Well, I'm pan," Maddie said proudly, "and Vicki claims she is too, but I totally think she's demi."

"What?"

"Demisexual? She only likes fucking people she's in love with, whereas I," Maddie said, moving closer to Jordan, "like fucking anything and anyone. Everyone has such hang-ups about sex, it's like pathetic, you know? We are just, like, totally animals after all, evolved monkeys. I'm all for giving in to my primal instincts."

Jordan shifted uncomfortably on the couch.

Maddie frowned. "Oh, you're like probably Christian or whatever. Victoria is too. Most people around here are."

"Wait. You don't believe in God?" Emma asked.

"Of course not. There have been like thousands of gods and the dude on the cloud with the beard is the only real one?" Maddie rolled her eyes. "We learned about Karl Marx in school. Religion's an opium for the masses to keep us in line."

"What about heaven? Hell?" Emma asked.

"It's just a story to keep us from killing each other, duh! Like all the stupid societal conventions they expect us to follow. Well, fuck that! Rules are totally meant to be broken. Bitch, there is just the here and now. Just us and the moment. Why do you think we're doing this?"

Emma shut her mouth. There was never any arguing with Maddie. Even Jordan seemed to realize this as he just continued nursing his drink without a word of dissention. But Maddie smiled at her friend to reassure her. "Isn't my best friend just like totally fucking beautiful, Jordan? I love looking at her, don't you?"

"Uh, yeah," he said, staring down at the floor, his eyes obviously growing heavy.

Maddie rose from the couch and sat in Emma's lap, throwing her arms around Emma's shoulders. "I, like, love her more than anything and anyone in this whole universe. We'd totally do anything for each other." She caressed Emma's cheek, and a shiver of lust ran through Emma. Even a light touch like that could garner a strong, wild, pulse-pounding, goose bumps–rising response. And when Maddie's lips touched Emma's, all was right in the universe. They kissed for several seconds, passionately, deeply, tongues exploring each other as they had a hundred times before, and Emma almost forgot about their guest, at least until Maddie broke the kiss and whispered, "Get into position. It's time."

Be it the always-expert kisses or the weight of those words, but Emma couldn't breathe for a second. It was as if she drifted out of her body and just watched as the person resembling her stood up and moved toward the bar to turn up the music. It was loud enough to wake the dead, but she could barely hear it. Maddie returned to the couch, all smiles for the slow-blinking Jordan. *Drink. Music. The baseball bat.*

When Emma bought the bat that afternoon, it was heavy in her hands; now she couldn't sense its weight. She was a ghost. Insubstantial. A robot with no emotions or free will. She thanked God for that.

"Are you okay, Jordan?" Maddie asked with her patented smirk.

"I don't . . . I . . ." the guy said quietly.

Emma's ghost walked toward the back of the couch. She couldn't see his face. She was glad.

"Feeling sick? Yeah, that's because of the drugs we slipped in your drink, you fucking pervert," Maddie said.

"What . . . ?" the man slurred.

Emma stood right behind him, bat in hand. She couldn't lift it. She just stared at her joyous friend, who practically glowed with excitement. Like she was a vampire feeding off her prey's fear and confusion.

"The drugs were Emma's idea, so you couldn't fight back. I kind of wanted you to fight back a little. But this is still . . ." Maddie shivered. "You're about to fucking die, Jordan. We're going to kill you and bury your body in the hole we dug today in the lake."

I can do this, Emma thought. *I can do this . . .*

"No one is ever going to find you. *Ever,*" Maddie said with glee. "But we'll know."

I can't do this, Emma thought as part of her soul returned to her body, as tears filled her eyes. *What the hell am I doing? I can't do this.*

"You're dying, and we're killing you," Maddie said, almost breathless in anticipation. "And there's nothing you can do about it. *Nothing.* You're powerless."

"Fuck you," Jordan slurred.

"Emma, do it now," Maddie ordered, never taking her eyes off Jordan.

I can't do this. I can't do this. I can't do this . . .

"Now!"

I can't do this. I can't . . .

Maddie's gaze whipped up toward Emma, determined, cold blue eyes connecting with the petrified green ones. Emma knew Maddie saw her terror, her reluctance, her weakness. A flash of disgust tinged those blue orbs, and in that moment Emma knew with absolute certainty that if she didn't obey, she'd lose Maddie forever. Nothing was worse than that. Not hell, not prison, *nothing.*

Emma swung the bat.

A sickening crack not even the music could drown out filled the room as the bat connected with the back of Jordan's head. He cried out in pain and doubled over on the couch.

"Again!" Maddie shrieked.

Emma swung again.

Jordan collapsed onto the floor, clutching his bloody, broken head and babbling, "Why? Why?" between his cries of pain. The moment he fell, Maddie retrieved the knife Emma had hidden between the armrest and cushion. Panting like she'd just run a marathon, Maddie fell to her knees beside Jordan, knife in hand. "Why? Why?" he kept asking, pleading.

Maddie stared down at him, eyes wild with bloodlust, with joy, with madness. "Because, why not?" She shrugged. *"We can."*

Maddie plunged the knife into his chest. Once, twice, Emma didn't know because she had to turn away. Had to drop the bat and cover her ears to muffle his screams. They seemed to last forever, but only really for ten seconds. Somehow the silence was worse. It wasn't until someone touched her arm that Emma opened her eyes and gasped. Maddie's beautiful face was spattered with blood, her clothes soaked. But she didn't seem to notice. She smiled bright enough to rival the sun before kissing Emma like a drowning woman. Emma let her, even tried to reciprocate the passion, but for once couldn't.

Maddie pulled away, smile still present. "I love you. I fucking love you forever and always. Thank you for doing this with me. I couldn't have done it without you, Emma. I really couldn't. Thank you. Thank you. I love you. *I love you.*"

Emma almost believed her. She almost believed Maddie believed it. "I love you too."

Maddie held onto both sides of Emma's face, hands still warm and wet from the blood. "I so want you right now, so fucking bad, but we need to keep with the plan. We're so not done yet, right? You get the bleach, I'll start wrapping him up."

"Okay."

After another long, lingering kiss, Maddie went to work. So calm. So collected. If they hadn't planned every step out the week before, Emma would have just stood there as Maddie did everything. But Emma found herself opening a plastic trash bag and collecting everything used that night. The knife, the bloody clothes Maddie shed revealing her flawless body, the drug-laced glass, the wallet, cell phone, and car keys Maddie removed from Jordan's pants. There wasn't a detail they hadn't discussed or overlooked that night. They covered the body in bleach before rolling him up in the plastic while wearing gloves. Everything, including their clothes and his wallet and cell phone, went into a trash bag Maddie tossed in a dumpster on her way to pick up Emma in the golf cart at Luther Glass Park after Emma had left his car at a nearby shopping center parking lot. Emma felt nothing, not even when she found a picture in the car of Jordan holding a little boy. She felt *nothing*.

It wasn't until they stood under Maddie's dock, across the filled-in grave, when Maddie smiled at Emma, truly smiled at her partner in crime, that Emma experienced a wave of elation. It was done. She'd helped kill an innocent man. And he *was* innocent. She had no illusions about that. She wasn't as stupid as Maddie thought. As gullible. She knew the true reason Maddie had wanted to kill the man. She was just bored. She wanted to prove to herself that she could. To prove to herself that she could get Emma to do anything for her. Poor insecure, pliable Emma, who worshipped the ground her goddess walked on. But what Maddie didn't understand was . . . Emma didn't care what the reason was. All that mattered was Maddie could never leave her now. Because Emma knew Maddie far better than Maddie knew Emma. Just the mention of prison, the thought of her loss of freedom—Maddie would do anything to avoid that. She could never leave Emma now. So it was just the two of them, only them, until the day they died. Alone. Together. Trapped in their own little bubble. What was the life of one stranger compared to her own lifetime of happiness? She was entitled to it. She *deserved* to be happy.

Emma held out her hand across that grave to her best friend, now her soul mate, and they walked back to the boathouse and didn't leave until it was time to watch the lake rise, toasting with rum and Cokes as the water hid away all their sins.

"To us," Maddie said.

"The baddest bitches in the PTC," Emma finished before clinking glasses with her BAE. "Together. Forever."

A MOMENT OF CLARITY AT THE WAFFLE HOUSE

BY Kenji Jasper

Vinings

for "Belle"

1. The Spark

"You sure you don't want it?" Cam had asked you twenty years before, while cramming chicken-fried steak into his mouth at The Beautiful. Despite its reputation for being Atlanta's best, the mac and cheese was always kind of bland to you. You preferred your Grandma Sally's, because she used cheddar *and* Velveeta. And it was dark and crispy on the top. So you got a little bit of crunch in every first bite.

Back then The Beautiful was the closest thing you had to an office during the week. Neither of you kept day jobs. But it wasn't safe to plan and plot anywhere other than places familiar. You knew both exits, where the parking lot let out to, and the intervals that the cops rolled by. The night manager sold smoke on the side (wholesale only) to cover what he owed to the bookies. They knew him well at Grady Hospital's Marcus Trauma Center. But that part ain't have nothin' to do with you.

The words were a young man's question, powered by his pumped-up ego. You'd pulled pistols on the right targets and walked away with some cash. No problems with the cops and you'd never done time because you only chose marks who wouldn't run to the Red Dogs the minute you burned rubber toward the closest freeway. Your thing was to never set up anywhere you could possibly get blindsided.

Even though you and Cam ran the show, Bebe was the slim end of your isosceles. She was studying chemistry at Spelman but had grown up in the Calliope projects in NOLA. She knew the game and she'd actually run the same hustle for her man back in high school. So it wasn't no thing to up the stakes. The *J.R. Crickets* tee and heeled ankle boots matched her silver shorts perfectly. The cocoa butter on her legs made them gleam.

Just the weekend before you'd been outside of Club 112 (this was in its last days). You'd sent her in with the tightest dress she could find at BCBG. And she had brought some college chicks with her, square broads from Carolina and J-Ville, chicks who only knew a setup when it came to place settings and blind dates.

All five of them went in there dressed to the nines, and in no time Rico Wade from Organized Noize was all up on Bebe. His platinum chain, covered in chunky diamonds, was at least six months of living expenses. You had seen him out a bunch of times before and knew that he always had it on ever since *ATLiens* had gone platinum. Word had it that he bought the chain right after he got the plaque for the songs he produced on the record.

Rico let Bebe and the girls into the VIP area and took them along for food when he left. You and Cam were parked in the lot and followed them when they all came out. You waited for their crew to peel down to four and then you hit the quartet in the parking lot at the IHOP on Peachtree, and hit 85 South with twenty grand worth of stones and precious metal in Cam's glove box. By the next day Webster's had a picture of Rico next to the word *slipping* in the dictionary.

You were a success . . . again. But something about it all just didn't sit right with you. It felt too easy, like you were missing something, like there was some thread hanging from the action that might choke you to death if you weren't careful. And you couldn't have been more right.

With hindsight being as clear as water, the truth was that you were starting to look for bigger game, for less attention, for something more than what you could snatch off some rapper's neck at the right intersection. You might have even been thinking about getting out of the game at twenty-one, which was probably what you should've gone with.

"Nah, man. I ain't feelin' it," you said, voting nay on Cam's next proposed jack move, which had something to do with breaking into Erick Sermon's house while he was off on the Def Squad tour.

"You know how much we could get outta dat?!" Cam had argued, desperately searching for interest in your eyes that just wasn't there. The look he gave you was cold and calculating, like he'd just solved some equation that had been stuck on the blackboard for as long as he'd been alive. You were too young to get that this was the moment when you stopped being the little man under him and started being a threat. To you there was weed in the air, Crown Royal in the belly, Scarface on the system, and nothing but time for you to make all your dreams come true.

"We need to step up our game, folks," you proposed as a counter. And after that the stakes went up like a city on fire.

You hit Body Tap with a six-man crew and walked out with a quarter-mil to split. You had taken Jermaine Dupri for a drawer full of platinum pieces at his crib in Parrot Cay. But your best work had been cracking the count room at the Gold Club and walking off with close to 350 G's while the entire floor choked on the exploding FedEx package filled with pepper spray.

Cop specialists were on the lookout. You got kinda notorious. But Cam was getting out of control.

He graduated from a BA in blunts to an MFA in H. And with that shift his money stacks melted like soft serve on summer concrete. You knew he had a problem. You didn't even trust him anymore. But you were so used to the whole Butch-and-Sundance thing that you made yourself believe it wasn't the biggest mistake of your life.

"I know where there's some real money at," you had proposed as an alternative that afternoon at The Beautiful, ready to reveal the secret that you should've kept hidden for just a little longer. You told him about Jamie, the dude who owned Club Garage, and the million in the safe at his crib, and all the jewels he rocked, and how his security system was, and well . . . that was ALL Cam needed to hear.

You did the job. Then Cam snitched you out to Club Garage security when you took the lion's share (because it was *your* plan and *your* contacts that got you the in). So you had to empty a .45 into the two dudes who came to your crib looking for the repo (and then safely tossed the pistol). But when the cops arrived, they matched up jewels to photos on file with Jamie's insurance company, and found your prints on a shell casing in the living room. You ate seven for the burglary and eight for third-degree murder.

Your years inside were not particularly pleasant. The environment taught you everything you needed to know about breaking bones and snatching limbs out of sockets. You welcomed those with size and weight advantages, as you were so thoroughly convinced of your imminent death that you got to a place where you literally feared nothing (other than the next day of the same).

You came in with a soul fat with hope and left with one as slender as Rihanna on a deck chair. You spent most of the first five years down trying to put it behind you. But you couldn't once Bebe started writing you the letters. She and Cam had a kid and got married, but somewhere in the middle of the *Family Matters* life she started thinking about you. She came all the way up to Augusta to see you on a weekend when he and kids were out of town.

It turned out that he was back on that shit, and he'd already hit her a few times when she called him out about the sixteen-year-old he was fuckin' at the house while she was at work. You were hesitant, clinging to loyalties shorter than the time you'd done. But that changed when she told you she was in love with you.

You didn't know what love meant outside of that high school bullshit, blood family, and what rappers said on the tapes you heard at the prison barber or what you read in the books to keep each grain in the hourglass of your sentence from killing you. She wore that same perfume that she had on when she used to run with y'all back in the world. But there was a tiny scar over her left eye and these cute freckles on her arms that she said ran in the DNA.

Back in the world you had known plenty about getting nuts off and breaking headboards in cheap motels off 20. But you wanted more than that. You wanted to spend a month with her, or maybe a year, or maybe forever. Time is an illusion behind the walls.

You wanted her to fry you catfish on Saturdays just in time to watch the college games and suck your dick when she was happy that you helped her keep the house in order. The partner who had kept you apart from her was the same one who had put you inside over nothing but ego. This time, even without your money or the hunter-green Impala sitting on Daytons, she made you feel powerful. She made you feel like she was where you belonged.

2. Thunder Rolls

Scarface's "A Minute to Pray and a Second to Die" oozes out of your earbuds as you weather the commuter tram from Concourse C to the baggage claim at Hartsfield. After parole was up you took the last of what you'd stashed in bonds and treasuries in Grandma's attic and bought a barber shop in Charlotte.

Bebe started selling Mary Kay for her cousin as cover, just to make the trips to come see you. She'd got him out of the house with a separation, but he wouldn't give her a divorce, threatening to name her as an accessory in some hustle she'd helped him run. So she kept the two kids and the condo in that tower sandwiched between Phipps Plaza and Georgia 400, with his name latched onto hers like a leech in swamp water.

You've only got one night to get it done. But you've been planning it for weeks. Greyhound is a shitty way to travel but they take cash and you can carry blades without getting searched. There is a car waiting in short-term parking. It has been rented under the name of someone else, someone with a face and credit history that is *not* yours, someone willing to look the other way just long enough for you to do what you need to do.

The 2014 Dodge Challenger came equipped with a leather overnight bag full of prearranged tools. Someone hacked the server at the rental car place and made some changes in the system records. Someone else filled in all the bogus details and made the pickup. The keys are in a small envelope taped to the inside of the wheel well. When you turn it over, Travis Scott's "Antidote" spills out of the speakers like you'd made a request (even though you can't request songs on the radio anymore). You turn it down while checking your mirrors, certain that you haven't been seen.

On the drive north toward the city you think about things: the length of your layover, the forty-degree temp outside, the *Empire* Christmas special on Fox, and your dinner date a few hours into the future. There was a time when this place was your home, when you might have kissed the cheap carpet at Hartsfield when you landed. You knew you were gonna be in the A forever. But Joe Louis said it best: "Everybody's got a plan until they get hit."

Thunder rolls.

It's midnight at the corner of Ponce and Federica. You watch the video feed from the nanny cam you placed in his crib a few weeks ago. Your perch is an empty studio apartment across the street. The rain patters like brushes on a snare.

Cam's watching *Stevie J & Joseline Go Hollywood* on the flat-screen and swigging Coronas in succession. It's the portrait of a divorcé working for MARTA when he once had millions. There is an enlarged poster from *New Jack City* in a frame next to a basketball jersey behind glass. It's been twenty years since the boss's glory days have passed him by.

The signal booster attached to the webcam keeps the image on the tablet stable as you enter the front door of the building. You copied the master key to the building weeks before, a gift from a well-paid "friend." You make a note of his status on the tablet. He's just taken a swig of his beer from the same sitting position.

It's a good thing Fellini's delivery guys don't need uniforms. All you need to look the part is the pizza box and the credit card receipt. The pizza you bought with the toppings you know he's a sucker for. No security in the building. The only cameras are in the lobby. Nothing a long brim and the shadows can't neutralize.

You slide the tablet into your bag. You don't need it anymore.

You ring his cell phone, using a Nigerian accent, with "pizza" and his apartment number as the only comprehensible words. He opens the door, his hunger the sole tool needed to bring about his demise. He eyes the pie before he sees your face. And when he looks up at where your face should be, you jab the blade into his gut and push him inside.

It's not personal when you slash his jugular. That's just to keep him from screaming. You stab him underhanded until he falls backward onto the floor. The blood is pooling, getting all over you and the carpet, couch, and coffee table. The bloody knife almost slips out of your hand. But it's okay; you planned for that.

There are two full bottles of rubbing alcohol inside the pizza warmer. You unscrew the caps, punch through the safety seals, and douse the body in a liquid that's 91 percent flammable. The clear liquid fuses with the blood. You remove one layer of clothing to reveal a shirt and pants underneath, unseen by anyone, and toss the bloody rags onto the pyre. Then you the light the match and close the door behind you.

You don't need his body to burn to a crisp. You just need to get rid of your own DNA and everything that connects you to the crime. The camera, the tablet, the pizza, and the clothes are best served as ash. You can hear sirens off in the distance as you climb back into the car you rented under someone else's name.

The sky is pitch black. The rain begins to come down, but

you know where you're headed—to that tower in Buckhead just past the Ritz-Carlton, on the other side of Phipps. She is waiting for you at the door when you arrive at her tenth-floor abode.

"You do it?" she asks, looking deep into your eyes to see if she still has that hold on you.

You nod. She loosens the belt on her robe and motions you inside.

"Good," she says.

Her condo is a series of glass walls framed by iron and steel atop a concrete floor and carpet. There's a framed pencil drawing on the wall, a sketch of a zydeco band playing for change on Bourbon Street done by a distant cousin. You know she misses the kids who are staying with Grandma. But you can tell she's missed you more.

The storm finally arrives. Lightning strikes, illuminating the endless rows of tall and slender trees that hide the 75/85 junction in dark and flooding rain. She speaks in French creole, doing it just to fuck with you (and because you like it). These moments are a decade and a half in the making, a tape on auto-reverse.

She has this scent that kind of reminds you of Lotus Flower Bomb mixed with Halston. You cut her panties off with a paring knife from the block in the kitchen.

You rolled the L in the ashtray that's now down to a half, and her second bottle of Veuve is almost empty. You trace the inside of her left thigh with your tongue. She giggles when you get to the ticklish place just above the knee. She touches herself before you can get to it, her ring and middle fingers brushing her clit gently until your tongue arrives.

Then your lips take over, drinking it in like she poured it for you in a glass. You hold her other leg in place over your shoulder. And out of all the times for talk, she decides to ask you a question.

"You don't get tired down there, do you?"

"Not when I'm motivated," you murmur.

Even in the dim light, with the rain hitting the glass like hail, you can see the thickness of her nipples in the darkness while she fumbles with your belt. One shoe is on the other side of the room, where she threw it on the way in.

You claw each other out of your clothes like warring leopards on a savannah. She gets your zipper down and reaches inside. Her grip is strong as she guides you toward her, rolling the rubber on in just the nick of time.

She exhales as you enter her, parting waters that begin to run down the insides of her thighs, which you hold open as you thrust deep, coming out slow and then slamming again. You find your rhythm but she doesn't let you enjoy it as she flips you over. You think of suggesting that you should move this to the bedroom. But the upholstery is soft and she straddles you, your hands all over a phatter ass than the one you remember. It's her show . . . all the way until the end.

Lightning flashes again.

She bites your nipple so hard that you think it's gonna bleed. Then you tell her to do it again. She rides you so hard that one end of the couch jumps up off the floor. You turn her over and enter from behind. She says she can feel your balls hitting her clit. She backs it up like the lethal weapon it is.

She comes out of nowhere, tightening around your Magnum force, her words smothered by the arm of the couch she's biting. Her thighs tremble from the effort and you climax along the way, hands on her hips until you collapse against her. You lick the crease in her spine. She reaches back and strokes your face with a soft and slender palm.

"What time's your flight?" she asks, turning her face away. She doesn't want you to leave.

You light the L in the ashtray, take a puff, and let out a cloud. "Not until nine."

"Let's get breakfast." She parts your lips with her tongue just in time to take in most of your second puff, and then lets it out of her nose. "Good boy," she grins.

"So I'm a dog now?"

"No. But I keep you on a tight leash. I ain't done with you yet."

You watch her feet pad prints on the finished wood as she wanders back into her bedroom. She has work in a few hours, the first of her four weekly shifts of fixing the skin of the rich and famous. She turns on the sixty-inch Vizio and your eye sockets burn in the face of a Geico commercial with an action star kicking and punching bad guys while on the phone with his mother.

Glenn Burns, looking more like a game-show host than weatherman, says that the rain will continue all week. The water in her condo runs scalding. Hence the bathroom is flooded with more steam than that in *Risky Business*. You kiss hungrily in the shower, wet hands wandering toward all the parts you just finished playing with. But you won't go all the way again because there isn't time. You both need to take your place and lock into preestablished alibis.

Rain ends despite the forecast. The sun rises into partly cloudy skies. Now the two of you are sitting at the counter of the Waffle House in Paces Ferry. It's just after three a.m. and the pecan waffle and side of hash browns with scattered onions, OJ, and coffee land in front of you. Her hand rests gently on your thigh. She takes a forkful of your hash browns and eases it into her mouth.

"Grease always tastes so good." She is gym-obsessed, worried about the fifteen she wants to lose. You tell her you'll take the weight off the next time she comes to see you.

You sip from her juice. It's all yours now. She will give you whatever you want. No strings attached. And you know this. That's why she's worth it.

You tell her about always stopping at the Waffle House in Durham, back when you used to rip-and-run 85 South for various parties, the days when you still needed heat on your hip, when you didn't see what was coming way before it got there. You tell her that you used to think of her on those runs before you went inside, back when you were all babies, and *loyalty* and *honor* were more than buzz words memorized by the chain of fools you couldn't cut loose from. As it turned out, the same link that brought the two of your together was the only thing keeping you apart.

Her hair is the same color all these years later, that jet black with integrated extensions woven with the Sacagawea mane hiding underneath. You flashback to the weight of her thighs wrapped around you, and the scent that covers you like the clouds bordering the gates to Nirvana.

You remind her of that tape she made you. It was all rappers from the NO. Early shit. P and C-Murder. Silk Tha Shocker. Big Tymers. Some voices you didn't know with that gumbo-thick slur that was so different from Georgia. She said she had made it for you because she couldn't officially get you anything for your birthday. So she waited two weeks and then gave you the tape in a case cover that was made out of "backshots" from *XXL Magazine*. She didn't think you'd like her because she didn't have a whole lot back there.

But Cam always got real jealous when he saw the two of you alone. So she did the tape on the sneak, hoping you wouldn't say anything. You tell her you kept your mouth shut because you felt guilty about having a crush on her. She smiles in a way that makes her blush. That was the secret you had kept from the world for what seemed like a century. You are both glad that it's all out in the open now.

The scar above her eye is gone. She says she used the aloe from a plant she bought, the only one in her house that didn't die from her forgetting about it. You ask her if she feels safe now that the problem is handled. She says she always felt safe when it was just you and her.

To her, you were the one who always kept Cam from popping off. You both knew he was prone to smashing shit, like a little kid throwing a tantrum. She says he punched her four times in ten years, always in the face so the world could see the swelling and the bruises and know who it came from.

"He ain't gonna do that no more," you say. "He ain't here no more."

She lets out a deep exhale, the kind that comes once you've finished an exam, and it is what it is. Her eyes cut away from you toward the cheap steaks frying on the griddle behind the counter. They smell like they need salt.

"You didn't just do it for me, did you?"

You could tell her yes. But that wouldn't be true. Cam had it coming. He sold you out over his bullshit elastic ego. But as you look into her chocolate eyes you see that all the plans and the plots, all the moves and covers you made in those years back then, were about getting ahold of something you didn't have to steal, something you'd overlooked that might even have been yours to begin with.

You are not a killer. But you have killed . . . more than once. You feel more guilty about those dudes from Club Garage who took the door to your crib in Midtown off the hinges.

All they wanted was to get back what you and Cam took. But you were twenty-four and from Hope Homes. You weren't going out like that.

Those two big niggas went down whimpering like unfed puppies. Cam deserved something slower to remind him of all the years you lost. But when you saw him, broken and solo, without even kids to keep him warm, you realized that he had been dead for years. He just didn't know it.

She leans toward your ear and whispers it like a secret. "I love you," she breathes.

A knot that's been inside your gut for twenty years begins to relax. Then the two of you sync into each other. Your hand rests perfectly on the curve of her hip as you sit side by side in the booth, watching the cars streak by on the stretch of 75 just beyond the Motel 6 and the BP station. She puts her head on your shoulder and for a while you forget about all those years you lost.

Just then you are back at The Beautiful sneaking glances at legs that have miraculously remained the same, and chocolate eyes that instantly erase your misplaced loyalty and the foolish choices made in youth. You are not young anymore. But you are not too old either. There is time.

FOUR IN THE MORNING
IN THE NEW PLACE

BY JIM GRIMSLEY

Little Five Points

The girl who sold him five dollars' worth of pot lived upstairs; she would sell him any amount, really, provided she was holding, but he thought of her as the five-dollar dealer because she was willing to give him just that little, wrapped in plastic and stuffed into a paper sack. Sometimes five bucks was all he could scrape together. She left the bag at her door for him to pick up since she was not at home, and he shoved the money into her mail slot, a wilted bill he had picked up while bussing tables a couple of blocks away at the Little Five Points Pub. She was a rock star in the Netherlands. *Sort of* a rock star, she said. She had a band named Pony Pony, all women, and they sang alternative rock songs while wearing bright makeup and shaking their hair and sometimes jumping up and down. One of their singles got airplay in Holland, though nobody called it Holland over there. The name of the single was "Purple Night," and tomorrow she was traveling to the Netherlands with the band to play at a music festival. What a trip, she said, it was a trip to think about flying out of a country where nobody knew her, really, except in a few clubs around Atlanta, and then to land at an airport where the band would probably have fans, actual fans, to greet them, with signs that said, *We Love Pony Pony*, or maybe something more original than that. She hoped for something more original. But he got what she was saying, right?

She was telling him all this after she got home from work at the feminist bookstore; she had come down the stairs to his apartment for a visit and was pacing back and forth in front of the sofa he had found on the curb just down the street. The sofa was covered in orange velvety something-or-other with a brown stain along the front, but it smelled all right and was otherwise in good shape. She had brought a joint so he was relieved about that and happy to see her, because they were smoking her pot and not his tiny five-dollar stash. Which would have to last him till she came back from being a rock star in Holland, when he could buy more. She was walking up and down his living room and talking without stopping, Life is such a, a, wow, a thing, she said, with a gesture like she was trying to grab it, life, with both hands. So cool to think about the two of us in your ratty little apartment, you know what I mean, right? And one day I could be, like, this big rock star and you could be, like, this famous actor. I mean, there's nothing wrong with your apartment but these are all ratty little rooms in this house.

Here they were, talking like this and smoking, and over there in the Netherlands people were playing her record and listening to her sing that song about a night turned purple and hazy, and he wondered briefly why haze was always purple in songs but gray and dull in real life.

He had lived in the house on Sinclair Avenue for only a couple of weeks and he knew that the rooms were not especially nice, but he hardly cared to have her say so. He had been buying pot from Molly for a lot longer than two weeks, and when she told him there was an apartment downstairs that he could rent if he wanted—they had become chums by then, not exactly friends—he talked to the landlady and moved in as soon as he could pack all three boxes of his belongings. Molly's friend Winona, who also lived in the building, borrowed her boyfriend's Toyota truck to help with the move, which took about ten minutes of loading and about the same of unloading, including the boxes and his clothes. He had been hoping Winona's boyfriend would help them too, but he was at Georgia State modeling for an art class; Winona mentioned this at least three times, because she was proud to have a boyfriend who was so good-looking he could model for artists, though she didn't say that part so bluntly, of course. She was something of a dumpling herself—short, her body shaped a bit like a yeast roll and basically the same color, unbaked, pale. She had cheeks so plump a person wanted to pinch them—John James wanted to pinch them, certainly, and it was all he could do to keep from doing so to both Molly and Winona, they had such similar chubby cheeks. But they were helping him move into the new apartment so he refrained.

Later, they all smoked a joint out of Molly's stash, though Winona puffed it in short bursts as if she were trying to blow smoke rings, and coughed in a prissy way, laying her palm flat across her bosom to indicate that drugs were a struggle for her.

Now, after two weeks in the new place, with his boxes unpacked, he was watching Molly pace from one corner to the other, long strides ending with a little bounce. She was walking the length of the apartment, one corner to the other, including the room with no windows where he had put his bed. She had a round face, moonlike, and full lips with a natural pout, the kind of lips that appeared at their best when placed near a microphone; she had big, round eyes of a startling pale color, almost gray, and lashes that curved extravagantly upward, fine and dark. When you saw her you had to look twice, and it was easy to watch her in general. She was big-boned, tall, not fat but rather rounded and full. He found himself appraising her, considering what he might think if he saw her on an album or on the cover of a music magazine. She had brought her boom box and the room throbbed with her voice, the harsh guitar—"*Purple haze in a purple night*," she sang, repeated for the chorus.

He never thought of her as pretty, but if asked he would have said yes, she was, but not in any standard kind of way, with her moon face and pop eyes. He would have described her as if she were a doll with a bendable waist and long legs and a face that one wanted to watch; he would have spoken of her as though she were slightly disembodied. But he was not the kind of man who thought of kissing her or holding her.

He was the kind of man who thought of kissing and holding Winona's boyfriend, a wooly headed man with olive-colored skin of a rich, smooth texture, muscles stacked on him in tidy patterns head to toe. What drew John James to the boyfriend was the usual—the fact that the guy was self-involved and cocky, judging from his walk and general bearing, his way of shaking his long, dark curls. Such precise, clean, planned appearance, perfect and regular as a bouquet of narcissi. John James first saw the boyfriend months before he moved into the building, during one of the visits he paid to Molly to buy pot from her. He had walked through the front door, past the mailboxes, to the middle of the house where a staircase climbed upward. The boyfriend was there, knocking on the door of the apartment that would one day soon belong to John James, the boyfriend wearing navy-blue gym shorts, the rest of his body snaky with muscle and skin, glowing in the dim light. The door opened and he stepped inside quickly. For one second the boyfriend looked at John James, eyes that swallowed the house, and asked, Are you watching me? Are you pleased? A moment's rush, and then John James climbed the stairs.

But now he lived here. And in short: on Thursday, Molly packed her bags and the band's sound gear and headed to the airport to fly to the Netherlands. She was having her moment. Wearing tight jeans and a fake fur jacket, leopard print. Smoking cigarette after cigarette, lips bright red, like a tiny pool of blood. John James helped carry her luggage and trunks to the battered Toyota, once yellow, now mostly rust. Away drove the future rock star.

John James walked the local streets in the afternoon, looking for furniture that people dragged to the sidewalk. A cool, cloudy morning, rain likely. No luck that day, but on Saturday he found a coffee table in decent shape, sitting next to the curb; this was in the morning, John James out looking for the early worm, and here it was. He pulled the coffee table into a nearby hedge of sweet abelia and hurried home.

John James knocked on the door to the apartment upstairs and the boyfriend answered; yes, he would be glad to help get the coffee table with his truck, he said, his voice very deep, stiff at first, then more willing. He stood in the doorway with one hand on the lintel, his arm nice like that, showing off in a sleeveless shirt. Yes, he would be glad to help, and turned, heading back to a shadowy corner where he lifted a set of keys, Winona's high voice saying, Where are you going?

John wants me to help him move a table he found.

Winona asked, When are you coming back?

As soon as we move this table. He answered her questions in a flat tone, contrasted with the strained, bright sound of her voice. That okay?

Sure. I'll be here. Winona in a burst of light: she watched

the boyfriend with an expression at first placid, then hollow, tugging down the tail of her shirt with one hand, a reflex gesture that she repeated a moment later. Slowly, with fingertips, she smoothed one dark strand of hair across her forehead, behind her ear. Pressing that palm over her bosom again, as if she were having trouble getting breath.

So the boyfriend drove John James in the truck, the two of them shoulder to shoulder in the small cab, the boyfriend, whose name it turned out was Leonard, shifting gears with a bit of a grind. The truck was bouncy like a pony on the cracked and pitted streets. The day was too crisp for Leonard to be wearing a sleeveless T-shirt, but that was the point, wasn't it? Leonard hefted the table out of the bushes and carried it to the truck without any help, holding it in front of him like a shield, both arms flexed, with momentary glances at John James, the two of them meeting eyes, brief moments when John was aware of his heart pumping, a feeling of falling in the belly. He had not been making this up in his head after all, maybe, perhaps. It was possible that something would happen this time. But he stopped the thought there and they climbed into the truck together.

It was a cracking day in late autumn, leaves tumbling in a wind, high oaks and elms and poplars on all sides, the city as much a forest as anything else, greenery overwhelming every patch of untended space. Blackberry bramble covered the front yard of one of the abandoned houses on Seminole Avenue, beer cans partly buried in the fallen leaves under the thorny thicket. Wind ripped through the treetops. A drunk had fallen on his backside on the sidewalk at the back of Seven Stages—the man struggling to his feet, breathing heavily, bag wrapped around a bottle cradled against his midsection, the way he would have held a child. A modest knot of teenagers in leather jackets and dog collars stood near him, shuffling their big black boots, watching as he stumbled and cursed.

Never a word said by Leonard. He made a slight humming sound as he drove, a note of pleasure almost, so content was he to be himself. In the small space, one of his arms was constantly moving close to John James, who watched it, fascinated; why were some men's arms so much more pleasing than others? The exact tone of olive or bronze, the perfect arrangement of silky black hair, the triceps and forearm dancing as he steered. This was Leonard the boyfriend, speaking. He was a performance.

John James had a loud mattress, full of squeaks and groans, box springs gone aural, a noise that carried even through the old plaster walls of the house. He had a new coffee table and a thoroughly disciplined backside, all in one afternoon. Anybody in the house could hear it. Winona surely could hear it. She would know. But Leonard took his time and did a thorough job atop John James and afterward went nonchalantly home.

What pleased him most, in the quiet of the apartment after Leonard the boyfriend had gone, was the fact that something had happened this time, that he—John James—had lived through an event, something that was outside his head, where most of his romance had dwelled up till then. Cleaning and polishing the coffee table, he felt as if his life was coming together. He worked his shift at the pub in a state of hyperawareness, noticing details of smell, cologne hovering over the shoulders of the men as they sat at the bar or in booths, stale beer in back of the bar, spoiled food in the garbage can, wisps of cigarette smoke in the smoking section of the restaurant. Newspaper with a picture of President Reagan soaked in coffee sitting on one of the chairs. For some reason that image stuck with him, the president emerging from a plane and waving to somebody, that movie-star hair piled on his head, dressed just so, all soggy and drowned.

At home later, Leonard waited in the apartment, pacing back and forth, while Winona paced the floor overhead, steps clear and quick. She was wearing special clicking shoes, the sound had an echo. John James looked up at the ceiling where he expected to see the exact spot of each *tap-tap-tap*.

Leonard caught him watching. He blew out a long breath, his nostrils widening a bit.

You don't have to worry about her, okay? He spoke in such a deep timber, how could anybody question a voice like that? Overhead the *clip-clip-clip* faded into background noise and all John James could hear was the sound of his own breathing, the bass of Leonard's heartbeat, the ragged sawing sound the bed made, groaning back and forth. Yet still, his back on the bed, John James stared up at the ceiling, tracing the lines of old water stains in the plaster. He listened for the *step-step-step* in the aftermath, smelled the salty sweat on Leonard's shoulder, tossed in the dampness of each other, pulling apart gradually.

He was used to playing the part of Winona himself, so he could picture the tightness of her body as she walked from one wall to another, a hand across her waist, the other hanging loose. She had likely paced like this a lot of times in the past, every day that Leonard came home later than expected, every time he left the apartment and headed downstairs, every time he told her he was just stepping outside for some air, he would be right back. The frantic panic of the midsection, a hurt that can't be held. Sitting then standing then sitting again. Standing at the window sometimes brought rest for a moment. But Leonard would fuck anybody he liked, and he would always come back to her as long as she never complained. John James knew that feeling inside out, backward and forward.

But later in the night, when Leonard had gone upstairs again, there came a howling, an eerie sound that drawled on and on. Sometimes high-pitched words, sometimes only the sound. John James woke and heard it, a shivering through him, a feeling that his gut was sinking out of his body, his heart pounding then slowing, a smell of incense, sandalwood, biting his nostrils. All this time a stick of incense had been burning beside the bed. He snuffed it out with his fingertips. The fight upstairs grew quiet after a while.

He had a day and a night of the usual voice in his head, Love is the whole object, the sole purpose, the full flowering, and on and on. Thinking of Leonard was enough to pass an hour in a kind of drugged haze, the warm feeling, the returning sensations, echoes from close at hand. Later he met Winona on the stairs to the basement, when he was returning to his room from doing a load of whites and she was carrying a basket of towels in her arms. She looked pert and neat, hair brushed and glossy, cardigan buttoned over a white blouse, a single fake gem on a fake gold necklace. Only when she looked at him, a veil dropped over her face and she passed him with two quick steps.

Later that night came a knock at his door, and he leaped up from the battered armchair, straightening the rug in the foyer with his foot. There was Molly the newly minted rock star—it was Molly in the doorway, and she was already talking. She had a magazine rolled up into a tight cylinder, and she gripped it in her fist as if it were trying to escape.

I just need to dump all this on somebody, she said, and he said, You're back already, and she said, I've been gone like five days, dude, and he said, I guess that's right, and she said, Anyway, it was so wild, there's no way even to describe it all.

She flopped down on the couch, arms spread, legs spread, looking like a mannequin, for just a moment, splayed out there on the furniture.

All these kids who liked our song came out to meet us at the airport, and we had people, you know, at the hotel, like. She pulled back her hair so that it was bundled into a little bouncing ponytail. She was looking at the ceiling as she spoke, tapping that magazine on the cushion of the couch. The airport part was great. And the gig was great. But then this critic wrote this review.

Review?

You know. In a magazine.

Is that it? he asked.

He did not have to ask which part of the review in the music magazine had upset her, since she had underlined it in green ink. *Molly Harbinger is the lead singer of the band, striking if pudgy, round-faced like a moon girl, and she bounced up and down onstage like a happy puppy, thin hair flopping about, singing in that odd, striking voice.*

I'm pudgy, Molly said. And my face is round.

The guy liked your voice, John said.

I'm pudgy and my hair is thin, she said. She was looking right at him but she was not seeing anything at all. Her eyes were bloodshot. She sat oddly, with her elbows tucked close together and her hands on her cheeks; she looked as though she were trying to shrink herself.

So they sat there while he studied the plaster cracks in the walls and she told him details about the trip in bits and snatches—the size of the crowd, the oddly bare hotel room, the people who recognized her in one of the hash shops. Always returning to the review, the way it made her feel after-ward; singing in front of thousands of faces receding into the dark amphitheater, a moment like a dream, and then a couple days later there was this critique. And after reading it she was pudgy and moon-faced.

The problem was that, sitting there, her sweatshirt riding up her midriff, a lip of belly poking over her jeans, she was the definition of pudgy, and her face was oddly round and large, like an owl. He could still see her on the cover of an indie-rock album, eyes outlined in black and lips bright red, hair spiked in all directions, leather around her neck, wearing tight black this-and-that, owning her image, working with it. But instead, the sight of herself in someone else's eyes had frightened her, and here she sat.

Then: the moment shifted when Leonard the boyfriend opened the door, not bothering to knock, because men like Leonard burst into rooms as though afire; and then: he walked into the apartment with a cool look at John James; and then: on the stairs stood Winona, howling something, and she flung herself into the door too, and the whole apartment building was now in John James's living room, shouting and pandemo-nium, and poor Molly sitting in the chair looking lost.

Late in the night he woke in a strange room and had to think where he was and how he came to be there. Leonard lay beside him, smooth round shoulders, bare back in dim light from a television, the bright colors of a made-for-TV movie flickering over his skin. They were in Leonard's bedroom. Winona lay on the far side of the bed. For a moment John James was back in the midst of what had happened, the three of them in here together, Leonard with a blank, satisfied smile as he took the other two onto the bed. They had done what Leonard asked, without question. John James pushed the memory away and felt a hint of sickness. He was watching Winona's milk-dough bottom turned toward him, a slow slide of her buttock. He had never been so near a naked woman before.

He raised out of bed trying to stir the covers only slightly. Rippling light and shadow fell over everything, masking his bits of motion as he stepped into his clothes. Still, he knew Winona was watching him, he was sure of it, sliding his shirt over his shoulders, carrying his shoes. When he reached the door he turned back to face her. There she lay on the edge of the mattress. She said nothing, only watched him, a sheet across her breasts, Leonard moving unconsciously toward her as he slept, the two of them soon entwined. A line of beer bottles, perfectly spaced, stood guard on the floor. In each bottle was reflected a tiny television screen, mottles of dark moving in all the bright frames.

What if his face was in there somewhere, in that moving pattern of white and gray and black, the person he saw himself becoming someday, prosperous, generous, beloved? Whereas tonight, what the glass reflected: shamefaced, he skulked along a wall, watching the floor.

Easing the front door closed, he stepped onto the landing and heard a sound from Molly's apartment across the way. The stereo played Pony Pony, loud for four in the morning. Her front door was open. He almost sneaked past it, slipping down the stairs, but instead stepped over to her doorway and stood in it. She was still sitting in the chair, a fifth of bourbon beside her, tilted a bit but not yet enough to spill. She was looking out at the room heavy-lidded, both hands on her bare belly, rubbing like a Buddha. The music magazine lay at her feet, open to the picture of her at the microphone, one leg in the air, moving like a rag doll.

She had been crying but now her eyes were dry. She looked at him as if he had been standing there all along. I thought I would be so happy, she said.

For John James, the words cut into him as if he were speaking them too. He sat with her till she closed her eyes and drifted away. Kneeling at the stereo, he looked for the button to turn off the tape, and quiet flooded the room. No more purple night. He stood and watched Molly for a while, then walked down the stairs to his own apartment, and closed the door, and waited in the dark.

MA'AM

BY ALESIA PARKER

Midtown

Lorraine didn't know who could be knocking on her door that sunny spring morning. It never ceased to amaze her how many people came knocking on a person's door in the middle of the day. For most of her life, she had been at work from nine to five like all decent hardworking people, so she had no idea how busy a person's doorstep could get during working hours. She didn't miss her work, though, as being a secretary wasn't exactly her dream job. But truth be told, Lorraine had never dreamed of jobs. She dreamed of husbands, and she had done very well for herself. Councilman Nathaniel Booker Hightower was primed to become the next mayor of Atlanta, and Lorraine was more than ready to glide into the role of first lady.

She shook her head and smiled at the wonder of it all. Being a "lady" at all was something of a triumph, considering where she came from. She'd graduated from Washington High School forty years earlier with nothing but good looks and a paper certifying that she could type eighty words per minute. And now look at her, home at eleven o'clock in the morning ironing the wool suit she would wear to the press conference announcing her husband's mayoral run. Who could believe that she was once a fast-tail girl from John Hope Homes?

There was that knock again. It couldn't be the Witnesses. It'd been a long time since they'd come knocking. It was a waste of their time, as Lorraine never answered the door. Most of them knew not to even bother her, but every now and then one of them liked a challenge. She turned her attention back to the Italian double-crepe wool skirt. She had made it herself. Nothing pleased her more than being asked where she purchased her clothes and she could say, *This? Oh, I made it myself.* Domestic science is what they use to call this sort of thing, back in Jackie Kennedy's day, back when homemaking was still an art. The suit matched the soft lavender necktie that Booker would be wearing for the announcement.

Whoever was at the door wasn't going to give up. The knock this time was the age-old shave-and-a-haircut. The Witnesses were never so lighthearted. Lorraine set the iron down on the ironing board, walked over to the door, and parted the curtain sheers covering the door window with her finger. She froze, then she snatched her finger back from the curtain as if she had mistakenly touched the hot iron she'd just been using. She stood still, holding her breath deep in her chest, hoping he hadn't seen the movement of the curtain.

"I know you're there, Raine," a familiar voice sang. The low chuckle that followed was equally telling. "I hear the television on. You watching *The Price Is Right* like you always do 'round this time. And I saw the curtain move. So you might as well open the door."

Lorraine leaned her forehead against the doorjamb, more to balance her swirling thoughts than to still her needy body. This was the part of being a housewife they didn't teach in home economics classes. She slowly opened the door.

"Jonathan, I asked you not to come check on me anymore. We can't do this. We can't, you know that. You know I'm—"

"Yes, yes, I know you're the wife of the future mayor of Atlanta. I understand that. You made that painfully clear."

Lorraine's breath quickened at the sight of Jonathan; she hadn't seen him in six months. She only heard the steady whine of his mail truck as he drove from mailbox to mailbox. For a couple of months she made sure she was in the back of the house so she couldn't hear his approach. The very sound of that vehicle trundling down the road caused a beading of sweat on her forehead and in other unmentionable places.

There was a time she leaped with joy at the sound of his mail truck. She first heard it when he was delivering mail to the houses on the opposite side of the street. That gave her enough time to be waiting for him at her own mailbox with a glass of cold lemonade in the summer or a cup of hot coffee during the cold winter days.

And Jonathan appreciated her kindness. He flashed the same gap-toothed smile he had as a boy. He was a man now, a far cry from the little boy who played Little League at Adams Park and sang in the choir at Mount Vernon Baptist. She even remembered when he used to call her *Miss Lorraine*.

The provision of refreshments to her mailman was innocent enough. She enjoyed talking to him and reliving their early years, even as he placed bills and circulars in her hand. It was amazing how much he remembered, seeing that he was twenty-five years her junior. Jonathan even began circling back around to her house a couple of days a week to have lunch with her. Lorraine looked forward to his company, as her husband traveled more than he was home.

One day they were talking in the kitchen after lunch together, just before it was time for him to finish up his route. She reached over to brush a few crumbs of the coffee cake they'd just eaten from his beard. Jonathan grabbed her hand and gently kissed her fingertips. Kissed fingertips quickly and easily became kissed lips.

It was all very romantic, very *Postman Always Rings Twice, Lorraine Gets Her Groove Back*—every cliché in the book. Lorraine figured she was entitled to a little extracurricular affection, as Booker was gone from home so much you would have thought he was a traveling salesman, rather than a city councilman. And was there not a long tradition of refined ladies who took on discrete lovers? Maybe even Jackie Kennedy herself took special liberties, if only in her deep secret thoughts. And this thing of beauty could have gone on forever, but Jonathan, young and dumb, wanted to take it to the next level.

"We could be together, Lorraine," he said that night she told him the affair was over. "Like *really* be together. No more hiding."

Lorraine smiled at him the way you would smile at a child who tells you he wants to be an astronaut. "I'm going to be first lady of Atlanta, you know that."

"You're not happy," he said. "You know that." Suddenly he snatched the satin sheets from the bed, leaving her naked and exposed. "You think I don't notice the keloid scars, the bruises? The remnants are still there, even though you claim he only abused you early in your marriage. I can still see them. I love every inch of your body. How can I not see how much he's hurting you?"

Lorraine pulled the covers back around herself. "It's over, Jonathan. We had a deal: you don't ask me about my life and I don't ask about yours."

Now he seemed like the boy she had known and fallen for. "But I love you, Raine. How can I love you and not ask questions?"

That was over six months ago. And here Jonathan stood now on her front porch with questions swimming in his beautiful hazel eyes.

"Jonathan," she sighed, taking firm hold of the reins of her memories, of her desire for him, and resisting the urge to run her fingers through his curly hair that shone dark red in the sunlight. "You have to go. I just can't do this anymore."

"Not going before you sign for this mail," he said.

"What?"

Jonathan shook the bright yellow envelope. "Mail. You have mail. I'm the mailman, remember? I deliver the mail, rain or shine."

"You could've just left it in the mailbox," Lorraine said, her voice more heady than it should have been. She took a deep breath just to calm herself. "Next time, just leave it there."

Jonathan smiled. "Like I said, you have to sign for it. I have to do my job first. I have to love you later, from afar and forever."

Lorraine signed her name, her hand shaking like a drug user itching for another hit. *One more good time before quitting for good*, her body whined. This was another experience she had shoved far behind her, though. Drugs, hits, pretty young boys, the angst of just about every sad movie on any given cable channel made especially for women. Now she was living a new life that stretched out in front of her like a yellow-brick road. All she had to do was stay on the path, and stay out of the dusty back rooms of her heart.

She shoved the clipboard at him. And it didn't help that Jonathan was slow to possess it, taking the time to touch her shivering hand. His touch was like wind gently blowing on smoldering ashes, threatening to ignite them into the raging wildfire they once were. It didn't help that the actual wind carried the scent of his aftershave straight to her head. She had purchased the same scent for Booker, but on her husband's skin the scent was brackish and sharp.

Jonathan took the clipboard from her hands and backed away. "Thank you, ma'am." He stood on the top step of the porch and looked out over the street. "You know I have my differences with your husband, but I have to admit that he gets things done. Just look here at these streets. Bricks instead of asphalt. If I didn't know better, I would think this was a white neighborhood."

"Permeable pavers," Lorraine said.

"Say what?" He turned to face her.

"They're permeable pavers. They solve the flooding problems in our neighborhood."

Jonathan chuckled. "Solving problems. I guess that's a good thing, that's progress. Problems get solved when white folks start moving into the neighborhood, right?"

"Don't say that. My husband represents all the residents of this neighborhood. That's why he's going to be the next mayor." She wanted to say more, but she was suddenly captivated by the lone wiry gray hair in Jonathan's beard. She'd snatched it out many a night with her own teeth.

As if he could read her thoughts, he stepped forward and snaked his arm around her waist. He pulled her close. "Long live the new mayor and first lady. Is that what I'm supposed to say?"

His voice was at a frequency so low that she heard it with her bones, rather than her ears.

"You don't have to stay with him. Fuck high society. We could move to Birmingham, start over . . ." He released her and changed his tone back to ordinary mailman banter. "It's gonna be eighty degrees today. Can't beat that after it's been near a hundred all week."

"No, I guess you can't," Lorraine replied as she flipped the package in her hand. She watched a bowlegged Jonathan walk back down to his mail truck. She closed the screen door, but she didn't close the house door until she saw the mail truck disappear around the corner.

Lorraine sat down on the sofa. She touched her finger where Jonathan had touched it. Was she imagining it, or was her finger burning hot? Oh, that man. She grabbed a tissue from the box on the end table and dabbed at the sweat gathering at her cleavage. He was a dear boy, but couldn't he recognize when things were complicated? He, of all people, should understand. He had known her when she was living in the projects, sleeping on her grandmother's foldout couch, when "success" was finishing high school and not getting pregnant. If he knew how far she'd come, why couldn't he understand that she had to make sacrifices to keep what she had gained?

"Wonder if that girl won that car," she said aloud to herself as she squeezed the large bulky envelope. It was too late to know now. She would find out when the big wheel was spun.

Lorraine flipped the package over and over in her hand and examined the writing. Her name was printed neatly in large print, but there was no return address. The postmark was metered, and showed that it'd been mailed from the post office over by the Atlanta Civic Center.

The package opened easily. Booker's old wallet fell out onto the floor. "Well, well," she said. "I guess miracles happen after all."

The wallet had been stolen when Booker was robbed and beaten in Downtown Atlanta. He'd traveled all over the world without so much as a whisper of a problem, and yet he was robbed in the very city that he worked so hard to improve. It was so difficult to see her husband laid up in a Grady Hospital bed with his head bandaged and purple bruises dotting his swollen body. "God curse the man who did this to you,

Booker," she'd lamented as she fed him lukewarm soup from a small hospital bowl. "May God strike him down. May he reap what he sows a thousand times over." Lorraine wasn't much for religion, but religiosity was a second language to her.

She flipped open the wallet and glanced at the contents. Several credit cards were there, along with a plethora of business cards. There was also a picture of the two of them. Booker's driver's license and Social Security card were wedged behind the credit cards. It was like a DIY starter kit for identity theft, but here is was, untouched.

She stuck her hand inside the envelope, and pulled out neatly folded pages. They were yellow and lined, the top edges scraggly, like the sheets had been hastily ripped from a pad of some sort. She flattened the papers on her lap, and saw that it was a letter. She raised the reading glasses that hung around her neck on a thin gold chain to her eyes and began to read:

Ma'am,

I am returning your husband's wallet to you. I stole it. I am returning it, but I kept the money it contained. Yes, I kept the 1280 dollars that was there. I want to apologize for keeping the money. I am sorry, but I needed it. And after what your husband put me through, I deserve that money.

It was a Friday, 9 months ago, late in September. I was a bit down that week because I'd gotten a ticket for speeding and running a red light. (I'd only recently moved to Atlanta. I live in a nice condo in Midtown, but I only rent. I am not a person of means.) I tried to explain to the officer that I was still getting used to driving in the area, but he wouldn't listen. I later found out the fine for the ticket would be over 600 dollars. I am a secretary, and

I go to school at night. This was something I couldn't afford.

I'd just gotten paid that Friday and I decided to go out for a drink. My coworkers wanted to go out for drinks at Dugans. The price was right, but I am too old for such frat-boy hangouts. Anyway, I really just needed to be alone and have a good drink and a cigarette. I'd quit smoking, but stress always brings the worst out of me. So I went to the bar that's located atop the Peachtree Plaza. When I was little, I would come to Atlanta to visit my auntie and she always promised that one day we would have dinner up there and look down at the whole city. My aunt recently passed so I decided to go up there and keep her promise to me.

I felt self-conscious up there since I was the only person who seemed to be pinching pennies. I asked if there were happy hour specials and everybody looked at me like I had farted or something. I asked for a menu so I could see the price range. I am not much of a drinker. I usually have whatever wine is on happy hour and then I go home.

The bartender placed a drink in front of me and asked me if I would be a "test subject." He called it a Georgia Peach and since it was free, I drank it. It had triple sec, peach schnapps, Ciroc, and orange juice. He even put a few cherries on top. And they weren't none of those cheap fire-red plastic-looking cherries. I hate those. But these cherries had been soaked in vodka for days, and right there, I should've said no. I know good and well I don't deal with nothing like that. After drinking only half of the drink, I felt a little light-headed. I drank it too fast, I guess.

More people came in later that night. I had been sitting there for two hours, sipping my drinks. I was a bit lit and I knew I needed to sit there until I felt ok to drive. But by that time I had been test-subjecting all evening! That was ok because the bartender was keeping me company.

The bartender took my empty glass and gave me another. I told him no, I couldn't drink anymore, and that I needed to sit there another hour to sober up so I could drive home. If I drank another I would probably end up sleeping it off outside in my car.

But he said it was sent over compliments of a gentleman who had been admiring me from the far side of the bar. I looked down that way and the man smiled, lifted his drink, and nodded at me.

I didn't know what to do. I was taken aback because I am not the prettiest woman in the world. I am tall, real dark. I am skinny like Olive Oyl on a diet and I hadn't had a man pay attention to me in a long time. So it felt good to have this strange man send me a drink. That alone made my day.

Each time my glass was about empty the bartender would refresh it. I tried to tell him no, but the drinks were paid for. Each time the mysterious man at the end of the bar would raise his drink and smile wide and wink. I did the same even though I wished he had bought me something to eat instead of all that alcohol. But I was too shy to admit that I was hungry.

At that rate, even though I lived close by, there was no way I was going to be able to drive home. I'd closed my eyes and was enjoying the music when someone behind me cleared his throat. I opened my eyes and looked over my shoulder. It was the man who'd been sending me drinks.

Now, my grandmama told me never to trust a man who had conked hair, whose hair was prettier than my own. She said they were trouble and I should cut loose and run fast in the opposite direction. But I only thought about that for a minute. The liquor was running my mind so my mind wasn't quite running right, if that makes any sense.

The man was polite enough, asking if I minded if he sat and talked with me. I said no. He said his name was Johnny Bird and he was the youngest son of jazz great Charlie Bird. Now, I didn't know much about jazz but I had heard of a Charlie Bird.

Johnny said he was downtown on business. A bellhop at his nearby hotel recommended the bar. He thought it would be a good place to get a quick drink. He didn't know he would be so blessed as to meet a fine woman like me. Even in my less than sober state of mind I knew he was just flirting. I was happy to laugh.

What pulled at my heart strings was how he talked about his nasty divorce from his wife. She'd gotten everything and he'd gotten nothing. He said that they had a big house off Cascade and she was living in it with the mailman while he's living in a shack behind the baseball stadium. He said it wasn't the money so much as the betrayal. He was a little lonely and wanted to someday get back in the dating game.

We talked for a while and I told him about my traffic ticket woes and my trouble getting adjusted in a new city. He nodded every so often and stared into my eyes while he sipped whatever was in his tall frosted glass.

The music got louder and faster and more people came in. It was hot. Johnny Bird asked if I'd like to go someplace a little less crowded where we could continue talking. I saw nothing wrong with that. He was handsome and kind. I started thinking that maybe what they say about Atlanta isn't a lie—that there ARE nice men here, even gentlemen.

He slid off the barstool and removed his wallet from the breast pocket of his suit jacket. He laid two crisp hundred-dollar bills on the bar and told the bartender to keep the change. I was touched that he would tip the bartender so well even though he was having financial troubles of his own. Johnny Bird offered me his arm and we left the bar. I felt like my life had turned into a romantic comedy.

He suggested we go to his hotel. He said he was staying there because the little house he was renting was being fumigated. Under normal circumstances I would have been skeptical but the night felt magical. You, being his wife, must know how he can make a person feel. He took me to the Savannah Suites hotel in the south part of Midtown, over on Pine Street. Now I was a bit surprised by that. That was a sketchy area. I thought that hotel was "by the hour" if you know what I mean. I am not saying that I frequent such establishments but I know one when I see one. I was wrong, I suppose. I wanted to say something but I was afraid that I would hurt his feelings. You know how men are sensitive about anything to do with money.

He could see my apprehension. He reminded me about his terrible divorce and how that place was a nice extended-stay hotel and he needed to save his money for the lawyers. This hotel was cheap but clean. Why did I think I was too good for the simple things in life? I was drunk and this made a sort of sense. Like I said, I am a woman of modest means. And maybe this was some kind of test. You know how the man pretends to be poor to make sure the woman is not just trying to get his money.

We got to the hotel and sat on the sofa and talked. He

opened a bottle of wine and the taste was slightly bitter. Again, I didn't want to offend him so I drank it down without a word.

By 3 a.m. it was clear that I was not up to going back to my car, so I asked if I could stay until morning and sleep on the sofa. He said yes, if I'd allow him a kiss. That didn't seem like it would be a problem. After all, he'd been very nice to me.

The kiss was nice, as I expected from such a gentleman. He said he wanted to have sex. It was the first time in a long time that he'd been with a woman who helped ease the pain of his divorce. And it had been a long time for me too. And I did feel sorry for him. I felt a bit strange because I'd never been with a man old enough to be my father. We lay in bed and drank some more. I even fell asleep.

I awoke to him lying beside me. And my hands were tied to the bedposts. He proceeded to do things to me that I don't care to write about. If you are his wife, I imagine you know what I am talking about. A man like this does not control himself. Suffice it to say that he called me every horrible name besides my own and he more than injured my body, he raped my spirit. But ma'am, this is what happened to me. At least I am alive to write what Johnny Bird did to me.

This is how I choose to think of it.

I was able to escape when he allowed me to use the restroom. I stumbled into the bathroom and sat on the edge of the tub. All was quiet save for the hard knocking of my knees together. I didn't come out until I heard his loud snores.

Johnny lay on the bed spread eagle, naked to the

world, in a hard drunken sleep, which I unhappily am familiar with because of my stepfather. I quickly gathered up my clothing but I couldn't find my panties. I decided to leave them. The longer I stayed there, the more of a chance he'd wake up.

I happened to look up and catch the reflection of my face in a large mirror that hung over the sofa. My eyes were near swollen shut, my cheeks purple with bruises. A trail of blood flowed from my nose. I was grateful that I wasn't able to see the harm done to the rest of me.

I had to get out of there. I remembered him placing his keys and wallet in the pocket of his jacket. His jacket lay across the back of the sofa in the living room. I dug around in it and found his keys and wallet. There was money in there but what I noticed was the picture of you, ma'am, and your husband the so-called Johnny Bird. The date on the back of it said it was taken a couple of weeks before that awful night. It had your names and the date of your wedding anniversary, the day the picture was taken.

It was your face that did it to me, ma'am. You reminded me of my auntie, the one who said that she would take me to the Peachtree Plaza one day. She was like you, proper and respectable. She always wanted me to have the better things in life, like education and a good man. She talked the talk and walked the walk but it was not enough to save her. Like you, she was married to a terrible man. The reason I keep telling you how happy I am to be alive is because my aunt was not as fortunate.

The next thing I knew, I was standing over Johnny Bird with an empty wine bottle in my hand. For the life of me, I can't remember walking from that living room and into the bedroom. I never believed when someone

would say that they didn't remember committing a crime.
I thought they were lying.

Now I understand.

This is what I can piece together not from memory but
from the chaos in the room when I came to again. I think I
knocked him upside the head with that bottle so hard that
it broke, glass splintering and going everywhere. He woke
up with a start, his face bleeding from the broken glass.
He was handcuffed to the bed and duct tape covered his
mouth. I must've done that too, but ma'am, I can't say that
I remember.

I showed him the picture of you and him together. Told
him what he was doing wasn't right. I told him all about
my auntie and he didn't care. He kicked his foot out at
me, knocking me hard in the thigh. I knocked him in the
head with the lamp and the phone from the nightstand. I
smashed him in the face with the Gideon Bible. Blood was
everywhere. He passed out.

I ran from the room and saw the wallet on the floor
next to his keys. I snatched up the keys, trying my best to
find the one to his car. Then I remembered when he placed
the hundred-dollar bills on the bar. I looked in the wallet
and there was a stack of hundreds there. I shoved the wallet in my coat pocket and ran out the door.

I did my best to compose myself, walking among the
homeless people meandering around. I wandered among
them for an hour, watching to see if the police would come.
Some kind homeless woman even offered to share her water and half-eaten sandwich with me. I gave her one of
the hundreds from the wallet and she said she would pray
for me.

Ma'am, I was afraid for several days. I turned on the

news every day and night, expecting to see my face on the TV as a part of the crime-stopper reports. It never happened. But I did see a picture of your husband on the TV, and something about him being mugged and how he was recovering at Grady Hospital. He was a councilman, someone big in the city government. My heart stopped at the thought of it. I would be going to jail. I knew they were looking for me. I'd watched enough crime shows. There was enough blood at the scene to find me. I was so scared. I kept the wallet in the back of my closet as I was pondering whether to turn myself in to the police or not. No one ever showed up at the door.

Instead, some two weeks later, I went in for my court date and paid my speeding ticket in full and in cash.

I was afraid. I kept my head down as much as I could. The police didn't recognize me. They called me ma'am, showed me respect. I paid the fine and left with my record clear.

My conscience was not clear though. I kept thinking about the wallet and the cash. Your husband is a man with a problem but that didn't mean I should've taken money from him. That was money that he earned and I was taking food out of your family's mouth.

So, I am returning the wallet. I kept the money. I ask you to forgive me, but after all I went through I told myself that God was blessing me in the process. I know that this is a lie and I should not involve God's good name in this mess. But the least I can do is return this wallet and say that I am so sorry.

Ma'am, I just wanted you to know that your husband is a very sick man, but I imagine that you know this already. He needs to get help before somebody gets hurt *worse than me. God forbid he kill a woman. If you know him, you know that I am not exaggerating. So I am coming to you with this information in the name of my dearly departed Auntie Twyla.*

Again I am sorry.
Sincerely,
Jane Doe

Lorraine stared at the letter for a long time. Then she looked up at the television just in time to see the girl on *The Price Is Right* lose her showcase. She had overbid by just a few dollars.

"Too bad for her," Lorraine whispered.

The noon news came on after the game show. There was Booker, with a crowd of people around him, dignified as always, his hair neat as ever even in the blowing wind. She'd permed his hair the night before so that it would be perfect for the announcement. She'd ironed his shirt and carefully laid out his suit and shined his shoes. Lorraine never got used to looking at the television and seeing her husband there. This time she muted the set so she didn't have to hear his voice. She knew he was telling the reporters how he was outraged with this or that, laying the groundwork for tomorrow's big announcement.

Booker was standing next to his protégé, Charlotte Johnson. She was the one who actually ran things and came up with all those innovative ideas. Booker just took what she said and packaged it as his own. He gestured toward her, and Lorraine thought she saw the young woman flinch. She wasn't sure if she should feel jealousy or pity for Charlotte. Did Charlotte know what she and the mysterious writer of the letter knew?

She turned back to the lavender suit swinging from the hanger. She had designed it herself, imagining it as a nod to Jackie Kennedy, the first lady of all first ladies. Now, Jackie knew that being a first lady was all about keeping secrets and looking good at the same time.

Right there in the living room, Lorraine stripped down to her bra and panties, put on her suit, and stood before the mirror. She tugged at the hem to make the fabric lay flat. She turned to assess herself from every angle, and from every angle the suit appeared homemade. She looked like she had in grade school when there was no money to buy off-the-rack and her mother made do with needle and thread. Surely it would look better once she finished ironing out the seams. But what was the point? How had she come so far to get nowhere?

She lifted her chin and the ghostly imprint of Booker's fingers peeked out just above the collar. How could a bruise left years ago still be there? She thought of Jonathan and his promise to take her away from all of this.

At that moment, there was another knock at the door.

"Jonathan," Lorraine whispered. She nearly tripped over the cord of the iron as she ran for the door. "You came back for me."

She snatched the door open and there stood the Witnesses, prim and proper in their Sunday best.

"Do you know where you will be spending eternity?" the taller of the two women asked in a soft voice. She held a copy of their magazine out to Lorraine.

Lorraine looked past them, hoping Jonathan was there too. But of course he wasn't. Why would he be? "No, I don't," she answered under the eager gaze of the proselytizers.

The smile on the Witnesses' faces melted into frowns of sadness.

"Too bad for me," Lorraine added before they could speak another word. She stepped back and closed the door.

THE FUCK OUT

BY JOHN HOLMAN

East Lake Terrace

Here's a word: glorious. That's how it feels for Blur to be back. It's Friday! Folks standing around drinking in Uncle Card's yard, some sitting at the picnic table, some gathered near the shedding magnolia. Bobby "Blue" Bland on the boom box, pickups in the driveway and on the shoulder in front of the house. After work for these dudes. Blur, first weekend out of jail in six months of fall and winter and now it's springtime! Bobby "Blue" Bland! *Snort!* Because Blur and Uncle Card are of the Blue family and Blur is tired of the Prince music Joyce has been playing, and anyway for Blur this is like a family reunion. No relation to Bobby Bland, nobody thinks. Uncle Card and Blur, and Joyce, and Uncle Ron and Uncle Red who run the funeral home. Blur's mama down the road. Uncle Card the so-called black sheep 'cause he runs a liquor house. Ron and Red don't come nowhere near here. Busy with the bodies and the respect. Joyce has been playing Prince nonstop. Dead Prince.

But Blur is not in the yard right now, though he can hear the music outside. He's in Uncle Card's dark kitchen rummaging through shaky drawers and pressboard cabinets for a lock Card wants for the cage out front for some reason. He called from Augusta a half hour ago. Blur doesn't have any money to buy a lock, and he'd have to walk to the store, unless Joyce, his aunt, his mom and Card's younger sister, lets him borrow hers. And it might rain. "Got a surprise," Card said.

The kitchen has dark, fifty-year-old linoleum on the floor and dark, fifty-year-old cabinets and counters, and a couple of drawers that will fall completely out if you're not careful when you open them. Some hardly open at all. He rummages, finds screws, nails, thumbtacks, Post-it notes, twist ties, cleaning products, rubber gloves, plastic bags, rags, paint cans. He finds an old combination lock, locked, with no combination code on the back. There's a padlock with no key and that's too small, anyway. He looks through the back door to the screened back porch. There might be something in the tool chest out there. No. Just wrenches, hammers, and sockets. Back in the kitchen, a brown roach runs up the faded curtain over the sink window. Blur was supposed to spray insecticide while Card was gone. He swats hard at the roach with a folded magazine from the dinette table and the curtain rod falls. He reaches to put it back. He's cracked the pane. Maybe nobody will notice for a long time. The insecticide canister, like a big oxygen tank with a nozzle and hose, is on the porch, but first he'd better take a trash bag and clean up the empties out front, then figure out the lock—borrow money from Joyce, get a ride to the store. Or walk. After, he can spray the fucking roaches. Jail was full of them. And mold. And lice, which is why Blur is bald. It's 6:05, according to the clock over the stove, and it's still light outside, but getting dark soon, and the rain that could happen has dimmed things already. Patchy, itchy-looking clouds over the sun. Hopefully, Card is just now leaving Augusta, two hours away.

He takes a trash bag outside, maneuvers around the guzzlers gathered about, and grabs the empties off the picnic table. Then, just as Blur spots the doctor and his old drunk beagle walking down the road, *Smack!* A side glimpse and Blur sees Teddy fall like something big and heavy off a truck, or out of a tree. *Thump!* Facedown in the new grass.

"Shit!" yells Blur. "You just got knocked the fuck out!"

Big dumb-ass Wheatbread stands over Teddy, fist still clenched. Other guys whoop or don't do nothing, keep standing around like only the wind is different. Which it is, a little. Teddy, knocked the fuck out. The doctor half drags his beagle, Poon, into the yard, which looks 80 percent better since Uncle Card put in some seed and planted red and yellow flowers here and there. Still some dirt spots.

"Dudes," the doctor says, "help the man."

"Could be dead by now," old man Word in a lawn chair says.

Somebody else says, "Can't help him, then."

"Motherfucker, stop messing with me," Wheatbread mumbles, pouting.

Teddy stirs down on the ground among tossed beer cans and pony-size liquor bottles. He scoots up on his hands and knees, huge yellow work boots trembling at the end of his wobbly pant legs. Might be having a seizure.

"You all right?" says the doctor, bending with his hand on Teddy's shoulder. The doctor hardly ever stops by to hang out. Drinks at home. Does some kind of CDC work. Poon wanders the length of his leash, pees on a dead azalea at the porch corner. That azalea didn't make it. Blur missed Poon. Old Poon. A lemon-squeeze dog. Face whiter than dumb-ass Wheatbread's. First time Blur met the doctor he told him about his own sweet beagle he had years back. How if nobody could find Blur, like his old lady back then, all they had to do was follow his dog. Too good of a damn dog.

"God a'mighty," Teddy says, like mud's in his mouth. But

it's blood, where he got his lip busted or he bit his tongue or both. Tooth loose? He wags his head like a big sick cow. Teddy's a thick brother. He lets the doctor hold his arm while he scrambles to his feet. Shakes himself, and the doctor stumbles back. Drops the dog leash. Poon is under the picnic table nosing the dirt. "Fuck you," Teddy mumbles. To the doctor? Can't tell. The doctor chuckles.

"Called me Whitebread," Wheatbread says. "Too many times."

Teddy swallows hard and frowns. "Hagh," is the sound he makes next. "Fuck you, Whitebread." Now he laughs and then throws back his head and growls like a lion. Or a bear. Mouth looks like he's been eating an animal. Wheatbread's ears go red. But the doctor is between them. Not the ears . . . but maybe. Maybe the only one besides Uncle Card who can stop a fight around here. Maybe Joyce. Blur without his taser today, which he could zap a nigga with if he had it. *Growllll!* Teddy with his shoulders hunched back and his face at the sky, eyes like he's looking at something, but nothing's there except a bird and a plane. Gray clouds. He staggers and lurches out to the road, *Growllll!* a few more times before he sits down on the middle line, legs stretched out in front of him. Gotta be free, Blur gets that. Blur can see him between Birdie's black Ram and old man Word's green no-name truck. Maybe two cars come by, each way, and steer around him. There's speed bumps now, anyway. That happened while Blur was inside.

"Doctor," Blur says, "buy me a beer!" shaking an empty OE waist high.

"Buy *me* one," the doctor says. Ball cap pulled down low to his sunshades. Got on some mint-green cargo shorts and a Bob Marley T-shirt. Hundred-dollar tennis shoes, Blur bets. Blur already owes him money, or maybe he doesn't. Hard to know if the doctor expects Blur to pay him back from all the times he's bummed a couple of bucks off him. Doc doesn't even look sorry anymore when Blur comes to his door and says his mama's in the hospital and he needs bus fare to go see her. Last time he rolled his eyes and just gave Blur a five. Blur's mama is all right, but she does get sick sometimes. Blur thinks, I guess Doc ain't missed me while I was inside. Hard to tell if he really wants a beer, either.

"Let me borrow Poon," Blur says.

"So you can sell him?"

"My little girl wants a dog. I'm gonna make her think I got her one and then say it ran away. You'll get Poon back. Just a loan. It's her birthday next week."

"Shut up, Blur," Joyce says. She pats Poon's head over at the picnic table, where Wheatbread is now. "You always using shit that ain't yourn."

"You got a little girl?" the doctor says.

"Might as well be mine," Blur says.

"Humph," Joyce says. She has an arm sleeved with silver and copper bracelets to her elbow. Don't know how she can stand that, Blur thinks. Reminds him of handcuffs. She wears a new big braid across her head like a basket handle. Joyce is his aunt but they're about the same age, thirty-six for Blur. A little sweet on the doctor. A little sweet on Prince too, must be, in her satiny purple shirt. Been crying. Around last Labor Day, she spent days painting the picnic table all kinds of colors so she'd be outside whenever the doctor walked by with Poon. "Poon!" she'd sing. "Hey, Doctor, how you *doing*?" Took to taking her own walk early in the morning, but couldn't go on pretending she was out for her health with Poon stopping every few feet to smell something in the ditch. Pee on something and take a shit. Her out there in leopard-print slippers and sexy sparkly tights. Had to just walk on and leave the doctor behind. The picnic table does spruce up the yard. Blue benches with yellow legs; red, yellow, and blue-painted planks on the table.

Joyce'll never get no doctor, though, is what Blur believes, no matter how she smiles that gap-tooth mouth or slicks her side hair into flat sideburns. Wheatbread is on her case pretty hard, anyway. And the doctor's got white chicks coming and going from his house like he's running a coffee shop outta there. Funny, the doctor likes white chicks, or don't mind them, and big dumb Wheatbread, looking as white as his dead white daddy, likes black-as-midnight Joyce, who likes the doctor, who happens to be one them pecan brothers. Most of the crowd is dark as Jamaicans, though. Maybe two or three straight-up Africans come by sometime. Since Katrina, way back awhile now, all kinds wash up here.

What does Blur like? Beer and pussy, and don't care what brand, either one. They call him Blur because of his thick eye-glasses. Bottle bottoms. But he can see with them. He can see who is drinking what and he can spot possible pussy.

Beer is plentiful but pussy is scarce. Chicks come by on Saturdays, mostly, but with other dudes or dude-like chicks. And Uncle Card keeps strict inventory on the beer, with Joyce's help. Stingy Joyce. Blur is the runner—he goes to the store and gets supplies—and Joyce and Uncle Card are the cashiers. Blur can't even drink a free beer and he lives there, even though he's the one that goes down to Kroger to get the cases Card sells to these fools. At least he got the job back after getting out, and at least he can still stay with Uncle Card in exchange for working for him. He can't live with his mama, who's bossier than Joyce and Card. A lot of these guys bring their own quarts and half-pints, and that's all right because they run out quick and buy Card's anyway before too long. Blur might get a beer off one or two of them, like a tip. He has to borrow Card's truck to get to the store.

The doctor rounds up Poon. "Where you been, Blur? Ain't seen you," he says.

"Had to go away for a minute. Parole violation. You didn't know?"

"Damn, Blur. Welcome back."

"Thanks!"

The doctor takes Poon out to the road where Teddy is still sitting and laughing to himself as cars creep by, passengers looking at him like he's a big bag of interesting trash. He tries to pull Teddy up again, from the armpits this time. Teddy starts laughing and growling at the same time. Wheatbread curses and swings his legs from under the table, over the bench, and heads to the road. Maybe to kick Teddy. Who knows why half-and-half Wheatbread will take that name but not Whitebread. Wheatbread can't be his real name. Honors his black mama, Blur guesses. Basically, white ain't quite right around here. Lots of white people have moved in, though, even before Blur got incarcerated. Pushing their babies in carriages. None gonna push past Teddy now, though. Go the other way. Blur's seen signs stuck in the ground at the end of the road saying the East Lake Terrace community meeting is next Monday night. East Lake Terrace is a new name to him. Maybe folks trying to siphon some status from the golf club across the way. Used to be just Candler-McAfee, the intersection where the bus picked you up or dropped you off.

Wheatbread gets behind Teddy where the doctor was. The doctor stands to the side with Poon. Wheatbread hauls up Teddy, who laughs that private laugh he has, like he's the most clever man ever to get knocked the fuck out. Teddy

walks on down the road, must be to that house he's squat-
ting in. You can hear him howling and growling. The doctor
turns down the side street with Poon, who don't want to go.
Wheatbread pushes his sand-colored hair off his forehead and
brushes his hands on his jeans. Squints both ways on the road,
and at the sky. Clouds thickening the west now, out across the
street, behind those houses. Storm kind, which is what Blur
doesn't want 'cause then everybody gets in their truck and
stops spending, and stops tipping.

If Wheatbread won't come back in the yard, Blur's gonna
finish his beer. Fuck Joyce. If he does come back, whatever. At
least all the violence will be done before Uncle Card returns
from Augusta. Been gone two days. If Card gets mad, no telling what job he'll give Blur, like punishment, like making him
crawl under the house to change the furnace filter, which he
hates. Dirt and spiders, a cat carcass one time. Feels like a buried man trying to get somewhere in the dirt. Like everything
is Blur's fault. It ain't his fault, for instance, that the white
folks called the cops about the beer cans and loud music in
the yard, that he got arrested 'cause he had that taser under
his shirt and the cops called it a concealed weapon, that some
of Card's azalea bushes didn't take because Blur was in jail
and couldn't water them, that Wheatbread is such a sensitive
dummy.

"Come here, Blur," Joyce says, sniffling, teary-eyed again.
It was last week when Prince died. Blur heard about it in
jail. It was on everybody's radio and TV. A shock, sure, but
Blur tried not to feel it. He'd be getting out soon, is what he
wanted to feel. Joyce, she even went to the concert at the Fox.
Dude's last show ever. A three-hundred-dollar ticket! That
price pisses Blur off more than anything. She's looking away,
wet-lashed, to the old lantana bush at the border between

the yard and the neighbor's. Two little hummingbirds hover at one of the yellow-red blooms. "That's sweet, ain't it?" she says. "When's the last time you saw a hummingbird? See the purple in the tail feathers? Even birds paying tribute to Prince."

Blur can see they are hummingbirds, not big bees, but has he ever seen one, much less two together? You got to know they some free motherfuckers, he thinks. Them motherfuckers is just like me. Them motherfuckers like the springtime too. But they don't know from Prince, he thinks. Do they know from death? Free or not when you're dead? Ask Uncle Ron and Uncle Red, maybe. Son of bitch dying like that in the springtime sours the mood, all right. *He's* the fuck out, all right. All the way the fuck out.

Wheatbread comes on back, finishes his beer. Leans in to Joyce but doesn't speak. He's a plumber, whereas Teddy's a tree man, and nearly every other dude in the neighborhood cuts grass and cleans gutters. Everybody freelance. 'Cause everybody's a felon. Here, though, they drink and cut up with Uncle Card's friends who have steady jobs, like city sanitation and construction or some other blue-uniform work, and after work on Friday, and Saturday and Sunday all day, Card does good business selling drinks. Uncle Card does yard work too. He's done all right. Has a truck with a trailer to carry his mowers and Weedwackers. Does yards in "better" neighborhoods. White yards. Makes sense, then, for his own yard to look good. Card has a work ethic that kind of kicks Blur's ass.

Bunny Bone comes into the yard with a dude Blur's never seen before. Bunny who thinks *she's* a dude, and looks like a dude, and might be a dude except with big loose titties under her big T-shirt. And she's albino too. Whiter skin than Wheatbread's. Got her own thick glasses plus weird white eyelashes and nappy blond hair. Used to be Blur wondered how she hung with all the brothers without getting those dead-white titties looked at and squeezed. Blur used to imagine them, wondered if the nipples were white too, or like her thick pale lips. But then, because she's the scariest-looking and loudest of anybody during a fuss—face scrunched like a powdered knuckle—he wondered if *she* might be the one to rape some chick. And thinking about rape he felt bad for thinking about her titties. She's got a life supply of annoying wolf tickets to sell. Bragging about what she'd do if somebody said this or that to her, what she actually did to somebody who said this or that.

"What's going on?" she says.

"Bunny Bone," Blur says, "Teddy just got knocked the fuck out."

Other dudes don't pay her much attention. A couple of up-nods. They're talking about how sorry the Braves are going to be this year, or cursing about something else. One dude, Birdie, on his cell phone, says, "Man, fuck the United Way."

The new dude with Bunny must be about six feet nine inches up in the air. "Too Tall," Blur says, nodding. Bunny must have bribed a ride from the dude, 'cause Bunny can't drive.

Joyce says, "You know this guy?"

"Naw. He's too tall, though." Blur likes getting in that joke, 'cause he's short, for a man. Like Prince, he realizes. *How's the weather down there?*

"This here is James," Bunny says. Both wearing the same kind of outfit—navy-blue T-shirt, gray work pants, and gray-coated blunt-toed boots. Blur thinks, I must look like I'm on vacation in my flip-flops and shorts. Baggy shorts. Dingy T-shirt. Bunny Bone works concrete. Has a loud whiny voice like everything is an outrage. *This here is James*, came out like she's yelling at a referee.

"Gimme two," she says.

Blur grabs two OEs from the cooler behind Joyce. Passes them to Bunny, who drops some dollars on the picnic table where Joyce works the cash box. Blur's phone gurgles in his pocket. It's Uncle Card calling. He's been gone, but not for yard work 'cause his trailer's still here. A woman, Blur suspects. "Is it raining there?"

"Not yet," Blur says. "Clouding up, though. Heavy air."

Card says. "You got the lock?"

"When you getting back?"

"On my way," he says. Which doesn't tell Blur much. How much time he has to get a lock. He looks at the beer cans and pony bottles still on the ground. Card expects the yard clean, and he cashes in the cans. Trash bags full are stored on the back porch until there's enough worth selling.

Blur tells Joyce about the call, that he already looked in the kitchen. She gets up and walks around the front of the house—Blur can't fathom why Card hasn't done something about the way it looks, like paint it, or pay Blur to paint it, because its gray shingle siding is ugly and some of it's broken off along the bottom, showing tar paper. The cage is a chain-link cube with a flat tin roof to the right of the house, where Card stores his broken mowers and old lawn furniture. Junky. But Card didn't say to move anything in there.

Joyce says, "Maybe he got a new truck or riding mower."

People do steal, so the lock is for something of value, Blur guesses. Card keeps his good stuff on the trailer, locked all the time even when on a job, because somebody once stole a lawn edger when he was cutting somebody else's grass. If it's a new truck, then what about the old one, which is a vintage

Ford, blue with silver flecks, chrome recessed rims, and fat blackwalls? Blur hopes he didn't trade it. Blur could buy it on time, maybe. But Card can't drive home two trucks. Either way, Blur has to get a lock.

Joyce says, "Better clean up the yard first. Then go buy one. I'd let you take my car but you just got out of jail and you already don't have a license, Blur. Better hurry up, I guess."

Bagging cans, Blur frowns at Joyce when she puts on another Prince CD. He feels already saturated with Prince music, and figures it'll just make Joyce cry even while she snaps her fingers to the beat. But she smiles, starts singing along to "Do Me, Baby." Bunny Bone, sitting at the picnic table with Too Tall, Joyce, and Wheatbread, starts a story about a beggar on the MARTA train, somebody selling toiletries, but Wheatbread interrupts her: "Did he have any mouthwash, Bunny? Your breath smells like fish guts."

"Go to hell, Wheatbread," she says. "You think you some kind of comedian, but you ain't. All you is is a half-breed sissy. I don't know why you open your mouth. Anything you say is bound to be confusing."

Funny, coming from Bunny. But her irritating voice, crossed with Prince's high-pitched singing, makes Blur think, *Why can't Bunny Bone be dead now and not Prince?*

"I'm not a sissy," says Wheatbread. He looks at Joyce. "You know I'm not."

A lot of people laugh.

"That's right, Whitebread," Blur says.

Wheatbread is up fast before Joyce can grab him. He clutches Blur's T-shirt at the neck and stares down at him, his fist tight under Blur's chin.

"Oh fuck," Blur says to himself, perplexed by what is happening, by Wheatbread's pond-green eyes, pink face, and yellow teeth, by whatever Joyce is saying—something sort of soothing under Bunny Bone's hoot of a taunt, which is like an off-sounding high note on an electric guitar. Blur got through all the time in jail without getting hit, stabbed, choked. He squinches his eyes tight behind his black-rimmed glasses.

"Don't fight, don't fight," Joyce is saying.

"Oh yeahhh!" Bunny Bone wails.

"You made a mistake?" Wheatbread asks.

"No. I don't know," Blur says. "What did I say?"

Wheatbread lets him go. Pats Blur on the head, like he's a child. Blur lugs the bag of empties he's collected to stack with the others on the back porch. He can see the yellowed clock above the stove and figures he has time to spray roaches out of the kitchen at least, so he does. It takes his mind off what just happened with Wheatbread. He sprays the sulk away. Then he moves on through the house, the living room where his bed is a black sagging couch, Joyce's room girled up with purple and pink curtains and bedspread, and Card's room, as tidy as a monk's, white sheets tucked neatly and folded back over a gray blanket. Army man.

In the bathroom, spraying the cabinet under the sink where Lysol and Clorox are kept, then the medicine chest crowded with old Band-Aids, ointments, and out-of-date medicines, Blur hears Card's truck pull into the driveway. Fuck, that was way fast. The truck has four chrome exhaust pipes and sounds like a big-chested predator. Blur has long wanted that truck. The bathroom window looks out on the caged area where Card wants a lock. What the hell does Card want to lock in there?

Blur hustles the insecticide canister to the back porch, blasts poison on the floor there, then gets the combination lock out of the kitchen drawer. On the way around to the truck he rotates the dial, hoping to hit upon the numbers to spring the lock. He finds the crowd of drinkers surrounding Card's truck. Wind is strong enough to move people's pant legs. Bunny's high, grating voice sings, "Goddamn, Card, you done got a fucking *dog!*" Which is why Blur's been hearing barking since he came outside.

"What's her name?" Joyce asks.

"That's a boy," Bunny says. "Look at the sack on that sucker."

"Oops," Joyce says.

"Name's Prince," Card says.

Blur can't get a good view of it. He can see a large black tail whipping back and forth. Not a pit bull tail; he's afraid of pit bulls. A pink-eyed pit bull once chased him onto the roof of a car. Come to think of it, Bunny Bone reminds him of that dog. Too many pit bulls in the neighborhood already.

Wheatbread says, "That's a big-ass puppy, bruh."

Card turns to see Blur. Card is smiling big, his gray-speckled mutton chops arched back with his cheeks, his bald head full of furrows. "You got the lock? Gonna put him in the cage."

Blur puts the combination lock in his pocket. Better to have no lock than a useless one, he figures. "Not yet. Ain't really had time. You got back too fast."

"Jesus. Well, you got time now, Blur?"

"How am I supposed to get a lock, anyway? I need some money. I need a ride. What the fuck kinda dog that is?" Blur stares now at the dog's wide black face, alien amber eyes.

"It's a cane corso. Best guard dog on the market."

"Connie? Never heard of it," Bunny Bone says.

Something else for Blur to take care of. Feeding it. Shoveling up shit.

"Not Prince," Joyce says.

"Why not?" Card asks.

"'Cause," she says.

"It can be a dog's name too," Card says, annoyed. He clips a wide blue leash to the silver pinch-chain around the dog's thick neck, and lets it leap down from the truck's open tail-gate. It has stopped barking. It walks the leash around Card's legs, and after Card steps out, it moves toward Wheatbread and Too Tall, who both step behind Bunny. Bunny sidesteps it, and it goes toward Joyce.

"Oh, it *is* just a puppy," Joyce says. She's tentative, but puts her knuckles to its head. "God, it's big, Card. How much bigger will it get?"

"A little bit. About five months old now."

Birdie, the guy who hates the United Way, appears beside Blur. He spits on the grass and says, "Got a damn killer there, them brindle stripes," and walks back to the picnic table side of the house. He turns and yells, "Put motherfuckers in y'all's mortuary. Blue Brothers get *lots* of business."

"Come here, Prince," Card says, jerking hard on the leash to turn the dog back to him.

"Call it something else," says Joyce, tearing up.

"That's already his name. I didn't do it. Lots of dogs named Prince."

"Be original, then."

Card just looks at her, wraps the leash around his wrist. Blur ambles toward the cage, which will need to be cleaned out for that dog to have some roaming room. He looks around for a stick to slide between the latch handles, something to hold the dog in until Card decides to give him some money. He feels the weight of the lock he can't work in his pocket. Anger springs up in Blur as he toes accumulated tree fall at the base of the chain links. Here he is, just out of jail and being told to lock something in. Thinks of himself as a dog now. Following Card's orders, following jail guards' orders. If he makes a move on his own, something like a pinch-collar clamps down, puts the squeeze on his fucking brain so that he's like paralyzed, scared to move, scared to even think about moving lest somebody pinches some more. He picks up a sturdy short stick that might work to at least keep the gate from flapping open. It slips through the handles and stays snug, and despite his anger, this pleases Blur, meanly.

Suddenly the dog barks again, *Woofwoofwoofwoof!* Loud. Thunder booms out of the sky. The dog lurches on the leash that Card holds hard with two hands, its big front paws rising as its hind paws drag a little in the grass. Pinch-collar don't mean shit to that dog. Joyce, Bunny, and Wheatbread—everybody scatters back, and Blur can't figure what the dog is crazy for. Maybe scared of thunder. Can hear it before anybody else. Then Blur sees the doctor on the road with the old beagle. Must think Poon is food or something. The doctor is looking worried at Card's big dog, but Poon pays no attention, his head and tail high, with a little swagger in his walk. You can hear other dogs barking now in the distance. The whole dog neighborhood has gotten interested. Poon, dumb-ass, don't even know he's a tight grip from being mauled. Poon don't even know it's dangerous to be free out here. Every dog is dumb in some way or another, Blur thinks, and he is suddenly tired of what's dumb. He thought Card was smart, but it's dumb to buy a damn dog that needs to be fed and exercised and cleaned up after and kept from killing somebody. And the doctor, who ought to be smart, thinks it's safe to walk a house pet around in this neighborhood. And after it kills Poon it'll bite the doctor and eat a baby and it'll be put down, and anything left living will still be dumb.

"Holy shit!" shouts Bunny, laughing. "Doctor, you better get yourself a big stick or a rifle to walk with!"

Then Blur feels dumb too, because he doesn't know how to be free. He wonders what else in the world he could do to keep living. First time he's wondered this. Not day-by-day stuff, but something where he could afford a three-hundred-dollar show ticket, hundred-dollar shoes, a truck, his own dog if he wanted one. He had thought getting out of jail was the future, but something else is. How long before Card is dead? Prince dead already and nobody saw that coming. Bobby "Blue" Bland *been* dead. He doesn't like Card's dog, which is death on a leash. Funny idea. Maybe he can move in with Teddy in that abandoned house down the road. Cut down trees with him until one falls wrong and puts Blur the fuck out too.

Card wrestles the dog away from the road. "Shut up, now!" he fusses at the animal. "Blur, open the damn gate."

Too Tall follows behind Card as Blur pulls out the stick and swings open the gate. Card kicks Prince hard in the butt. The dog shivers against a dusty old mower set on cinder blocks, snuffs out his fury over Poon. "You just need to train it good, that's all," Too Tall says. "You got to show it who's boss."

Blur closes the gate and puts the stick back in place. "Dog eat motherfucking *dog*," Bunny says, like that's not already obvious.

"You all right, Doctor?" Joyce yells, wiping her eyes.

The doctor raises his hand in thumbs-up, but looks skeptical. Blur calms a little as Prince explores the limits of the junked-up cage, and the others go back to the drinking side of the yard. Dark purple clouds break in the west and show a smear of yellow and red. Sunset. Looks like iodine on a giant dirty wound. The wind feels kind of scary on Blur's bald scalp.

He fingers the lock heavy in his pocket. The barking in the distance keeps on.

ABOUT THE CONTRIBUTORS

DANIEL BLACK is professor of African American Studies at Clark Atlanta University. He is also the author of several novels, including *They Tell Me of a Home, Perfect Peace, The Coming,* and *Listen to the Lambs.* Alice Walker said, *"Perfect Peace* is a spellbinding novel that kept me reading late into several nights . . . It is a gift to have so much passion, so much love, so much beautiful writing so flawlessly faithful to the language of ancestors . . ."

TANANARIVE DUE'S short story collection *Ghost Summer* won a British Fantasy Award in 2016. The novelist and screenwriter has also won an American Book Award and an NAACP Image Award. She lives in the Los Angeles area, but she spent three years in Atlanta while her mother was ill, where she served as a distinguished visiting scholar at Spelman College. During that time, she was awarded a Lifetime Achievement Award in the Fine Arts from the Congressional Black Caucus Foundation.

JIM GRIMSLEY has lived in Atlanta for over thirty years, having debuted his first play in the city in 1983. He is the author of a dozen books, including *Winter Birds* and *Dream Boy.* In 2005 he was awarded the Academy Award in Literature from the American Academy of Arts and Letters. He teaches at Emory University.

ANTHONY GROOMS has lived in Atlanta's Inman Park neighborhood for nearly thirty years. When he isn't teaching, he writes novels in his spider-ridden cellar. His novel *Bombingham,* set during the Birmingham civil rights movement, won both a Lillian Smith Book Award and a Hurston/Wright Legacy Award. His novel *The Vain Conversation,* about redemption for race crimes, will be published in 2018. For more information, go to anthonygrooms.com.

JENNIFER HARLOW earned a BA in psychology from the University of Virginia. She has worked as a bookseller, radio deejay, lab assistant, and government investigator. She is the author of the F.R.E.A.K.S. Squad Investigation series, the Galilee Falls Trilogy, and the Iris Ballard series. She lives in Atlanta and is hard at work on her next book.

Alexander Fedorov

JOHN HOLMAN is the author of *Triangle Ray, Luminous Mysteries,* and *Squabble and Other Stories.* His fiction has appeared in the *New Yorker, Mississippi Review,* and *Oxford American,* along with other journals and several anthologies. He is a Whiting Award recipient, and has taught at Georgia State University in Atlanta since 1993.

Jen Barnis

DALLAS HUDGENS is a native of Atlanta and a graduate of Duluth High School and Georgia State University. He is the author of the novels *Drive Like Hell* and *Season of Gene* and the short story collection *Wake Up, We're Here.* He is the founder of Relegation Books, a small press based in Washington, DC.

Dafna Steinberg

KENJI JASPER wrote the best-selling novel *Dark* in Atlanta just after finishing his degree at Morehouse College. His articles for *Creative Loafing, Upscale,* and *Rappages* helped to take the careers of groups like Outkast, Goodie Mob, and Arrested Development national. His novel *Cake,* written under the pseudonym D, takes place on his college stomping grounds. Jasper's next novel, *Nostrand Avenue,* will be published by Kensington Books in 2018. He lives in Los Angeles.

Beowulf Sheehan

TAYARI JONES was born and raised in southwest Atlanta. A graduate of Spelman College, she is the author of three novels, including *Silver Sparrow,* an NEA Big Read selection. Her work has been supported by the National Endowment for the Arts, Radcliffe Institute for Advanced Study, and the United States Artist Foundation. She is on the MFA faculty at Rutgers University–Newark.

Brad Fairchild

SHERI JOSEPH is the author of two novels, *Where You Can Find Me* and *Stray,* and a cycle of stories, *Bear Me Safely Over.* She has been awarded an NEA fellowship and the Grub Street National Book Prize in fiction, as well as numerous residency fellowships including MacDowell and Yaddo. She lives in Atlanta, where she teaches in the creative writing program at Georgia State University and serves as fiction editor of *Five Points.*

Ruth Collins

BRANDON MASSEY has lived in Atlanta since 1999. He is the author of several novels, including *Dark Corner, The Other Brother,* and *Don't Ever Tell.* Visit www.brandonmassey.com for the latest news on his publications.

Kenyaneé Releford

ALESIA PARKER, a native Atlantan, is a happy chemist by day and closeted writer by night. She has honed her craft through various writing workshops in the Atlanta area over the past decade. Her story in this volume, "Ma'am," is excerpted from her manuscript-in-progress, *Always Watching.* This is her first published story.

Ashley Inguanta

DAVID JAMES POISSANT is the author of *The Heaven of Animals: Stories* and winner of the GLCA New Writers Award and a Florida Book Award. He was long-listed for the PEN/Robert W. Bingham Prize, and was a finalist for the *Los Angeles Times* Book Prize. His stories and essays have appeared in the *Atlantic, Glimmer Train,* the *New York Times, Playboy, Ploughshares,* and the *Southern Review.* He grew up in Gwinnett County, Georgia.

Migdalia Braithwaite

GILLIAN ROYES was born in Jamaica and furthered her education in the United States, completing a doctorate in communications at Emory University, where she initiated her love affair with Atlanta. She is the author of the cozy mystery novels in the Shadrack Myers series published by Simon & Schuster, and her film script *Preciosa* was recently shot in St. Croix. She is currently working on a film adaptation of her novel *The Man Who Turned Both Cheeks.*

Also available in the Akashic Noir Series

NEW ORLEANS NOIR
edited by Julie Smith
288 pages, trade paperback original, $15.95

BRAND-NEW STORIES BY: Ace Atkins, Laura Lippman, Patty Friedmann, Barbara Hambly, Tim McLoughlin, Olympia Vernon, David Fulmer, Jervey Tervalon, James Nolan, Kalamu ya Salaam, Maureen Tan, Thomas Adcock, Jeri Cain Rossi, Christine Wiltz, Greg Herren, Julie Smith, Eric Overmyer, and Ted O'Brien.

"*New Orleans Noir* explores the dark corners of our city in eighteen stories, set both pre- and post-Katrina . . . In Julie Smith, Temple found a perfect editor for the New Orleans volume, for she is one who knows and loves the city and its writers and knows how to bring out the best in both . . . It's harrowing reading, to be sure, but it's pure page-turning pleasure, too." —*Times-Picayune*

MIAMI NOIR
edited by Les Standiford
334 pages, trade paperback original, $15.95

BRAND-NEW STORIES BY: James W. Hall, Barbara Parker, John Dufresne, Paul Levine, Carolina Garcia-Aguilera, Tom Corcoran, Christine Kling, George Tucker, Kevin Allen, Anthony Dale Gagliano, David Beaty, Vicki Hendricks, John Bond, Preston L. Allen, Lynne Barrett, Jeffrey Wehr.

"For different reasons these stories cultivate a little something special, a radiance, a humanity, even a grace, in the midst of the noir gloom, and thereby set themselves apart. Variety, familiarity, mood and tone, and the occasional gem of a story make *Miami Noir* a collection to savor." —*Miami Herald*

D.C. NOIR
edited by George Pelecanos
288 pages, trade paperback original, $15.95

BRAND-NEW STORIES BY: George Pelecanos, Laura Lippman, James Grady, Kenji Jasper, Jim Beane, Ruben Castaneda, Jim Patton, Robert Wisdom, Norman Kelley, Jennifer Howard, Jim Fusilli, Richard Currey, Lester Irby, Quintin Peterson, Robert Andrews, and David Slater.

"From the Chevy Chase housewife who commits a shocking act to the watchful bum protecting Georgetown street vendors, the tome offers a startling glimpse into the cityscape's darkest corners . . . Fans of the [noir] genre will find solid writing, palpable tension, and surprise endings . . ." —*Washington Post*

BALTIMORE NOIR
edited by Laura Lippman
304 pages, trade paperback original, $15.95

BRAND-NEW STORIES BY: David Simon, Laura Lippman, Tim Cockey, Rob Hiaasen, Robert Ward, Sujata Massey, Jack Bludis, Rafael Alvarez, Marcia Talley, Joseph Wallace, Lisa Respers France, Charlie Stella, Sarah Weinman, Dan Fesperman, Jim Fusilli, and Ben Neihart.

"Baltimore Noir dresses the city up in engrossing storytelling . . . [with] perversely horrific twists, hard-bitten clichés, and portraits of the truly deranged." —*Baltimore City Paper*

RICHMOND NOIR
edited by Andrew Blossom, Brian Castleberry, and Tom De Haven
280 pages, trade paperback original, $15.95

BRAND-NEW STORIES BY: Dean King, Laura Browder, Howard Owen, Yazmina Beverly, Tom De Haven, X.C. Atkins, Meagan J. Saunders, Anne Thomas Soffee, Clint McCown, Conrad Ashley Persons, Clay McLeod Chapman, Pir Rothenberg, David L. Robbins, Hermine Pinson, and Dennis Danvers, with a foreword by Tom Robbins.

*"Richmond Noir'*s collection of diverse voices, interests, period pieces, present-day reflections, architectural insights, cultural commentary, and the pervasive sense of mortality that characterizes an urbania so bound to inherited nostalgia, capture the indefinable nature of what it is to live in Richmond." —*RVA Mag*

BROOKLYN NOIR
edited by Tim McLoughlin
320 pages, trade paperback original, $15.95

THE INAUGURAL TITLE in the Akashic Noir Series, *Brooklyn Noir* features Edgar Award finalist "The Book Signing" by Pete Hamill, MWA Robert L. Fish Memorial Award winner "Can't Catch Me" by Thomas Morrissey, and Shamus Award winner "Hasidic Noir" by Pearl Abraham.

BRAND-NEW STORIES BY: Pete Hamill, Nelson George, Sidney Offit, Arthur Nersesian, Pearl Abraham, Neal Pollack, Ken Bruen, Ellen Miller, Maggie Estep, Kenji Jasper, Adam Mansbach, Nicole Blackman, C.J. Sullivan, Chris Niles, Norman Kelley, Tim McLoughlin, Thomas Morrissey, Lou Manfredo, Luciano Guerriero, and Robert Knightly.